JEFFREY'S LONGER SHORTS

Geoffrey Crees

ARTHUR H. STOCKWELL LTD
Torrs Park, Ilfracombe, Devon, EX34 8BA
Established 1898
www.ahstockwell.co.uk

First published in Great Britain, 2017

British Library Cataloguing-in-Publication Data.
A catalogue record for this book is available
from the British Library.

By the same author:
Where Was God Last Friday? (Hodder & Stoughton, 1995)
Jeffrey's Shorts (Instant Apostle, 2013)

ISBN 978-0-7223-4802-4
Printed in Great Britain by
Arthur H. Stockwell Ltd
Torrs Park   Ilfracombe
Devon EX34 8BA

DEDICATION

To friends at Forest Gate Church, Mitcheldean; and the Chaplaincy Team at Gloucester Royal Hospital.

ACKNOWLEDGEMENTS

Every author, however modest in output, is indebted to many others before the printed words become a reality.

I am grateful to Pam Britton and Wendy Stephens for their original comments in the initial stages of this book.

To Pam and Malcolm Britton for their Author's Profile, to Mark the photographer, and to Dave Stephens for the loan of his three-quarters shorts. To Steve D. Cook for imaginative illustrations. To Richard Stockwell and Rose Nicholas for proofreading and preparation for printing. Not least to my wife, Jean, for her love, patience, computer skills and pertinent criticism and comments which have contributed to and shaped this work.

CONTENTS

INTRODUCTION

Why write another book? Won't two do? Strangely, it is difficult to put into words, but talking to other authors there seems to be an agreement that there is a compulsion to always want to write more! It comes with an inner (I believe God-given) desire to communicate some of the hopes, dreams, fears and desires of every human being and, given the warm reception I have received for *Jeffrey's Shorts*, I decided a sequel was in order – fewer stories, but double the length.

I make no apologies that *Jeffrey's Shorts* was oblique in its Christian message while this current book is possibly more direct!

In 1871 Anthony Trollope, the author of *Barchester Towers*, wrote *Anna* on the SS *Great Britain* en route to Australia. Many of these stories were conceived on the way to and from France via Brittany Ferries. Such situations can concentrate the mind wonderfully well!

It is often said the printed word says a good deal about the author. If this is so, I trust the reader will judge me kindly.

Geoffrey Crees, summer 2017

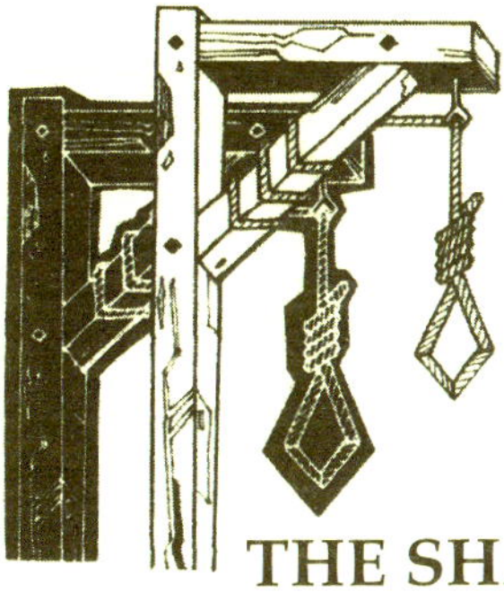

THE SHADOW OF THE NOOSE

A FANTASY STORY

Social media had been buzzing. Many people believed him to be innocent, including those in semi-secret Churches, such as Olivia; but all appeals exhausted, Harri stepped out of his cell with his prison officer beside him for the very short walk to the scaffold, where the noose was facing him, and he could espy a coffin in the corner. Beside the governor was the chaplain and one other jailer.

"Anything to say, Janze, before we carry out the sentence of the court?"

"No, sir!" Harri had grown accustomed to respect authority.

"Take one step forward."

At that moment Harri bent down, whipped out his taser gun and fired it rapidly at all four men, who before they could press an alarm were writhing on the floor. For good measure Harri shot off the noose, which dropped off with a plonk on to the governor's nose. Harri got the bunch of keys from the officials and sped down the corridor, unlocking several cells as he went out into the prison yard. Just then he caught sight of a Fresco delivery van, jumped in, pushing the driver out with force, rendering him unconscious in the process, and at the last moment Harri grabbed the driver's cap. The gates having been opened already, he sped out wearing the cap, so the gate official assumed Harri was the delivery driver. Once outside in the cobbled street, he drove across to what, in fact, was the top of a steep hill with steps on its narrow sides.

Back in the prison chaos reigned when, at last, the panic button was pressed; in the meantime some twenty prisoners had escaped, though only two got outside the walls, and another three sat outside their cells not knowing quite what to do.

Eventually some sort of order was restored, but most assumed that Janze had been 'topped', and it was a long while before his escape had been realised.

Having steered the electric van to the top of the hill he let it go, whilst he jumped out, forgetting to take the cap with him. Rushing straight into the nearest shop, a hairdresser's, he grabbed a gown, draped it round himself and sat in a chair.

The assistant, who was engrossed in the happenings outside the shop, did not realise his presence for quite a while. She turned, realised she had a customer, and asked if she could be of help.

"Just a trim of the beard, please."

"Certainly, sir."

Harri was also in a state of shock now, as being addressed as 'sir', and in the presence of a young woman, were never in his thoughts in the long years of planning his escape from captivity. He noticed her name was 'OLIVIA' with 'hairdressing assistant' on her badge, which made him wonder if she was the assistant, who is the boss?

He soon got the answer when she called out, "I've got a customer, Mrs Trinkwasser."

"Carry on, dear" came a slurred voice from the back of the shop.

For Mrs Trinkwasser, drinking water was always last on her mind, and she spent most of her days in the back of the shop with her favourite vodka bottle.

Outside, the delivery van careered down the steep hill,

with a few early morning shoppers leaping out of the way, until it shot out into the muddy, murky waters of the river, where it slowly sank with just the top of the cab showing. A passing police officer, wondering as to the fuss, shouted for the small crowd to keep back, to no avail.

"Was the driver in it?" and "Where did it come from?" were the questions circulating among the bystanders.

The officer duly called for backup, which was delayed because of the chaotic scenes inside and outside the prison.

"Could you deal with a couple of blackheads, please?" asked Harri.

"Certainly, sir. I'll just get my plastic gloves and tweezers."

Olivia was wondering, 'Who is this guy? It can't be Harri Janze, who was hung this morning; maybe it is his twin brother come to watch the notice being put on the prison wall.'

Minor operation over, Harri whispered, "Can you help me? I haven't any money on me," at the same time noticing that Olivia had beautiful olive-coloured eyes.

'Oh, oh, oh,' thought Harri.

"That's OK. Come back later today when the bank is open."

"No, I haven't any money anywhere, and my urgent need is somewhere to hide."

At this the penny dropped in Olivia's young mind. Yes, it was the famous/infamous Harri Janze, but what was he doing here? Why wasn't he dead? Did the hangman's rope break? She had heard such stories in the past.

"Quick – while Mrs Trinkwasser is asleep!" (Which in fact she was most of the time.)

The shop was built into the hillside with plenty of rooms downstairs. A room was found, unkempt but lockable with a toilet inside. In fact, Harri could not believe his luck – he had escaped the noose, escaped prison and now was smitten by Olivia, his saviour. He gladly assented to being locked in and for extra security shut himself in the toilet.

"I shall have customers waiting – but trust me, I'll come back with some food and a spare key so you can go your own way once the fuss is over."

'Trust me' – Harri had not heard such words for years. Food was, of course, the last thing on his mind since his last requested meal was fillet steak, fresh broad beans, new potatoes, Yorkshire pudding and gravy followed by a large helping of plum duff, custard and ice cream.

The prison chef was not really pleased to get up earlier than usual and thought to himself that, with all that food, either he would swing quickly or the rope would break!

The civil guard having been called out, some sort of order was restored, interrupted by numerous TV camera crews, whose personnel soon set up their satellite dishes and put their vans where they thought fit in the narrow streets. Many of the residents desiring their moment of fame queued up in front of the cameras to tell their stories, many of which were elaborated and embellished with "I saw him – such a wicked look in his eyes" and so on.

At 10.30 a.m. a statement was read on national TV to the effect that there was a brief delay in the execution of Harri Janze and that no one in the prison service was available for interview. "Another last-minute appeal" was one passing comment.

The regional administrator appeared from some thirty kilometres away, but found it difficult to get through the crowds. When he did eventually get to the governor's office he met with the four officials, who were still confused and bemused by what had happened.

"Have you any explanations before I sack you – including you, Mr Chaplain?"

The chaplain thought this a bit harsh as he only came into the prison for executions. No other religious practices were normally allowed.

Crowds gathered above the riverbank, and spotlights and floodlights were soon shining on the delivery van or as much as was above the murky waters. Then the delivery man's cap floated to the surface.

"Poor Tom, he must have drowned when the van went into the water."

"A judgment on him, I say – he was always late with his deliveries" was a more severe comment.

The TV crews rushed down the hill, slipping and sliding on the cobbles as they went. Inside the prison it was discovered in the confusion that Tom, the delivery driver, had been taken to the prison hospital, where he recounted his story of being thrown out of his van by an escaping prisoner. The head of the civil guard put two and two together and concluded that, in his attempt to escape, Harri Janze had, in fact, driven the van into the river and had drowned.

At noon a press conference was called outside the prison gates and a statement issued to the effect that Harri Janze due to be executed that morning had escaped and commandeered a delivery van, but had lost control down the hill, plunged into the river and had been drowned.

Heavy lifting gear was to be employed next day to recover the van and the body of the prisoner. Media questions flowed thick and fast.

How many prisoners had escaped? Were they still at large? How did the condemned man get his gun? Did the governor die when he was shot? And many more as well. The media were beside themselves in their frustration and asked anybody they could find for their story.

The regional administrator held up his hands and shouted, "That is all." Then he turned on his heels and disappeared inside the prison.

Harri, of course, was quite oblivious to all this, though he could hear hurried footsteps in the street and distant raised voices. All there was to read was old hairdressing magazines and a dirty old Bible, which he ignored apart from noticing the words 'Trust in Jesus' in the latter.

He thumbed through each edition of the magazine until his attention was caught by the heading 'Young Hairdresser of the Year Awards' and saw a picture of Olivia receiving her prize. He could not believe his eyes!

The sound of a key turning in the lock distracted him.

"Harri are you there?" It was Olivia whispering to him. With hurried breath she recounted all she knew of the day's happenings, much of which came from the seemingly endless TV interviews. "Nobody knows you are here. They think you drowned in the river. Tonight I will borrow my uncle's pickup truck and take you to a place of greater safety."

True to her word, in spite of the armed police around, Olivia came with the pickup truck, loaded with bales of hay for delivery. She had chopped a couple of bales in the yard, which smelt strongly of cow dung and urine.

"Climb in the back under the bales," she instructed.

"Not in this suit - they smell a bit high."

"You have no choice," she remonstrated.

Soon they were on their way out into the country.

Olivia should have explained that her uncle's farm was divided in two when the country was split apart, so his pickup was a familiar sight crossing the border. The guards, who had taken a few drinks to celebrate, as they saw it, Harri's death by drowning, rather than hanging, did not look twice as they saw the vehicle approaching.

When it duly stopped they gave it barely a glance, and drew even further back when they smelt its load. Waved on through, Olivia sped along the side road by the river, stopping outside some small farm buildings, and a cottage used as a gîte.

"Harri, help me with these bales."

Despite Harri's reluctance, the van was soon unloaded.

Keys to the gîte in her hand, she showed Harri his new abode. He could hardly believe his eyes - it was small, clean and comfortable.

"Here is a box of food for four or five days and some clean clothes. Just lie low and give me Mr Trinkwasser's suit. I will get it rapidly cleaned and hang it on the hook in the office and Mrs T. will never know."

He took all the precautions he could, such as not switching on any lights, refusing to flush the toilet and so on. On the second night there was a knock on the door.

'Oh no, the police have tracked me down, even if I am across the border.'

He looked through the spyhole and saw a small elderly man with an even smaller elderly lady. The man wore a rough woollen coat with a strange hat. Obviously not the police, but it might have been a trap to lure Harri to open the door. Lie low Olivia had said, so without more ado he silently crept back into the room.

Old Mr Smykna had always been curious about who stayed in the cottage, and sometimes popped in to say hello. However, he assumed the place was unoccupied despite his dog having great sniffs around the door. He eventually surmised that whoever unloaded the hay bales had popped into the cottage to see all was well.

'Still,' he thought, 'there is something strange. I'll try again in a day or two.'

But he never did.

The repercussions of the escape were far-reaching. Prison Officer Vadka was summoned before the authorities. He had not dared say he had lost his stun gun for fear of reprimand, yet when Harri had found and later used it he knew worse was to come.

The new governor was incandescent with rage. "If it was left to me, I would send you to the gallows instead of Janze, but imprisoned you will be until a trial can be arranged. GET OUT!"

The media began to lose interest in the story, all except a young British journalist called Danny. As he was confined to a wheelchair it took longer to arrange a flight and a hotel suitable for his needs. His sister-in-law, who acted as his carer, knew that Danny had a good 'nose' for a story.

Very few doubted that Harri had drowned in the delivery van, and that his body had been washed down to the sea. The district and national authorities really wanted to cover it up, so it was officially decreed that, whilst the escape of a condemned man was regrettable, justice of a sort had been done, and it was said that when Janze's body was eventually recovered a proper inquest would take place.

Harri, of course oblivious to all this, was now getting rather bored, but he dared not step outside even if the sun was shining. The literature in the cottage was a pile of farming and holiday magazines, but tucked at the back was a book entitled *Bibllia*.

'Strange,' he thought. 'That's similar to the book among the hairdressing magazines at my previous abode.' He, of course, had not been allowed any reading material, let alone girlie magazines in the condemned cell.

He was taunted by other prisoners along the corridor: "Cor, Harri, you should see this one! But where you're going you won't want pics of any sort."

The key turned slowly in the lock and Harri's heart missed a beat. It could only be his rescuer, his saviour. It was. There was Olivia, dressed in a very smart olive-green coat and skirt to match. Although he was still wondering why she had never shopped him to the authorities, knowing that the penalty for her actions could also lead to a death sentence. He stood in the half-light of a full moon, full of admiration for her, and realised, for the first time, how beautiful she was.

"Quick – get in the car. All you need is in the boot."

Harri did not need telling twice, and soon they were on their way. The autoroute to Valge appeared. Harri was dumbfounded. Perhaps he had died, and in the company of Olivia was now in heaven – which he hardly believed in, but if this was it, great!

"Fish in my bag, and you will find your new passport."

Harri did so and, to be sure, there was his picture, minus beard, with a different hairstyle, looking quite unlike his prison self. He looked at the name: Henry Zanje. He was a new person! This new person had many questions.

"What did you do with my prison clothes, especially my boots?"

"Oh, I separated them out, making sure I had plastic gloves on, and threw them separately into the river, where they will sink to the bottom. They may find other items and just assume you struggled to free yourself when the delivery van went into the river. The River Sle stinks. Our city needs a modern sewage system like other countries."

"Where are we going?" asked Harri. "I notice we are on our way to Valge. It's getting late."

"Well, do you know I won a hairdressing competition?"

"I certainly do. I saw it in the mags on my first day of freedom."

Olivia was now full of pride. "The prize was three nights in a five-star hotel on the outskirts of Valge. The Forest Park Hotel is just about the best in the Trek Republic. The only problem was I had no one to go with and the authorities were reluctant to let me go alone. The Police Superintendent offered a sort of bribe and said I could go if he could come with me. However, I did meet this British guy called Danny, who is in a wheelchair. He finds it difficult to get about at the best of times what with the cobbles on our ancient streets. His sister-in-law, Rachel, is a fantastic girl (I thought at first she was his wife!). She managed to get the booking. I, too, now have a fake passport, just in case. Eric, a man in our village, has a thriving business so many people want to escape. I had no problem crossing the border to get to the gîte. The guards recognised me and merely said, 'No hay bales this time, lass? Boy, don't they stink! Quite unlike the perfume you are wearing.' So they let me through in our little Fiat. I shall need both documents, just in case."

It was quite late when they got to the hotel.

"Shall I put your car in the garage?" asked the doorman. He was thinking most people did not arrive in Fiats, but said nothing.

"George will show you to your rooms," said the receptionist.

'Rooms?' thought Harri. His idea of heaven had extended to spending the night with Olivia.

Olivia could see how his mind was thinking. She said, "Sorry, Harri, I like you a lot, but I don't love you. Sleep well - see you in the morning. How about a swim before breakfast?"

What a room! It had everything. Fresh fruit, fresh flowers. Harri could not believe it at first. The room below the hairdresser's, then the gîte, but now this was like a palace. He drew back the curtains and looked at the lights of the city he had only heard of and never dreamed of visiting.

He called out through the wall, "Olivia, are you there? Look at the view."

But Olivia was exhausted and was sound asleep dreaming of—?

Before long Harri was also comatose.

A knock came at the door, and after enquiring a maid came in with a trolley, drew back the curtains and asked him if he had slept well.

Fifteen minutes later, there was another knock and Olivia enquiring, "Are you ready, Harri? Your swimming trunks are in the bag."

With some reluctance, Harri changed, noticing the olive colour to go with the olive tracksuit and trainers.

"Harri, are you ready?" This girl was getting a little impatient, not realising, of course, Harri was not looking forward to getting in the water.

However, before too long he opened the door and Olivia was also attired in an olive tracksuit, so together they went down to the lovely heated indoor pool.

"Not bad, if I may say so," said Harri as he admired himself in the full-length mirror.

In all his time in prison he had done at least twenty-five press-ups morning and night plus various other exercises, which had kept him very fit.

"Don't know why you are doing that," said Vadka, his officer for his last morning on earth. "You won't be able to run from those gallows!"

But that is exactly what Harri did.

All the training did very well when he needed to sprint through the prison yard and climb aboard Tom's delivery van.

He thought to himself, 'Perhaps there is a shallow end' as he emerged from the shower on to the poolside. It was empty apart from Olivia, who emerged from the ladies' changing room in the most microscopic olive bikini, which left little to male imagination.

"Stop gawping; in we get!" cried Olivia, pushing him into the deep end, not knowing Harri's fear of water and that he could not swim. However, his fears were cut short as she got under his arms and hauled him to the side, which he clutched in terror, spluttering out the chlorine water as quickly as possible. "Stay there, Harri. I'll help you out when I've done a length or two." And, with that, she swam off with the agility of a seal.

'Rescued again,' thought Harri. 'Is there anything this girl cannot do?'

The three days passed very quickly – sightseeing, the ballet and a great concert were all part of a heady exotic mix. Anyone watching would think they were lovers, but Harri soon got the message that any physical approach would be rebuffed, so he tried with great difficulty to play the brother/cousin role. He was so grateful for his freedom.

All too soon it was time to say goodbye.

"Look, Harri," said Olivia, "Mrs Trinkwasser has given me notice and I now have some money to help you. Here are the keys of a flat and a map showing how to find it. I suggest you enrol for, say, some English lessons and perhaps a job-assessment course. I really have enjoyed helping you – it has been the most exciting time of my life. When you get to the flat ring Mrs Staplex. She will come and clean once a week, change your sheets and do your washing and ironing. Her number is by the phone."

"I don't know what to say," he replied somewhat tearfully. "You are indeed my saviour" – not knowing what it really meant. "One thing more: I'm very intrigued – you surely don"t want a passport to get home."

"Oh, all right, then." It was Olivia's turn to show reluctance, but she passed it over. "Have a look, then."

Harri was indeed gobsmacked – he had a new name and now this woman had his name on her passport. And, with that, he grasped her in his arms and kissed her passionately on the lips. She tried to resist, at least for a short while.

"I don't think I shall be back and you can't leave" were Olivia's parting words.

'I guess if they ever come back, they won't want single rooms,' thought the receptionist as they left.

All too soon the little Fiat was on its way. Tears were the order of the day as Harri packed his own bags and found the keys to the flat that was to be his home for three months.

"No need for security now," he said to himself. "All the same, better be careful," he added as he patted the stun gun in his left sock.

He duly enrolled in the English classes, where his hunger to learn made him top student. Fortunately no one wanted to know his background, and when he went for a drink with his fellows he kept quiet about his past and concentrated on knowing more about the others.

The vocational course proved more of a problem, but eventually his tutor, a woman in her late fifties, suggested journalism.

"What me?" cried Harri, who all along thought being a PE teacher might be his forte.

So he enrolled in the journalism course, finding that the money Olivia had left him was more than enough. Nobody questioned that he paid in cash or asked whether he had a bank account.

When the course duly assembled there were fifteen students, all from different backgrounds, some in their early fifties. The tutor, who was obviously well versed in the media world, made sure everyone introduced themselves and said why they had come. One or two said a great deal about themselves, but all Harri could say was that he was interested in the stories of other people's lives. ('If only you knew what my story is,' he thought to himself.)

The tutor outlined the structure of the course, about the principles of journalism, etc. "Next week I intend to introduce you to a young British friend, Danny, who is, in fact, disabled, and is staying in Valge. He will enlighten you about the press in the UK, and tell you what it is like to succeed in journalism against the odds."

Harri thought little about this, but looked forward to using his new-found knowledge of English.

The arrangement with Mrs Staplex worked very well. She was a friend of Olivia's mother, who had fled Valge many years before. Harri slept a good deal better. Gone were the nightmares of prison life and fleeing from the police. Instead he dreamed of Olivia and her minuscule bikini in the swimming pool.

As Mrs Staplex changed the sheets on his bed she noticed the stains and concluded, 'The young man needs a wife. I'll try to find someone for him.'

"Oh, Harri," she called, "how are you getting on with all that learning?"

"Oh, Mrs Staplex, I really enjoy the English lessons and I have enrolled on a journalism course."

She had no idea who Harri was – just a friend of a

friend, and that was good enough for her, even if she did wonder how he could afford the rent of the flat as well as her generous wages. 'Students', she thought to herself, 'are more likely to be poverty-stricken than well off, as this chap seems to be.'

"Oh, by the way, this came for you," said Mrs Staplex.

Harri was delighted to take the parcel.

"Expect it's all you need to be a journalist."

Without opening it, he put it to one side.

Olivia knew her fake passport would not cause her problems. She had assumed that the railway security staff would be less intrusive than those at her road border. However, this turned out to be the opposite. One inquisitive control guard took one look at the name and called his superior officer. Olivia gave him her most beguiling smile.

"You're related to that arch-criminal that escaped the gallows only to be drowned."

"Oh no," cried Olivia in mock distress. "Oh no, he was my brother-in-law." Tears rolled down her cheeks and she explained she had been in the Recht Republic for the past two months.

"What were you doing there?" The officer duo were getting more and more suspicious.

Olivia, who had done more than her fair share of lying in recent times, replied, "Oh, I was running a course."

"What in?" asked the senior official as he realised that he was the senior official and had his role to fufil.

"In hairdressing."

"Hairdressing!" he uttered, with disbelief written all over his face.

"Haven't the people of Recht anybody else to teach them?"

However, the younger official was now beginning to feel really sorry for this young lady. The flow of tears had dried to a trickle, and Olivia gave him the most winsome of smiles.

"Captain," he said, "if I may offer an opinion, I think this young lady deserves our sympathy. It is all very distressing for her and there is no reason for us to detain her or even arrest her. I suggest we search her and let her go."

The Captain's hard heart was also beginning to melt. "OK, we will get Lieutenant Podka to do it."

Olivia was very unused to being searched and was startled for a moment, but obediently picked up her case and followed.

Lieutenant Podka was everything Olivia was not. She was of vast build and had been a successful shot-putter in her youth.

"Many people think that by travelling by train to our beloved country they can be smarter than the border guards?"

"It is not so."

"Will you undress to your underwear?"

Olivia found this acutely embarrassing since there was no cubicle to offer any privacy, but under the officer's watchful gaze she removed her outer garments.

"And what is that?" Her interrogator was becoming more and more aggressive as well as curious.

"That is my gold cross. It belonged to my grandmother."

"Here."

So reluctantly she handed it over to this woman, who was becoming her captor.

"You know we don't allow these obsolete symbols in our country. And what do I find here?" she added as she pulled a New Testament from inside Olivia's pocket. "Stay here – I will report this to my superiors."

Olivia, now feeling cold, dejected and almost naked, thought, 'Harri would know how to get out of this. He escaped from something far worse.'

But she simply prayed, "Lord, help me. I need You now!"

Lieutenant Podka returned with the two other officers,

who could not believe their eyes at Olivia's state of undress let alone her acute distress.

The Captain said, "Olivia Janze, you will be charged with bringing subversive material into our beloved country, but to avoid that let me make you an offer - an offer that will give you your freedom." There was a long, long pause. "Spend the night with me, and any charges will be forgotten."

Olivia could not believe her ears. She had been praying before, but now it became earnest. Should she sacrifice her virginity for freedom? Not for someone she did not know or care for.

"Come on, young woman, make up your mind. This is your escape route."

"OK," she said, not realising what she was saying. It was the Captain's turn to be surprised, his lips almost salivating at the thought of sex with so lovely a woman.

Olivia was beginning to sense some sort of empowerment.

"OK, on these conditions: first, could I have my clothes back."

The thought of the prisoner dressing again certainly disappointed both men, but not Lieutenant Podka.

"Yes, we agree for now," said the Captain, dreaming of what might be ahead, having viewed Olivia in her underwear. "And the second condition?"

Olivia, emboldened by what she later described as God's Holy Spirit, replied, "My second condition is that I have back my Cross and New Testament, and that all four of us read it together for at least half an hour."

This was too much for Lieutenant Podka, who disappeared as other passengers were being detained.

The Captain thought long and hard and realised the initiative had now flowed from himself to the captive and did not know quite what to do. Gone was the swagger and bluster and the thought of sexual bribery, which he would have kept from his superiors - along with his younger subordinates, who would have to be silenced. Although a brutal regime ruled the land – hence Harri's false imprisonment – the border guards were trained to give a smarter, gentler image. Yes, corruption, greed, lies, torture and harassment might be the order of the day, but the so-called 'beloved' country tried, as best it could, to soften the image in dealing with the outside world. There was a real reluctance to embrace forgiveness – hence the problems. The Captain, who had the power to detain Olivia for just one night in a prison cell instead of a hotel bedroom, simply had to admit defeat. He was baffled. What had this lovely young woman got that he did not possess? Here was a dilemma indeed. He knew his subordinates would gossip; his potential liaison with Olivia would soon get back to his wife and family, let alone his superiors.

He called his junior and Lieutenant Podka together and outlined the problem. Lieutenant Podka was all for taking the matter to a higher authority, thinking there might be some money to be made if they all kept quiet, as she had neither the nous nor the experience to deal with it; all she knew was that the Captain really fancied Olivia, and she was jealous of the power her boss had since he and Olivia were almost the same age.

Olivia, meanwhile, sensing her spiritual and psychological victory was almost at hand, sat in a corner, wrapped herself in a blanket and tried not to shiver.

After long discussions, in which the phrase 'We must hush this up' was used more than once, the Captain indicated that his juniors would also be implicated, especially as he noticed how his sergeant behaved towards Olivia.

Eventually it was agreed that they would let Olivia go, but only after a night in a cell, as that way they could be seen to have been doing their duty, and no one would be implicated in any wrongdoing.

After a time, Olivia felt bold enough to pray. The

shivering stopped. She shut her eyes, folded her hands and said, very quietly, "Lord, I have got myself in this mess; can You, please, get me out as soon as possible. I pray for these border guards, who do not know You. Soften their hearts, not because I want to be free, but potentially they are Your children."

The Captain found her and thought she was asleep in the chair. Then he noticed her lips moving, which he decided was most odd, and so he coughed loudly. Olivia was startled.

"What are you doing?" he demanded.

"I was praying – and praying for you especially."

The Captain was taken aback. "Praying? Is that what you Christians do?"

"Yes, much of the time, and not just in tricky situations like this one, but thanking God for all His love."

"I see." The Captain was searching for appropriate words. "Here is an answer to your prayers, if that is what you want. You know I have the power to detain you without trial, indefinitely, on a charge of bringing subversive material into our beloved country, but we will put you in a cell for one night, and you can go in the morning. I am confiscating that New Testament, but you can have that Cross back since it is of such sentimental value to you."

In spite of the hard bed, Olivia slept soundly. The cell was surprisingly comfortable, with a shower and a toilet. In her dreams she thought of Harri – the first time she had thought of him for such a long time. Was it thirty-six hours ago she last saw him?

Next morning, after a reasonable breakfast, another guard showed her the way out and, surprisingly, she found a taxi to take her to her home village. What a story she would have to share with her small church, which met in secret, and not least with her pastor, who often had to be kept in hiding. She counted her money, which had all been returned to her, and decided to ask the taxi driver to take her through the city.

They bumped along the cobbled streets, much to the annoyance of her driver, who was thinking what might happen to his vehicle's suspension.

Olivia saw her old hairdresser's, now boarded up, and then they continued down to the Sle river.

"That's where that Janze chap drowned after escaping the gallows," said the driver, not knowing, of course, that his lovely passenger knew him.

On they sped until, at last, she was being greeted by her parents and sisters.

Meanwhile, at the border post, the Captain locked himself in the toilet and began to read the confiscated New Testament. His report would contain some half-truths, but he felt he could get away with it. He found a plastic bag, put in the book and hid it in the cistern – the last place anyone would think of looking for it, and anyway his report would say it was burnt.

After a couple of days' home rest, Olivia tried to consider her future. Her father worked in a factory owned by the government which made military uniforms. He possibly could get her a job there, but her hairdressing skills would not be much use.

Eventually she opted to help on her uncle's farm. She knew that she would be recognised as she crossed the border, but after a while she was usually waved through since she always returned at the same time each day.

One night her pastor came to see her. It was a risky business, but he made sure he was not followed. Could she help? He explained that some Christians in the Recht Republic wanted to send some books they had printed in their own language. "Can you pick them up?"

Olivia thought long and deep. "Yes," she said, "I'll risk it. I am such a familiar sight going with bales of hay and straw in my uncle's pickup."

And so she was able to do this several times. She even looked at the books, and one copy seemed to stand out – it had a strange picture on the front. It was called *Jeffrey's Shorts*. 'Doesn't look very Christian to me,' she thought. However, her pastor was very happy for her to keep it as she said she was sure she knew someone who would enjoy it.

The spring turned to summer and the farm work grew less and less as her uncle decided to sell his cattle, and so there was no need for Olivia to make her trips across the border. Every day she thought of Harri, but there was no way to communicate with him. Only government-approved telephone calls were allowed and all private letters were opened and most of them confiscated. She found some money she had hidden under the floorboards and booked a train (now reduced to one a week) to Valge. Amazingly it was the same taxi driver who took her to the station.

"Not going to drive over the cobblestones again. (They are worse than the potholes, and they are bad enough.) Don't get many bookings these days; money is so short – the land is going from bad to worse."

Olivia was aware of the dire economic problems her country faced, and in some ways felt she was becoming a burden to her family. There were lots of hugs and tears as she said goodbye, maybe for the last time. Her father pressed a small copy of the New Testament into her hands. It was not dissimilar to the one the Captain in the border control room had confiscated. That copy was now becoming quite dog-eared, as every time he was on duty he fished out the plastic bag from the cistern.

"Our Captain must have had prunes for breakfast, or he has constipation" was the Sergeant's comment, observing his superior's frequent trips to the toilet.

The taxi driver switched on to the state radio (that was

all there was) and to his surprise he could hear church bells, which got louder and louder as they approached the city.

"Stand by for a solemn announcement. At 8.21 this morning our president died of a sudden heart attack. . . ."

('More like a condemnation,' thought the taxi driver.)

At the risk of being late for her train, Olivia asked the driver to stop so they could listen to the ancient crackly radio.

"The Vice President has declared a national holiday, political prisoners are being released and border controls abandoned. Stand by for further announcements."

"Let's dance," Olivia said to the driver, and before long he was hauled out of his cab and they twirled around together. Soon many others joined in; flags and bunting were found and music echoed from many a home. The church bells so long silent just got louder and louder. Breathless with joy and excitement, Olivia and the driver got back in the cab and resumed the journey.

"Praise the Lord!" exclaimed Olivia.

"Praise the Lord indeed!" he echoed.

"Are you a Christian?" enquired Olivia.

"Yes, I am, but in secret for many years. If the authorities knew, I would lose my job."

"That's all in the past," she said.

With much honking, and also waving to the increasing crowds, they made it to the station, and to her surprise the train was still there. She paid her fare and said goodbye, sealing it with a kiss on the cheek.

"The train driver is probably celebrating the news somewhere nearby. I just hope he doesn't have too much to drink!"

As she walked along the platform, out of the corner of her eye she noticed the border control captain – he had a coy smile as did Lieutenant Podka. How could the Captain be so happy? After all he was losing his job. He waved as the train drew out of the station. In his hand was the New Testament he had purloined from Olivia.

The journey to Valge was uneventful except for the continual noise, some of it alcohol-related, as the freedom of her country was being enjoyed and celebrated. She wondered about Harri. How was he? Was he still keeping fit? How was his English? Had he completed his journalism course? And so on.

After a tiring but exhilarating journey she found his flat and rang the bell, and Harri, looking fitter than ever, opened the door. They fell into each other's arms.

"Come home, Harri, and marry me," was all Olivia could say.

The wedding took place on a beautiful spring day in a small country church where the scent of flowers in the air and the heady oxygen of freedom still abounded. The Captain was Harri's best man and the pastor excelled himself in the conduct of the service.

The reception also had the feeling of new life and exultation, with many commenting that this could never have happened in the old regime.

Harri and Olivia spent their honeymoon in a small hotel not far away. Their wedding night was all any young married couple could have wished for.

As they eventually settled down to sleep Olivia remarked, "Are you keeping your socks on, Harri?"

"Have to keep my stun gun somewhere" was his sleepy reply.

ENOUGH SAID

Cedric was one of those characters, perhaps one in a million, the sight of whom for most people produced more than a smile, and sometimes a real laugh. He had a laugh like Tommy Cooper and a chin like Tommy Trinder.

His family, and not only his family, were often saying, "You should go on the stage, Ced."

"No way," he replied. "They would only laugh at me."

Instead he became a plumber.

Ced grew up an only child. The neighbours suspected, though they never said, that his parents did not feed him properly. This was not true. When he was around eleven his mother decided to take him to the doctor, as his rapid growth in height was beginning to worry her.

His mother was reassured by medical opinion that she had nothing to worry about and that nature must take its course.

As they left the surgery Ced enquired, "What was that all about? Are you worried?"

"I'm not."

With a grunt the eleven-year-old expostulated, "Well, I feel a foot taller than when I went in," which made his mother wonder if she had a budding comedian on her hands.

Of course, there were practical problems, not least that Cedric's bed was too short.

"I'll fix that," said Cedric's father, whose DIY skills fell way below his claims and ambitions.

So, with a lot of banging, hammering and so on, Cedric's sleeping arrangements were improved, even if it meant propping up one side of the bed with a small wooden chest, which invariably slid away some time in the early hours, much to Cedric's discomfort and dismay.

The time came for Cedric to leave school with a trail of reports which, as well as the usual 'Could do better', gave full recognition to the possibility that he was unemployable except as a funny man.

His sports master thought he might make a good goalkeeper, but he couldn't kick a ball straight and even slipped over when taking a goal kick much to the amusement of the other players. Cedric got up with a big grin on his face, and wiped his hand across his chin, which made him look like someone who had just finished an assault course.

The PE teacher, not to be outdone, thought he could be a good high jumper, but, when Cedric tried, his legs got mixed up with the bar and he collapsed in a tangled heap of arms and legs. Fellow athletes just fell about laughing.

"This guy is so funny" was the general view, though one or two just thought him a real twit.

Girls? Well, one or two admired him for trying, but didn't fancy him as they thought they would look silly in his company. Anyway at this stage Cedric felt too shy to ask any of them out. He tried flexing his muscles, but his biceps looked like mere pimples on his arms.

Teenage gossip among the girls considered his physique and then dissolved into giggles, especially when Babs said, "He may not have any muscles, but I bet he has got a funny bone!"

However, Cedric managed to get a job with a local heating and plumbing firm, Lush & Co. Unlike his father, he became good with his hands, but it proved tricky for him when working in awkward places. He quickly became pals with Sebastian, who was a couple of years older than him. Seb, as he liked to be called, was always willing to help out, and before long the two became good friends both at work and in their spare time.

The firm's boss, Frank, recognised their companionship, and arranged for them to go together on jobs. 'At least he will calm young Cedric down a little,' he thought.

One day Cedric was left on his own and somehow he forgot to turn a valve off with the result that water flooded through a ceiling and Mrs Thompson, whose house it was, angry and distressed at the mess, spent some time ringing the firm and demanding compensation.

"She was in floods of tears," recalled Cedric as he met up with Seb at the local where they went once a week.

"I bet she was!" replied Seb. "Mr Lush wants to see you tomorrow at 8.30 a.m. prompt. I guess you are for the high jump."

Cedric with his memories of disastrous events at school merely grunted, "I'll talk him out of it."

The next morning Ced presented himself outside the manager's office, which was marked 'Lush & Co.' Such a description was not lost on Ced.

Mr Lush was in his most irascible mood. He stared Ced in the face – in fact it was a repeat performance of a confrontation with his wife an hour ago. Ced stood before him – in fact, towered over him.

Frank Lush felt rather small. He had been with the firm many years and had followed his father, Samuel, into the business. Many remarked that F. Lush had followed S. Lush in the trade.

"It was like this . . ." Ced began his explanation. Ced, in addition to his jokes and comic skills, had developed what his parents called the gift of the gab, or, more strictly true, the gift of the gob.

"Good," said Mr Lush. "I'm listening," but he had decided on his way to work that Ced deserved the sack.

Ced was now at his most eloquent as he explained that

the plumbing system in Mrs Thompson's house was very old and that it was surprising it hadn't leaked in the past. Before long Mr Lush noticed what he thought was the merest twinkle in Ced's eye. The five minutes Mr Lush had allowed for the interview extended to half an hour as Ced was in full flight. Ced leaned forward and caught Mr Lush eyeball to eyeball. He was now the one who felt intimidated, and ever so slightly slipped back in his chair as Ced almost bent over him with his lucid explanation.

"That stupid woman! Why didn't she say her system was so antiquated?"

"Enough, Ced." Mr Lush plucked up courage.

"Enough said?" replied the villain-turned-hero. "I thought I was the one who cracked the jokes, not you, Mr Lush."

The latter was, in fact, so intimidated that he merely whispered, "Perhaps you had better get back to work, Ced."

Cedric stood tall. "OK, Mr Lush, I knew you would understand."

On the way back from lunch Ced and Seb were standing by the side of the road when a hearse came by.

"Bow down in respect," uttered Ced, and the two of them bent low. "How sad," whispered Ced, "but - do you know what? - I can't straighten up."

Seb, who had easily got back in an upright position, replied, "So you can't, Ced. You look like one of the giant pins my gran used to wear in her hair."

"Never mind your gran, get me out of this. All I can see are my size-14 boots and the pavement, and there don't seem to be too many gold coins to make my stay worthwhile."

By now a small crowd had gathered wondering why Cedric was in such a position.

"Still breathing," said one man.

"That's encouraging," said another.

"I had an uncle who got like that. He were like it for years. When 'e died they 'ad to cut 'im in 'alf and put one part in one coffin and the other in another; but the undertaker charged double."

"Are you in pain?" enquired the earnest Seb.

"No, not exactly, but it's not what I planned to do this afternoon."

"Isn't that the lad who works for Lush, the plumbers?" asked a newcomer to the group, overcome with curiosity at Ced's plight. "I know what you are trying to do – give the impression of a U-bend. It looks like a publicity stunt."

Ced shouted between his ankles, "This is no publicity stunt; it's for real. Can't you see I'm going red in the face?"

Nobody knew what to do.

After about twenty minutes a police car drew up and the officer enquired as to the problem.

Seb and Cedric shouted in unison what had happened, and Sergeant Moore, an experienced officer, said, "I have never seen anything like this before. I'll call for backup. Perhaps the garage down the road will have some heavy lifting gear which we can put around your waist."

By this time a female police officer had arrived and, anxious to help, lay down by Ced and looked up at him.

'This is all right,' he thought. 'She is about my age and blond too. This is the sort of sympathy I appreciate.'

Their eyes met, albeit in a strange position.

"Do you usually meet young women like this?" enquired Seb.

"Shut up, you nut. She only wants to help," replied Ced.

The older officer now wanted info. Info was what he liked.

"How did you get in this position?"

"Well, it was like this," replied Seb: "we saw this hearse go by and Ced said we should pay our respects, and that's all we did."

"But the hearse was empty! It passed me at quite a lick

and I was just about to book it for speeding!" replied Sergeant Moore.

"Oh, crumbs!" said Ced, as much to the young female officer lying at his feet as to the pavement.

The speculation and comment by the now sizeable crowd increased quite volubly when they were startled by the sound of an ambulance siren. At this point Cedric slowly but definitely drew himself out to his full length – all six foot seven inches of it.

"Praise the Lord!" ejaculated one woman. "A miracle! I've never seen a miracle."

However, the young woman who had been lying at Ced's feet, almost, but not quite, gazing into his eyes, was not so impressed. The Sergeant had thoughts about wasting police time as a TV crew and newspaper reporters drew up. One reporter dashed up to Ced, another to the young female arising from the gutter. The TV producer, wanting the story for the six o'clock news, made sure a mike was in Ced's face.

"What was it like down there?"

Cedric smiled. "Oh, it was nothing really. I enjoyed looking into that lovely police officer's eyes. Where is she?"

But she had quickly stood up and adjusted her clothing, and was quickly bundled into the police car by the Sergeant.

"Not much of a story here," shouted the producer, indicating to his staff that they had better news to report. "Not much of a story!" Ced's ire knew no bounds. His idea was his chance of five minutes of fame and he was not going to be denied. At this point the cameras were rapidly switched on again. Here, indeed, was a local story as Ced went into overdrive about how he had wanted to show his respects to the deceased, been locked double, how he had drawn a crowd and been smitten by the young female officer.

The reporter just managed to suppress a smirk, saying, "Well, it does seem a bit funny."

"Funny!" exploded Ced. "I want to be a comedian, but this was not funny."

In the end it did go out as the very last item on the local news under the title "Traffic held up whilst tall plumber makes a U-bend", but few people took much notice.

"Must be short of news today and they need to fill in the space" was the general verdict.

A week or so later in the bar of the Slagthorpe Working Men's Club the regulars - and there were not many of them - gathered for their usual pint or two.

"What are we going to do about the annual entertainment show?"

Now, the entertainment show had been a yearly ritual for as long as anyone could remember. Always taking place two weeks before Christmas, it had, in the past, drawn large crowds, but in latter years had seen numbers fall rapidly.

"We 'ave to 'ave a committee meeting," commented Edgar.

"We are the committee," said Wilf. "We're all here except 'Arry."

"Better get 'Arry and quick sharp too," said Edgar, drawing himself out to his full width, which was indeed quite considerable.

So Harry was summoned to the meeting, away from the TV which he habitually fell asleep in front of most evenings.

"I've called this meeting of committee to discuss the entertainment we put on for the old folks each year."

(The casual observer might have thought that most of the committee qualified under the latter title.)

"Let's draw up a list," suggested Wilf, presenting pen and paper.

Edgar warmed to his task (this was as much ritual as the show itself).

"Let me see. Last year we had The Treehouse Trio to sing."

"Not much cop," offered Harry.

The determined Edgar said, "They do sing some of those old songs and most people like to join in. We will start with them – that should warm everyone up." Edgar was very aware that this committee meeting was eating up his drinking time and he said so.

"Ha very ha ha," interrupted Sandy, who had said nothing up to this point. "Eating-up or drinking time?" he muttered.

"What about Suzie the stripper?" offered Wilf.

"No, she's past it!" responded Edgar.

"I don't think so; I think the old folk enjoyed it," responded Wilf, "especially the men!"

"'Arry here forgot to switch the lights off at the crucial point in her act, and she vowed never to come again." Sandy was now in full flight. "Don't suppose she will. We saw all we needed to twelve months ago, didn't we, 'Arry?" He gave Harry a nudge in the ribs.

"Didn't see nuffin'. I was floundering around looking for the light switch."

"OK," said the now impatient Edgar, "we will have to put her in. We've got no choice. We can't afford anyone else and she wouldn't get a booking at any other club, especially at 'er age. Is that all?" Edgar's voice was more a statement than a question.

"Just a mo," said Harry. "That young chap on the TV news the other night said he wants to be a comedian. Could give him a break. What's 'is name? Cedric something. Anyone know 'im?"

"Yes, I do." Edgar was now at his most expansive. "My sister 'ad 'im round. She's always used Lush & Co. for all her plumbing needs. Young Cedric came to unblock a sink, but when he did he managed to get water everywhere and she found her kitchen flooded. She was furious, but Cedric explained to her that because of modern plumbing systems there is something called a retro pressure valve which, in conjunction with the special pipework in the house, had failed to stop the leak. Ced didn't say anything about leaving a stopcock open. In full flight, Cedric had continued that this retro pressure valve was at fault, and someone near here had actually drowned as a result. In the end Doris felt really sorry for Cedric, with 'im not being able to get into tight corners cos of 'is 'ight. She readily offered £10 to the Distressed Plumbers' Society when, without a flicker of an eyelid, Cedric produced the appropriate envelope. It took her quite a while to get over her guilt, but she consoled herself with the thought of her generous gift to the Distressed Plumbers' Society."

"Book 'im, then. 'E'll come cheap, and by the time Suzie 'as finished there won't be anyone left. They'll be off to bingo as soon as they can."

So someone contacted Cedric. He was delighted with the offer, but said he would only do it if Seb could come too. 'Ced and Seb - I can see it in lights in the West End,' he thought.

"Didn't all the great comic acts start this way?"

"Not in the Slagthorpe WMC," commented his mother when she heard the news.

"Just one other item, gentlemen," remarked Edgar to the assembled group, who were half out of their seats on their way to the bar.

"What is it, then?" Impatience was, indeed, Sandy's strong suit.

"Well, gentlemen . . ."

The committee all thought it must be important if Edgar was addressing them as 'gentlemen' - not once, but twice.

"Out with it, man," cried Sandy, his voice hoarse with unslaked thirst.

"Well, a church wants to use the club on a Sunday."

"A Sunday! A church!" the group shouted in unison. "Whatever next!"

"Hear me out, chaps." 'Chaps' had now replaced 'gentlemen'. Edgar read out a letter which he had concealed from his fellow members. The relevant parts consisted of a request to use the bar room, but not other facilities, every Sunday.

"What are they willing to pay?" Harry, the treasurer, was always mindful of the debt the club was in and that bar takings had been dropping in recent years.

"Doesn't say," replied Edgar.

"Don't like it." Sandy was keen to end the meeting. "I've heard some of these religious groups are very odd - very odd indeed."

"Well, this chap calls himself Francis Wethered, and says he would like to meet us. Says he is the church pastor, whatever that is. Like a vicar, I guess."

"I've an idea," said Wilf, waking up at last. "Invite 'im to the entertainment. He'll love Suzie, the stripper."

"OK, let's get ourselves back to the bar, chaps. I'll ring Pastor Wethered at the Praise Be Fellowship, as they call themselves - PBF for short - but not to invite him to the entertainment. It's too risky."

The following week, Pastor Wethered and two of his fellow church members met up with Edgar and Wilf. The meeting turned out to be quite contrary to whatever Edgar expected it to be. The trio were smartly dressed and seemed genuinely pleased to find themselves in surroundings so unlike many church buildings!

"Before we start" - Edgar was back to his belligerent best - "I don't want any of my members getting involved in your religious antics."

"No fear of that," replied Pastor Wethered. "We just want to discuss what facilities you have, etc., and on what terms you are willing to let the bar room to us. But, before all that, I am going to ask Simon to lead us in prayer."

Edgar and Wilf, who had hoped for a brief meeting, and hadn't allowed for anything such as prayer, nearly fell off their bar stools.

"Lord, if it's Your will that the PBF use this club, please show us."

Secretly, Wilf thought that if this was all there was to this so-called prayer, he might investigate further as he had a mountain of problems he could use a bit of prayer for.

Before any further discussion could take place, Edgar produced a document which he said they could all agree to and each of them could sign.

"'Old on a bit!" said Wilf and Pastor Wethered in unison. "Let's see what we are all letting ourselves in for."

So five heads bent over the proposed agreement.

Wilf was baffled by the language, which consisted of plenty of *heretofore* and *in consideration of,* and so on.

"Could I examine it? I used to be a solicitor before I became a pastor."

It was Edgar's turn to be gobsmacked. He had persuaded a friend to draft the agreement. The friend had a father who had been a probate clerk, and so had absorbed a certain amount of legal know-how, forgetting the truth that a little knowledge is a dangerous thing. So the pastor read through the document and, in the end, there were a considerable number of corrections – so much so, that the pastor offered to mail the revised document.

"Don't do emails," replied Edgar and Wilf. "Why can't you use the old-fashioned phone?"

A week later they met up again, documents circulated, and before long it was agreed. And "Praise be, I'll make sure the bar is securely locked" was Edgar's whispered comment to Wilf. "Don't want my favourite beer to go down their throats. Talking of which, let's get some in before the rest arrive."

As they got to the bar, they realised the three church leaders were already there.

"What are you drinking?" asked Pastor Wethered.

Edgar, who had received enough shocks, replied in a somewhat deflated manner, "My usual," knowing that Terry, behind the bar, would know what 'usual' was.

After a while the company relaxed.

"Another?" asked Edgar.

"No, thanks, but how about a game of snooker?"

Edgar, who had been club champion for many years, thought it would be a way of showing who was boss!

"Well, Carlisle here can play a fair game. He's only twenty-three, but his father taught him. Carlisle, who had said very little up to this point, muttered, "OK, but I can't be much of a match for someone as experienced as you, Edgar."

"Carlisle - that's an unusual name. Is that where you come from? Didn't know they had sex in Carlisle," whispered Harry.

Those who heard the comment preferred to ignore it.

Now Pastor Wethered felt he had to comment: "You see, Edgar, our church is like a rack of snooker balls."

"Eh, what?"

Edgar was keen to get on with the game and show Carlisle who was champion.

Pastor Wethered continued, in full flight: "We have white people; we have Chinese, like Won Luke, that's the yellow ball; we have a German who is all for God's conservation, he's the green ball; we have some Indians, they're the brown ball, a fantastic guy called Sanjay, but he is from Sri Lanka."

Edgar had heard of Sri Lanka, but guessed it was in India somewhere.

"The blue ball is a bit more difficult to identify. Hildegard from Sweden has the most beautiful blue eyes."

At this Harry woke up. "Only blue people I knew were the Smurfs, but that dates me."

"Pink represents all the babies in the church; and black, that is me and Carlisle here."

Carlisle now had a brief moment to say that his parents came from Carlisle in Pennsylvania.

"Does that make him a Yank?" Harry was heard to mutter.

Again most people ignored the comment. They went through to the snooker room with its one very worn table and some layers of dust showing it had not been used for some while.

"You can break," encouraged Edgar, believing a minor triumph was in his grasp.

Carlisle carefully picked up a cue, looked down the line, and took up a very odd position, aiming to hit the balls Harry had racked by aiming for the cushion with the white ball. To everyone's astonishment, not least the pompous Edgar, the white ball caught the outside red, and it slowly went into the pocket. His break eventually faltered on sixty-seven.

Edgar could not believe it, but rode his luck as Carlisle had left him an easy red. Duly potted, Edgar looked for a colour. There wasn't an easy one, but he took on the black, hoping for as much fortune (as he saw it) as Carlisle had amassed. In his excitement his cue slipped. The white ball did indeed hit the black, but went in off - seven extra points to Carlisle, who duly cleared up.

All Edgar could manage was a begrudging, "Well done, young man."

He soon made his getaway, leaving Harry to tidy up.

"Thanks for the game," responded Carlisle. "See you on Sunday."

"What, me?" replied Harry.

"Yes, you are very welcome," intervened Pastor Wethered. "Edgar has lent us his spare key, so we shall be here at 8 a.m. to pray and set up."

"Don't know about that," replied Harry, wishing in some ways that the ground would swallow him up.

And where was Edgar when you needed him?

"Don't get up till ten-ish on a Sunday, and then I go to the Lion before coming on here for another and then getting home for one thirty. Missus has my dinner on the table by then; woe betide me if I'm late. By the way, you'll be gone by twelve - we don't want our regulars put off by religion!"

Harry gained assurances that they would all be gone by

the time the bar opened at midday.

They went their separate ways with Harry's parting shot: "See you on Saturday for the entertainment."

"We will have to see. I'll check with my deacons and we will pray about it."

'There they go again,' thought Harry, pausing to reflect, and slipping into his more cynical mode. 'If they come to the entertainment, I might just go to their church. If they play ball with me, I'll play ball with them.'

Cedric and Seb met up in the Lion to plan their act.

"Where are we going to start?"

Ced knew lots of jokes, and had brought lots of joke books to supplement his own ideas.

"Stories," whispered Seb, slipping into his fertile mode and downing his first pint. "Let's tell them stories."

"What sort? Sexy ones? Clean ones? Political ones? Outrageous ones? What do you think?"

"Tell them the one about us in the street – how you couldn't get up, and all the palaver of getting you straight. They'll laugh at that. Let's have a re-enactment."

"What, here and now? Not in the Lion. I might get stuck again and then where will we be? And there will be no beautiful policewoman's eyes to look into."

"But we'll have to do it on the night."

"OK" was Ced's grumpy reply.

After an hour or so they felt they had enough material for ten to twelve minutes of their first comedy act.

"I'll get Shona to type this out for us."

Shona was Seb's very new, diminutive girlfriend, who had divulged on their first date that she was a dab hand on a computer keyboard.

"She said she will come and see our act. At least one person will laugh."

'And also my mum and dad,' thought Ced.

"Let's meet at my place and rehearse."

"Rehearse!" exploded Ced, loud enough for several of

the other drinkers to down their glasses and stare at the sight of this seemingly odd couple of men.

Charlie, in the corner, mumbled, "What on earth are they going to rehearse? Are they some comedy act? Looks like one big joke to me!"

The pair ignored the jibe. However, despite Ced's reluctance, thinking that just to stand on the stage would be all that would be needed to make people laugh, they fixed rehearsals for 7 p.m. each night for the next ten days or so to finalise their performance.

Seb's closing remark was "What are we going to wear?"

"Now, that is a problem," replied Ced, having given no thought to the matter beforehand. "Hey, why don't we rehearse in the lunch break at work? We could somehow arrange to be back in time together."

"And leave Mrs Granger's taps running?"

"You know I'll do whatever I can to make Lush break into a smile – I bet he has never smiled or laughed in all his life."

"Well, he certainly wasn't smiling when he threatened to sack you."

"Well, I managed to talk him out of that, didn't I?"

So they went their separate ways.

On Monday morning, they duly reported for work.

"I hear you are going on the stage; is that true?"

"Well, we have got a gig at Slagthorpe Working Men's Club on Saturday week. Are you going to come?"

"Not very likely," replied Mr Lush! "And I don't want you larking around here, or annoying customers for that matter. Off you go – we can't make money standing around here!"

So the pair went to their jobs, each trying to remember their lines, and they coped with the rush hour in their van with 'F. Lush, Plumbers and Heating Engineers' emblazoned on the side. They did manage to meet up in a couple of lunchtimes. Frank Lush did grudgingly allow the use of the directors' room, somewhat euphemistically so-called as he and his wife were the sole directors.

"Take your overalls and dirty boots off" was his parting remark.

Other employees were mightily curious to know what was going on.

"Why are Ced and Seb being allowed to use such a room?"

Ced had stated that not even Mr Lush was allowed to be privy to their act and he had been requested (ever so politely) not to disturb them. In such a situation gossip was bound to arise.

"Are they forming a trade union? Heaven knows, this company needs one. Why is Mr Lush, who is not known for his generosity, willing to allow two of his lower employees to use the directors' room?" And so on.

Eventually someone hit on the idea that the pair were engaged in putting together a company newsletter, and that seemed to satisfy most, if not all, of the staff. Winnie was not convinced! She had been with the company many years, and on one occasion had put her ear to the door and heard laughter!

'What a strange situation,' she thought: 'two junior employees using the directors' room for goodness knows what and sanctioned by Mr Lush.'

She timorously enquired of the latter, only to be told it was a private arrangement.

Now, Winnie's church had been having a series of talks on 'Grace', but this was stretching it a bit. The boss allowing the most junior of staff access to the holy of holies, especially in view of Ced's track record – i.e. bowing down to an empty hearse and getting stuck, let alone flooding Mrs Thompson's house when he left a valve open and escaping the sack.

However, she reminded herself, "It's not my business, but all the same . . ."

Meanwhile Pastor Wethered met with his deacons,

Marion Allsop, Samuel Jenkins and Brian Clun. He shared the discussion with them that Harry at the club and possibly others were willing to join them in worship in the club bar, but on the condition they came to the entertainment the night before, which by now most people knew included Suzie the stripper. Marion had never heard the phrase 'If you play ball with me . . .', but she knew about compromise and trade-offs.

Pastor Wethered explained, at some length, "If we want people to hear the good news of Jesus Christ we have to meet them where they are," etc., etc. He'd had considerable difficulty in persuading them to allow Sunday worship at the club, if only on an experimental basis.

"This is going a bit too far." It was Brian's turn. He had, at best, been lukewarm about the project. "We need to keep ourselves to ourselves. Let's not get too ambitious." Then he added under his breath, "We don't want others intruding into our lovely fellowship."

It was now Samuel's turn. By far the wisest of the group, he thought, and prayed, very hard about the proposed move, and in a moment of inspiration uttered, "Why don't we go and see Suzie?"

"Whatever for?" cried the others. "To find out why she does it, and whether she needs to do it. There must be easier ways of earning a living."

"I don't agree," responded Brian. "She is a sinful woman. I don't suppose stripping is the only thing she does."

Pastor Wethered reminded them that they were not there to sit in judgment.

Eventually, after a long discussion, it was agreed that Marion, Samuel and the Pastor would attempt to visit Suzie. Marion because she was a woman, Samuel because of his seniority in the church, and obviously Pastor Wethered.

Brian uttered, in a somewhat sarcastic tone, "Count me out. I don't want to be seen going to a house of ill repute," and he left before they could pray about it.

Suzie's home was a second-floor flat. She was amazed to

get a call from Harry at the club informing her that three people were coming to see her.

"Perhaps it's something about a backing group. I have to admit my act does need livening up."

Harry did not disclose the purpose of the visit, still less who the three visitors might be.

The group prayed before they knocked on the door, noticing the crack in the small window. Suzie, in her late forties, but looking at least ten years older, nervously let the trio into her front room. All three were aware of the smell.

"Sorry about the pong. It's Sheba, one of my cats." (There were five.) "She can't go out and has to pee indoors. Find yourself somewhere to sit if you can."

Finding somewhere to sit was not easy in spite of her previous efforts to tidy up. However, the threesome were eventually settled. The Pastor cleared his throat, looked at the children's photos on the wall and quickly cottoned on to the fact that the pair had different fathers, and that there was no indication of a male in the flat.

Eventually Marion came to the point and explained the situation.

"I did not fink you were musicians." (Which wasn't strictly true.) "Nor are you from the council, cos the council don't work on Sundays, and you don't seem like those who want my unpaid rent."

Marion plucked up courage, glad that Brian wasn't with them, and enquired, as gently as she could, why Suzie did this.

"I does it cos I need the money. My kids need a little treat or two, but it's 'ard enough since the club is the only gig I get now and they only pay a pittance. All my other venues have dried up. I HATE IT! I HATE IT! DO YOU UNDERSTAND? I HATE IT!" Suzie cried out, loud enough for the neighbours to wonder what she was shouting about, and a couple, having seen the three go into the flat, wondered if they could offer assistance.

'I'm glad Brian isn't here,' thought Samuel. 'We haven't much clue what to do next, but he'd be apoplectic.'

Maureen wrapped Suzie in her arms and the tears began to flow.

"I don't know who you are, but you really seem to care about me," she mumbled. "No one else does, apart from the kids."

Marion did not ask where the children were, but guessed they were with their respective fathers.

Eventually Suzie calmed down and murmured, "I could sing, instead of stripping, couldn't I? I used to have a reasonable voice. I like music-hall songs. Have you got anyone who could accompany me?"

"Oh yes," cried Marion, "lots of people play music in our church. Carlisle is very able. I'm sure he can help." When Suzie's attention was diverted, Marion whispered to Pastor Wethered, "Looks like a job for Mike and The Crew."

The Crew, as they were known in the church, were a group of six or so who tried (not always successfully) to put the Christian message into social action.

"Suzie . . ." Marion hesitated. "Suzie, I wonder if we could help in other ways?"

Suzie's eyes widened even more.

"We have a group in our church called The Crew. They can do all sorts of practical jobs, like decorating, cleaning, etc. Would you like them to come?"

"Oh yes, please." Suzie couldn't believe her luck.

So it was arranged for Mike to make a preliminary visit to assess Suzie's needs, and a couple of days later The Crew arrived with paint, wallpaper and cleaners. Within a few hours the flat was looking a different place. Marion had arranged for Suzie to go out on an extended trip with the kids, and when they returned Suzie was gobsmacked by the heretofore-mentioned makeover and new furniture.

"Just like those TV programmes!" she exclaimed. Her eyes watered. "Isn't it wonderful, kids?"

The kids, it must be admitted, were not quite as

enthusiastic. They did admit it was a great change, but thought to themselves, 'I wonder how long it will be before Mum gets it in a mess again, especially with all her cats.'

Carlisle arranged to practise with Suzie songs which he had never heard before. He took his keyboard round to the flat.

A loud knock on the door interrupted their rehearsal. "Can you keep the noise down?" was the neighbour's cry.

"Sorry, but we are rehearsing for the show" was Suzie's response.

"What show?"

"Why, the one down at the club."

"Well, you'd better get down there and rehearse. I want some peace and quiet!"

So the rehearsal was cut short. Carlisle wasn't very happy about this, but agreed, in the circumstances, it was for the best.

Pastor Wethered called the elders for prayer.

Brian was at his most truculent. "We haven't even got there for worship yet and here we are supporting these immoral acts. Whatever next?"

"Calm down, Brian." Marion was in her most conciliatory mood. "All we are doing is applying some Christian love to a tricky situation."

"Well, you can apply some of your so-called Christian love to me." And with that he stalked out.

"I thought we were here to pray," piped up Ken, who did more observing than speaking.

"And so we are," responded the Pastor, at last exerting his authority.

Like many other local buildings, Slagthorpe Working Men's Club hall had seen better days. Income from the bar and the members was dropping month by month, so Edgar could not wait for the income from the Praise Be Fellowship to arrive. Were they to be the salvation, at least in financial terms, of the club he had served and dominated for the past twenty years?

The entertainment evening came. A number of people decided to patronise the bar facilities, with one or two complaining.

"The beer isn't what it used to be. They're probably watering it down, I reckon," grumbled one customer.

The minibus carrying the rest of the old folk duly arrived, but they seemed a good deal less in number than last time. Out of the corner of his eye Edgar could see others. Yes, there was that pastor fellow and quite a lot of strange faces. Then he remembered the church leader saying the church was like a rack of snooker balls - yellow, green, brown, etc. Would they know what they were in for?

Harry, who was watching from behind the curtain, muttered, "You play ball with me . . ." and trailed off when he realised that the newcomers far outnumbered the so-called regulars.

Edgar stepped into the spotlight, adjusted his bow tie, coughed slightly and announced, "Ladies and gentlemen, we have not one, not two, but three wonderful acts for you tonight. The Treehouse Trio I know are your favourites; Suzie the stripper has a new act . . ."

"Couldn't be worse than the last time" was the universal comment, to accompanying mocking wolf whistles.

"And finally a new comedy duo, Seb and Ced."

"I know that Ced - hope he's a better comedian than a plumber. You should 'ave seen the mess he made in my cousin's house," cried a loud voice.

"So, without further delay, I give you our first act: The Treehouse Trio."

"Can they come and duly perform the same songs they always sing - the old folk like it" was the general comment.

After ten minutes or so (for some it seemed a lot longer)

they embarked on their final number, 'When the Saints Go Marching In', and the curtain closed to less than rapturous applause.

Edgar stepped into the spotlight once more. "Now, ladies and gentlemen, someone who is your real darling favourite - Suzie."

The curtains opened again and there stood Suzie in her usual blue gown, which, on closer inspection, had seen better days (so had Suzie, for that matter). A few wolf whistles and cheers greeted her.

"Ladies and gentlemen, before I begin my act, I want to dedicate my performance to that group sitting over there on the right."

Harry immediately switched the spotlight on to some twenty members of the Praise Be Fellowship, who had come to watch the show and now included the truculent Brian. Embarrassed and blinking, they did not know what to do or say.

Suzie, who was in full verbal flight, continued: "I want to say a big thank you to them for sorting out a bit of my life, and cleaning and redecorating my flat as well as looking after my kids."

A medium-sized round of applause rang round the hall, because the Praise Be Fellowship certainly comprised the major part of the audience, and they were not clapping.

Edgar audibly cleared his throat and muttered, "Get on with it."

As the spotlight switched back on to Suzie she continued: "Tonight I would like to sing for you, accompanied by my good friend Carlisle on the keyboard."

At this, of course, the Praise Be Fellowship members loudly applauded. The audience had now grown a little, and the male club members who had been ensconced in the bar and whose throats were well lubricated shouted, "We came to see you strip."

They were ignored by Suzie as she launched into 'We'll Gather Lilacs'.

The few OAPs there loved it. The church members did not know what to think. The beery group began to be more annoyed.

Edgar nodded to Harry as Suzie finished her song to hearty applause from the church group, including Brian, sympathetic claps from the OAPs and muted boos from the rest.

Edgar stepped out in front of the closed curtains saying, "Thank you, Suzie," although he didn't mean a word of it.

Suzie, meanwhile, in floods of tears was helped backstage into the arms of Marion, who said, "Let's get some coffee."

The other church members stayed.

Edgar continued: "Now for something special - a newcomer comedy act. Seb and Ced."

'Bet they're dirty,' thought Brian.

"Hope they're not as clean as they look," muttered the beery ones.

"A big round of applause for Seb and Ced."

Ced stepped forward into the spotlight. Of course his very appearance was enough to make people laugh - not least Brian, whose guffaws could be heard across the room.

"Thank you. I haven't started yet," uttered Ced, "but keep it going, you may not feel like it after the next few minutes."

"It says 'a few hours' in my script," intervened Seb. "Isn't clapping a funny thing?"

"Don't know - never been to Clapham. It's all junk, son! Is Clapham Junction near Waterloo?"

"Want to go to the loo! No, I don't."

And so it went on, most of it trivial and inane, but the audience loved it. It was half clowning, half quick repartee. At the end Ced pretended he could not get up and asked for a volunteer from the audience to help.

Up stepped a young blond lady, who said, "I've met

Ced before and he isn't pretending," and within seconds she had rolled on to the floor and was staring into Ced's eyes.

The audience were transfixed. Was this for real or all part of the act? They had no idea. Ced's heart melted. Yes, it was the blond policewoman he had met in the street. He had a real dilemma: whether or not to stay as he was and gaze into her eyes.

Edgar began to fume. Their act was already overrunning. He wanted to get to the bar. Harry had been given the job of leading the sing-song. The audience loved it; here was a real-life love story being played out in an unusual way, for quite a few of them knew WPC Blick.

Shouts of "Give 'im a kiss!" started to erupt from the audience.

Edgar called, "Pull the curtain, 'Arry," in a stage whisper loud enough for the front row to hear.

"I can't," shouted back Harry. "It's stuck!"

Suzie, who was just creeping out at the back, said to herself, "So I am not the only one to have been put in an embarrassing position by this decrepit club."

Harry fiddled with the ropes and pulled. Ced just smiled and smiled and managed to bend an inch or two lower. Eyes transfixed on each other. Were they going to kiss? The suspense was building. Closer and closer they inched towards each other. The more romantic ones in the audience purred. Others thought, 'This is better than Suzie the stripper. What is going to happen?'

Suddenly the lights went out, the fire alarm went off and a certain amount of panic ensued. Ced helped the young woman to her feet and stood up as well – at least, he managed halfway, and they embraced in the dark.

'This is all right,' thought Ced.

"I don't even know your name!"

"Janice," she responded, "but call me J." Then, realising her professional responsibilities, she found Harry getting the lights back on.

Edgar, resuming his rightful role, shouted, "Please calm down, everyone."

It did not take long for order to be restored.

"Ladies and gentlemen, I have just one more thing to say. We have been privileged in two ways tonight. First we have witnessed three wonderful acts, so put your hands together in appreciation."

The participants were nowhere to be seen and Ced was certainly not going to bow down again!

"Secondly," - Edgar, knowing he was missing drinking time was in full flight - "members of the Praise Be Fellowship have joined us. I think we should join them tomorrow when they have their worship here at 10.30 a.m. I for one will - not up here on the stage giving instructions, but sitting down there in the front."

"You play ball, etc.," muttered Harry, still fiddling with the curtain ropes.

Wilf, who had been at the back throughout the show, thought that if it hadn't been for these religious weirdos (he thought all religious people were odd) they would not have had an audience at all.

Just as Ced and Seb were leaving through a side door, with one or two appreciative slaps on the back, a man stepped forward.

"I, Hector Maclain, leave my card."

Seb took it and read, 'Hector Maclain, theatrical agent'. There were various phone numbers at the bottom.

"By the way, who's the bird?"

"Oh she is just called 'J' that's all."

"Give me a bell. Be in touch sometime."

Before the pair could explain, he was gone.

"I reckon the Lion is where we should be heading."

Sunday morning dawned sunny and bright. Members of the church assembled early to get everything ready for their new place of worship, leaving a very small group to pray. Pastor Wethered suggested they meet in a circle, and all except Brian agreed. When 10.30 a.m. came they were the only ones present. A feeling of disappointment was evident. They had prayed, they had attended the entertainment - or some of them had - and now, in spite of all their efforts, there were no newcomers to their worship, not even Edgar and Harry despite all their promises. The disappointment, if not disillusionment, became more obvious.

"Should have stayed where we were - it was cosy in the old chapel and we didn't have the lights of slot machines flickering away, or the smell of stale beer to distract us" were the unuttered thoughts of several, especially Brian.

However, Pastor Wethered started the worship. He had chosen one or two more traditional hymns and songs which newcomers might just be familiar with.

After about five minutes the door flew open and in strode Suzie.

"Thought I would give it a whirl," she stated in a loud voice.

A quieter voice murmured, 'Different from your usual whirl, eh!"

She picked a seat far away from other people, but had hardly sat down when Edgar joined her.

"Well, that makes two of us from the club," he muttered. "Thought there might be more."

The theme of the worship was that God lives in the lives of people, not in buildings, and that He can be worshipped anywhere.

"Haven't seen much sign of Him in the club lately," muttered Edgar. "Could do with His help the way membership and the finances are going."

"Shut up and listen," exploded Suzie in a voice that Pastor Wethered at the front could hear.

Around halfway through the worship the door opened and in came Brian, looking sheepish; he looked round for somewhere to sit and the only place vacant was next to Suzie and Edgar. He summoned up what reserves of courage he had and put himself next to two people who, at other times, he would describe as 'sinners'.

The worship drew to a close with the Pastor gently inviting anyone who wanted to discover how God could live in lives to discuss it with him over coffee.

"B----- that!" shouted Suzie.

She made efforts to leave, only to find her way barred by Edgar and, of all people, Brian, who could not wait to engage Pastor Wethered in a 'real' conversation.

And what happened to Ced and Seb? Ced's career as a comedian had its ups and downs. The agent did get him bookings, but sadly they did not amount to a great deal – mainly in working men's clubs and one to give a talk to the Women's Institute with the title 'My Life: Plumber to Comedian', but it was never enough and, in spite of increasing back pain, he returned to his old trade as a plumber. Once, however, he called into the office, where a pretty girl introduced herself as Belinda and gave him a job sheet.

"Oh no, not Mrs Thompson – I remember her from long ago."

Mr Lush, who with some reluctance had re-employed Ced, more out of sympathy than because of his plumbing skills, overheard and said, "On your way, lad, or you'll be back on your failed career."

With that, Ced left, but not without giving Belinda a wink, which got the response of a radiant smile.

Seb left the firm to set up his own business. He saw very little of Ced. He had supported Ced when he first set out on his professional career, but now their lives had different paths.

Ced, meanwhile, with not a little cunning, made plans to waylay Belinda, but for a long time their paths did not cross. Then even when they did he was hesitant about asking her for a date, though eventually she agreed but limited it to just a picnic in the park.

"What lovely food your mum provides."

"No, I did it. My mum died several years ago. But you know my dad – he's the boss of the firm."

"You are Belinda Lush!" exclaimed Ced. "I bet that makes you blush!"

"Funny, ha ha," replied Belinda in her best sarcastic tone, but nevertheless she grabbed Ced's hand. "I know your ambitions as a comedian have ground to a halt, but I like you very much. You must come and meet my friends."

"Who are they? What may they be?"

"Well, we meet in what was the old working men's club. It's called the Praise Be Fellowship."

"Eh, what?" responded Ced, who was in the dark about developments at the club. "I'm not sure I want to go there. I expect there will be people who will know my comic career didn't really take off. Lots of people don't take too kindly to failures, and especially so-called comedians."

However, when Belinda, her eyes sparkling, said, "Well, I think you are my hero," that was enough for Ced, and, suitably dressed, they met outside the newly refurbished former club. Belinda kissed him with a peck on the cheek.

'This is all right,' Ced thought. 'My career might have faltered, but it's taking off in new directions.'

However, he did feel uncomfortable as most of the others wore jeans, and some of the men were in shorts.

A man who introduced himself as Brian said with a smile, "I'll show you a seat."

But Belinda had forged ahead and introduced Ced to her group of friends.

The theme of the evening was 'The people God puts across our paths', basing it on the Good Samaritan.

'How odd!' thought Ced. 'That's the sort of thing that seems to be happening to me.'

Belinda, who contrived to cook lunch as well as going to worship, invited Ced back home. The introduction to her father was embarrassing.

"I know who you are, lad," he said with a suspicious Yorkshire accent. "We don't need any introductions."

"Dad, we are going to get married."

At this her father nearly exploded. "He hasn't asked my permission."

"I haven't even asked her myself!" responded Ced.

However, several months later they were married. Mr Lush duly gave his daughter away. Seb was best man and Beth, Belinda's best friend from the Praise Be Fellowship, was the one bridesmaid. Seb excelled himself in the best man's speech with a lot of play on Belinda no longer being 'Blush'. Some of the jokes fell on deaf ears - especially Belinda's father's.

Ced duly replied with zest and humour, all the while trying to avoid Frank's eye as he wasn't sure what his relationship with his new father-in-law might be.

A few months later it was quite clear that as Ced's promising career was beginning to falter. Belinda, now pregnant with their first child, sorted the situation and suggested to her father that a more secure future might be best for Ced.

"Oh, I don't know about that" was his muted response.

However, a few days later he rang Ced and asked him to come and see him. Ced was surprised, but the outcome was a job as a sales rep for the firm.

"With your personality you could do wonders for our image, selling plumbing requirements. Mind, you will have to keep your jokes in check."

"I certainly will" was Ced's reply. "Thank you, Mr Lush."

"Oh, call me Frank.."

"Aren't God's ways wonderful!" was all Belinda could say on hearing the news.

Ced could not contain himself and launched into a long tale using every pun he could about lush sales experience and so on.

Eventually all Belinda could say was "Enough, Ced."

ONE OF OUR SOCKS IS MISSING

"I've lost a sock," said Jill as she prepared supper.

"You can't have. You don't lose things; it's me that mislays all sorts of objects. Remember the watch last summer, and you found it at the bottom of the bed?"

"No, seriously, I put them both on the radiator and there is only one there now."

Ben looked with only half-interest as he was engaged in writing a play, which had come to a blockage about halfway.

"OK, I'll get behind the radiator and look."

And search he did, but to little avail.

"I'll have to get down on the floor."

Getting down now proved a good deal more difficult than it used to be, but he struggled to look behind the radiator; no sign of a sock. So he put his right hand between the skirting board and the radiator, and to his surprise pulled out a lady's sock.

"No, that's not it," cried Jill.

Ben searched again and to his greater surprise found another. He said, "Well, that makes a pair."

"But you still haven't found the one I'm looking for!"

Ben felt around again and brought out a tea towel. They dissolved in laughter and surprise. Ben searched again for the original missing sock, but there was no sign of it. However, he was aware that now he could not extricate his hand. He did manage to move his hand along the length of the radiator, and at last he located another sock, but was only able to touch it with his fingers. He pulled as hard as he could, but only succeeded in making his hand sore and a trickle of blood began to flow down his arm.

"What are we going to do? Shall I ring 999?"

Without waiting for a reply she picked up the receiver and dialled 999.

"Which service do you require?" enquired the operator, who had years of experience of such calls, both genuine and otherwise, and could usually detect from the caller's voice, how grave the situation was.

"I – I'm not sure," stammered Jill. "I guess it's the fire brigade. You see, my husband has got his hand stuck behind a radiator, and those fire fighters are used to getting cats down from trees."

"OK. Please give me your name, address and postcode and we shall send someone round as soon as possible."

With that, Jill rushed back to the kitchen, and Ben was glad to see her, lying as he was on the floor virtually immobile.

A ring on the doorbell announced the arrival of Leighton, Ben's nephew, from up the road. Leighton was struggling with A levels, but was graduating very well in the school of cynicism.

"Hello, Uncle Ben. Are you drunk again?"

"No way!" replied Ben. "I was looking for Auntie's sock and have got my hand caught behind the radiator."

"The only thing to do is move the radiator," said Leighton, "or amputation. Radiators are difficult to move, especially if they have been in place a long time. Amputation it will have to be."

Ben knew his nephew was joking, but nevertheless felt his blood run cold at the thought.

"What do you mean, amputation?" It was Leighton's sister, aged eighteen, on her way home from work. Isla was very different from her brother and she was soon kneeling beside her uncle. "Poor you! Is it hurting? Let me look." Isla worked in a local office, but harboured dreams of nursing one day. She was indeed full of solicitation.

Jill stood back as the kitchen was getting crowded.

"No sign of the fire brigade," muttered Ben, who had now got cramp in his left leg to add to his troubles.

"'Fraid not," replied his young nephew. "Got to get back."

Isla added that she had a date tonight and she must be on time.

'Not that Samson chap, I hope,' thought Jill.

With that they disappeared.

"I'd better dish supper up," said Jill.

"Dish supper down, if I can eat some," replied her prostrate spouse. So Jill provided some peas, mince and chips and laid the dish on the floor; and with a spoon in his hand Ben attempted to feed himself. It was a difficult process; he gingerly picked a chip up, but they were hot; so he tried the peas with the spoon, but again it was marginal success. At that moment Scuby, her lovely Old English sheepdog bounded in, saw Ben on the floor and began to lick his face. Jill managed to stop him, but then he spied the plate of food on the floor, thought it was his and it was very quickly devoured. Ushered out into the lounge, the dog wondered what it was all about, but was soon distracted by the flashing blue as the fire tender arrived.

"Sorry to have kept you waiting, madam, but it's been a busy night. What's the problem?"

Jill led two officers into the kitchen and explained the problem. Ben looked up as the fire officer towered over him. This bloke seemed huge.

Rankin, the fire officer, looked at his fellow officer, Annette. "I think we have a problem here."

"*You* have a problem!" uttered Ben with an uncharacteristic outburst, and perhaps thinking that his nephew's suggestion of amputation might be the solution after all.

Rankin suggested they put a wrench behind the radiator, but soon thought better of it. "It might crack and cause a leak. No, missus, you will have to call a plumber," and with a polite "Goodbye" they left.

However, a passing police car saw the flashing blue light, stopped and decided to investigate. PC Brodie indicated that he would go in, leaving his PCSO to control the crowd of neighbours and other onlookers who were now gathering in some strength.

"No need to bother, officer," said the fire officer, Rankin, as he was leaving. "Only some idiot got his arm stuck behind a radiator and they are calling a plumber."

PC Brodie, thinking of the report(s) he would have to make, decided to see for himself, and, kneeling beside Ben, asked, "What seems to be the problem?"

"Problem? Can't you see?" Ben was the nearest he had been for some while to anger.

"OK, it is not a crime scene, so I'll be off. I see you have been able to eat your supper."

"No, the dog pinched it!"

Jill interrupted: "Look, Ben, I made some jelly. Would you like some, officer?"

"No, thank you," retorted PC Brodie, and with that he left, instructing his PCSO to remain at the door, and addressing the group outside: "Ladies and gentlemen, there is nothing to worry about. Your neighbour, Ben, got his hand stuck behind the kitchen radiator, that's all. Please go home."

With that he got into his car, ignoring a ribald comment: "Is that where he keeps his cash?"

He drove round the block and came back to the house again. Then, seeing the crowd had dispersed, he collected his colleague and they reported back to the station.

"Lush Plumbing Services here," said the recorded message. "We are closed until 8 a.m. Monday morning. However, if it is an emergency Mr Lush will come. His mobile number is 0079 222 6543."

Jill contemplated if it was an emergency. The thought of Ben lying there another thirty-six hours did not appeal to her in the slightest. 'Yes, I can feed him, I can bring the sleeping bag down and make him comfortable, but he will need to go to the loo.'

With little hesitation she dialled the number.

A gruff voice replied: "Lush Plumbing here. I'm busy at the moment, but I will call you back as soon as I can if you leave your name, address and telephone number."

If Jill was at desperation point, Ben was even more so.

"I'll try some marge – that might do it," she said, putting the pack next to Ben.

After half an hour, though it seemed much longer, the phone rang, and Jill hurriedly grabbed it.

"Have you got a burst?"

Jill answered, "No," and went on to explain that she had dialled 999 and the fire brigade and the police had been called, though not an ambulance, but she was thinking an ambulance would have been needed if Ben's clever-clogs nephew had got his way.

"I'll be with you as soon as I can. I'm fixing some tap washers for Mrs Dorrien in Calchester and she does like to talk a bit."

"She does like to talk a bit," agreed Jill as she knew the lady, and her reputation for engaging in lengthy and meaningless conversations had spread far and wide. Jill reported back to Ben, who was desperate for a wee.

"How long?" His voice had a note of distress in it.

Suddenly the door opened and Isla appeared, dressed for the evening. She knelt down and, with Jill and Ben looking on, asked gently, "Have you tried prayer?"

Ben replied, "What good will that do? It's a plumber I need, not a priest! It's obvious that dressed like that you are not anything of the sort."

"Nevertheless," Isla said, "the youth-club leader says that it works for him and I guess it will work for you. Lord, we get ourselves in all sorts of 'sits'. Please help Uncle out of this mess and keep his temper defused."

"Hello, Lush the plumber here," came the voice.

"Wow!" said Jill and Ben together as the plumber passed Isla on the way to her date.

"What seems to be the problem?"

"Can't you see I've got my hand stuck behind the radiator" was Ben's angry reply, realising Isla's prayer about his temper was taking longer than he thought to be answered.

Lush knelt down beside Ben. "You know, I have to charge double for call-outs at the weekend."

Ben wasn't interested in his charges, only his freedom.

"I'll have to drain the system, and that takes quite a time and then dismantle the rad. I could be here for at least a couple of hours."

Ben said, "Do what is necessary," with a note of hopelessness in his voice.

At this point Jill interrupted: "Try turning your hand to the left."

Ben, desperate to try anything, found he could in fact move his fingers, and in a trice freed himself. Then, jumping to his feet, he rushed to the loo. The plumber and Jill looked at each other in wonder and disbelief.

"OK, I won't charge you for tonight. It is a humanitarian job. Goodnight."

As he went, passing Isla on her way back in, he said, "Some people do get themselves in a mess."

"He didn't turn up," she said glumly, but her gloom evaporated into joy when she realised Ben had got out of his trap. "I told you prayer works!" she exclaimed.

"Come and have some supper with us," invited Jill. "I expect you are hungry and I know Ben is as he's only had jelly to eat all evening."

Next day, Sunday, at worship their minister asked people for items for prayer.

"Go on," whispered Jill into Ben's ear.

Ben was reluctant to air his good news. "I can't," he quietly replied.

"Uncle Ben's got some good news" came a female voice. It was Isla on her feet.

"Come on, tell us," said the Pastor, inviting Ben to come to the front.

"Well, it was like this," he explained as some eighty to a hundred heads turned in his direction in expectation. Uncontrolled laughter took over and the minister, mindful of the occasion, managed a smile or two.

When everyone had finally calmed down, except for a dozen or so teenagers in the back row, Josephine, a redoubtable lady of Afro-Caribbean origin, cried out, "Praise the Lord!" and continued for some time so that others began to think a major crisis had been averted and not someone's trapped hand had been released.

The minister's sermon said it all: "We have been looking at the promises of Jesus, as in Luke 4. Last week it was preaching good news to the poor. This week we are thinking about freedom for prisoners." Ben and Jill's minister was a faithful servant of God, but no matter how he tried, and he spent many hours preparing, he had the unfortunate ability to make an exciting subject dull. Officiating at weddings, the service became something like a funeral – so much so, that one or two couples managed to ask for another minister to take the service. Ben looked round the congregation, who, with few exceptions, respected God's servant without really loving him.

He noticed, out of the corner of his eye, Joel and Cindy; from what he knew of them and guessed (and it was no more than that) they were locked in a somewhat loveless marriage. Even to the casual observer their body language gave more than a clue as to what happened behind their closed doors.

Then there was Babs, sitting in her usual place in the back row, a prisoner to her past. She had known minor fame on the stage until parts dried up, and she had to exist on her meagre pension, and sometimes handouts. The more Ben thought about it, the more he realised that, without exception, everyone is a prisoner to something. It may not be drugs or a power of some kind, but something that holds people in its grip.

The preacher was saying that Jesus wasn't in the business of opening all the prisons and letting all the occupants out. Ironically, Ben felt trapped but by what or by whom he didn't really know. Perhaps the person the preacher was talking about did provide a way of escape; was it possible?

Sermon over, final hymn sung, coffee and biscuits devoured, they were on their way home.

"That was interesting," said Jill.

"I suppose so," said Ben, his mind more on his lunch than the past hour or so.

Over their traditional Sunday meal, Jill, who had absorbed more of the sermon than Ben had done, casually offered, "You know Leighton came round last night to help, and offered to cut off your arm? I think we should offer to help him."

"In what way?" asked Ben, busy enjoying his lunch.

"Well, since his mother left, he has had to live with your brother and that cannot be easy as being on shift work, at seventeen, Leighton has to do a lot of fending for himself."

Ben, who had spent a lot of time with his brother when Sal had left the marital home, wasn't overkeen on revisiting the situation.

Jill, who still pined after Alan, the son they had lost many years ago, after which they adopted Harriet, who was now grown-up, married and living in France, still had a concern for young people who seemed lost and lonely.

"Let's invite Leighton round tomorrow night."

Before Ben could reply, the phone rang.

"Leighton here. Is Uncle there?"

"Yes, Leighton, what can I do for you?" Ben was not too keen on his Sunday lunch being interrupted.

"I just want to say how sorry I am for what I said last night. I didn't mean it. It's just I have a somewhat sadistic side to my nature. Isla told me the whole story. Guess it might be in the local paper on Friday."

Ben was horrified at the thought, but remembered that Danny, a local journalist, was sitting in the back row of the church and he was always desperate for a story.

"Look, Leighton, we were thinking of inviting you round for a meal." (The 'we' being something of a half-truth.) "Are you free tomorrow night?"

"Sorry, it's karate."

"Tuesday, then?"

"No, thanks – football training."

"Wednesday maybe?"

"No, I go to the gym after work."

By now Ben was ready to give up. Leighton's social programme was so full that there didn't seem to be any scope for family time. However, they eventually managed to settle on Saturday evening.

"By the way, I am called Ley by my mates. You can call me Ley."

"And you can drop the Uncle bit if you like" – something Ben only half-heartedly meant, as he was acutely aware of the gap in their ages.

Saturday duly came and Leighton appeared, scrubbed and polished but more than a little tired after his football match.

"Did you win?" was Ben's greeting as he ushered Leighton across the threshold.

"Look, Ben," Leighton was somewhat breathless, "I'm sorry. I didn't really mean cutting your arm off when you had it stuck behind the rad. It's just so many people are getting at me right now."

"OK, Ley, it's all right," replied Ben as he saw the lad was close to tears. "It was quite funny in the end. In fact, I can use it in my next book of short stories."

"Yeah," replied Leighton, "I read the last one - very funny they were. Did you make a lot of money?"

"No, not really," said Ben, wishing to change the subject. "In fact, we did cover our costs and hope to soon be able to give some away."

"Give it away?" Leighton could not understand such thinking. "Give it away?" he muttered. "What's the point in that? You are an almost famous author - you could make a tidy pile for yourself."

Ben was about to explain that, as a Christian, any money he has is really God's and he was only looking after it, but he stopped himself just in time. This was not the time for sermons, since he surmised the real reason Leighton had rung was not to apologise, since he knew that the teenager wasn't really into that sort of thing. He didn't have to wait half a second before the lad burst into the house with his mobile phone clasped to his ear.

"Uncle, my mates, or so-called mates, are always getting at me because I am black, and they think I'm gay!"

With that the tears began to flow - so much so that Jill in the next room nearly burst in to try to find what was wrong, but decided not to do so.

"OK, mate," said Ben, aware of the unusual situation of a grown man and an almost grown man clasped in each other's arms, one sobbing his heart out. Ben said, "You talk; I'll listen."

Ever since Ben had become a Christian he had tried hard to perfect his listening skills. He had heard countless times that he had two ears and one mouth and should use them in that proportion, but had found it easier to say rather than do.

"I know that I am adopted. I've known that for many years. I always thought it was odd that Mum and Dad were white and I was not, and when Mum left so suddenly I found in a drawer my adoption papers. I must have been six at the time. I didn't understand things like court decrees, etc. Mum and Dad did their best to make me welcome – at least they did at first, but then things changed, and I felt very much the outsider or – what's the word? – even patronised. Ben, where do I go?"

Ben thought long and hard. He wasn't, like his niece, into instant prayer; he considered drawing in Jill, but felt this was a 'man to man' situation.

However, his thinking was quickly interrupted by Leighton saying, "It's becoming bad at school. One or two of the guys are saying, 'Ley's a gay,' which isn't true. I like girls, but don't get many dates at the moment. Tash is quite friendly and tries to accept me even though I'm black and adopted, but she was warned off by Vince, her brother, and somehow believes 'Ley's a gay!' What am I to do?"

Ben thought back to his own teenage years. Certainly he had known something of his nephew's angst, but nothing like this.

Leighton continued, feeling that his uncle was at least listening to his problems and wondering what he could do about it all: "I tried going to church with Isla. She has many friends there and gladly introduced me, but even there I felt like a fish out of water."

Had the rumours from college got around?

Ben pulled himself to his full uncle height. "Ley, let's summarise the situation. There are things we cannot change." (Ben had never had any formal counselling training, but felt this was what one should do.) "What do you think they are?"

"Well, I'm black and I am adopted."

"Anything else?" Ben was at his most solicitous.

"No, I can't think so."

"What things could possibly change?"

"Mum and Dad get back together? Better friends with Isla? I try and cope with rejection and ignore the taunts?"

"Go on, what else?"

"I try that church again? They were really quite nice. I become a better footballer and show on the field I'm as good, if not better, than the rest of them. Somehow I have to answer the loudmouth Liam, who says his cousin Jonnie is willing to prove I'm gay. 'Meet Sammie behind the bike shed to prove you're not gay' is the shout from some of the more arrogant and vocal lads. I don't like Sammie and I know she doesn't like me, but if that's the way then I have to take it. I shall have to take precautions not to get her pregnant."

Ben realised in a slight state of shock it never happened like this when he was seventeen – or if it did he could not remember it.

At this point Jill thought that the 'man to man' conversation was possibly drawing to a close. Women could talk to each other for hours, but blokes, after half an hour or so, went back to the same old subjects: football and women.

'They must be getting hungry, thirsty or both.'

She tapped politely on the door.

"Go away, Auntie." Leighton had not got round to calling her Jill – it seemed too familiar.

She beat a hasty retreat. Nothing like this had happened before and so she busied herself around the house, her imagination trying to work out what kind of conversation was taking place. She longed to know more, but knew she must not interrupt. How was it that Ben, her husband of so many years, whose patience threshold was never very high, should be ensconced with Leighton, who only a few days ago had made sinister threats?

'I know, I'll ring Meg and try to get her to ring back, asking for Ben.'

"You have reached the household of Meg and Len Moulding," said the answerphone. "Please ring back later or you can leave a message after the tone."

"Meg, it's Jill." (She was trying to supress the anxiety she was feeling, not least because her nephew had rebuffed her in her own home.) "Can you ring back? It's rather urgent." She paused and then continued: "Please ask to speak to Ben." She sat back, expecting the phone to ring immediately. "Come on, come on, Meg," she muttered to herself. "Why don't you ring?"

A degree of rationality had evaporated from her thinking – she hadn't considered that Meg might be out shopping or even on holiday.

Ben and Leighton sat in silence – a strange silence, not of boredom or of tension, but each in their own thoughts. Even with their age difference, and different backgrounds, Ben felt a lot of fatherly feelings Leighton had never really experienced with his dad, or if he had they were buried in the past. His adoptive father had seemed too preoccupied with work, keeping the home together and the loss of Sal to another man. To Ben it meant, at least in part, recapturing the wonderful days with Alan, when they watched football at QPR and enjoyed summer days together. Neither was willing to break the silence. It was indeed a precious and poignant moment. The void was broken by the phone ringing and Ben got up to answer it.

Leighton was thinking, 'I don't do this praying business, like my sister, but this must be a bit like it, only she doesn't do silence.'

"Meg here." The voice was more than a little abrupt, as if something important had been interrupted. "You want to speak to me."

"Hello, Meg."

Ben could not know why she had rung and he too was a little cross that his precious time with Leighton had been disturbed.

"Jill said I should ring as it was urgent."

Ben was quite nonplussed, but at last the penny dropped and he realised that Jill, in perhaps a moment of jealousy, had found it hard that her husband and his nephew should be bound together in a conversation without her being party to it.

"It's nothing" was all Ben could reply.

"Doesn't sound nothing to me." Meg had not been a

college vice principal without gaining some experience. "Look, I'll come round and sort it out."

Since she had retired Meg had specialised in 'sorting other people's lives out'. Sadly the situations were left in a worse state than at first. She was, indeed, a determined woman and rarely took no for an answer.

However, in a moment of unusual courage, at least for him, Ben replied, "Thank you, Meg, for your trouble and kindness." (The word 'kindness' was something of an afterthought.) "I reckon I can cope." With that, he put the receiver down, but not without a twinge of guilt regarding his rudeness.

"Who was that, darling?" It was Jill in the next room.

Ben was always suspicious when Jill used that word. It was not unintentional on her part, but was something of a lever to solicit her husband's favour.

"Oh, it was your interfering friend Meg" was his tired reply.

Leighton, as a third party to all that was being said, was both amused and puzzled, but kept quiet as he considered he had enough of his own problems.

A ring on the doorbell was answered by Jill.

"Why, Meg, how nice to see you! What brings you here?"

"You know very well," was the grumpy reply. "Are you going to let me in? I want to talk to that husband of yours."

And without further ado she swept past Jill into the lounge, where her tracks were cut short by the sight of Leighton, whom she had known as a student, and Ben, on their knees in prayer.

"I – I can't believe it," she uttered as she rapidly closed the door.

"What is it, Meg?" enquired Jill.

"I – I – I . . ." For once Meg had had the wind knocked out of her sails. Gone was the bluff almost masculine authority; instead a mere whisper and eventually, after what seemed an eternity, Meg muttered a reluctant, "I'm sorry."

"That's all right, Meg." And leaving Ben and Leighton to their privacy Jill said, "Let's get a cup of tea."

"It's been six months since I retired and I hate it. The principal was away a lot, goodness knows where, and I had control of the college. We had governors, but they were useless. We never got through a meeting without politics intervening. But since those days I have had no one to boss about – except perhaps the dog, and he doesn't take much notice."

"What about Len?" Jill knew the answer, but asked the question all the same.

"Oh, Len keeps himself to himself. He has his own bedroom and cooks his meals on a stove in his shed. Weekends are different – we do have Sunday lunch together and some sort of conversation ensues, but it's not what I expected. I dreamt of exotic holidays, of visiting historic places, of sun-drenched beaches, and so on, but they were just idle aspirations. It won't happen, nothing will change."

Whilst this tirade was taking place, Jill realised that if anybody needed sorting out it was not Leighton or Ben, but Meg. She was at her wits' end to know what to do. Her thoughts were interrupted by Ben and Leighton emerging from the lounge, laughing and chatting together. It made such a contrast to Meg and her problems.

"What on earth have you got to laugh about?" muttered Meg. It was more of an antagonistic statement than a question.

Leighton was the first to reply: "I expect you heard how Unc got his hand stuck behind a rad looking for a sock and we had to get the fire brigade and so on. It makes quite a story. I suggested amputation, which was idiotic of me and I came to apologise and we ended up kneeling on the floor and forgiving one another. Isn't that funny?"

"No, not really" was Meg's response. Amusement and laughter never entered her world.

Jill was aware that the conversation was becoming more embarrassing by the minute, but kept her counsel. The tea had long been poured out and was getting cold.

Determined to break the ice, Jill said, "Look, Meg, why don't you ring home, say you are with Ben and Jill and Ben's nephew and you are staying to supper? And, by the way, invite Len to join us."

Meg was not used to being ordered about like this, but it seemed at least a partial way to face her multitude of problems and she dialled her home number.

It seemed ages before a voice said, "Len Moulding here. What do you want?"

To Meg's ears his voice seemed gruffer than ever.

"It's me." Meg was on the point of adding 'darling', but hadn't used that word for years so she shut up immediately. She explained the situation as briefly and kindly as was possible. "Jill wants you to join us for supper."

"I'll think about it." And with that he put the phone down.

Meg replaced her receiver and fell into Jill's arms in floods of tears. It was now Ben and Leighton's turn to be embarrassed. So with a nod and a wink they crept back into the lounge, where they knew kick-off in the footie was in ten minutes.

"I can never understand women," Ben uttered.

Leighton looked at his uncle and, from his teenage standpoint, exclaimed, "Nor do I!"

So they sat and watched TV. It was QPR versus Hull and Ben, a lifelong QPR fan, soon became quite animated.

Jill, detaching herself from Meg for a brief moment, put her head round the door, exclaiming with mock severity, "What is all this noise about? Leighton, are you fighting with Ben or what?"

Ben said loudly, "They nearly scored."

"What do you mean, they nearly scored? Why didn't they?"

Leighton thought he was in some kind of tennis-match type of argument, only he soon realised it was more of friendly banter not a full-blown row. He had heard enough of those in his young life, but he could tell the difference. There was something different about this household. He felt a bond with Ben which he found difficult to put into words, but it was great!

"Supper in five minutes," Jill finally called. "Can you do drinks, Ben?"

Now the urge to eat for two healthy males was becoming quite strong, so they dragged themselves away from the TV and joined Jill and Meg around the dining table. Leighton found this rather strange. He had existed in a 'grab and go' culture. Eating was about food and no more, and yet here was his uncle forsaking the TV to eat with others.

'Seems strange to me,' he thought. 'Why don't they put it on a tray in front of the box?'

A less tearful Meg sat next to Leighton, who could not make her out. It seemed strange to be eating at a table with someone who was so authoritative when she was at the college and now appeared, to his young eyes, almost a broken woman.

Jill took the lead: "We hold hands to say grace."

The shocks were coming thick and fast to both Meg and Leighton. Meg cautiously held Leighton's hand. She had never held a black man's hand before and was not sure she wanted to. Leighton for his part had never held a sixty-year-old woman's hand, let alone one for whom he had considerable respect in the past.

Jill said briefly, "Lord, thank You for each other, and thank You for providing for all our physical needs."

'All our physical needs? That is strange,' thought Leighton.

Meg was beginning to have similar thoughts, but kept them to herself. She was beginning, if ever so slightly, to forget about Len and feel wanted and secure in this household. It was so different from all that she had experienced in her long marriage, which for the last part had been far from happy. Meg and Len had tried to ignore the differences and absorbed themselves in their careers, but now they had retired that had all changed, and they lived in a state of armed neutrality.

They were halfway through the first course when the doorbell rang.

"That will be Pat returning the books I lent her. Shan't be a moment," announced Jill, jumping up from the table.

It wasn't; it was Len, standing stock-still with not one, but two, bunches of flowers in his hand.

"Come in, come in, Len," cried Jill.

"This is for you," he countered, handing over one bunch, "and the other bunch is in Meg's name, I guess. I want you to give them to her and say I'm sorry."

"Why don't you give them to her yourself?"

"No, I can't."

"Why not?"

"I – I just can't."

Meg, with the other three at the table, could not understand why Jill was taking so long at the front door. Ben took the initiative and, mumbling that her food would get cold, took Jill's plate into the kitchen. As he did so, he caught a glimpse of Jill talking in animated terms with a grey-haired man at the front door. He was tempted in more ways than one to intervene, not least as it was delaying his and Leighton's return in front of the TV. So, plate of half-eaten food in hand, he came up behind Jill, who turned round, glad that he was there.

"This is Len, Meg's other half. I invited him in to give the flowers to Meg. I got some too!" she exclaimed.

"No, I'm interrupting your meal. I must be going."

"No, you're not!" Ben, for once, became quite authoritative. "Come in and eat with us, and give the flowers to Meg yourself."

Len did not know what to do. For all his years, he just wanted to run. What possessed him to buy those flowers, he could not explain. The cold, austere Len, always in charge of his feelings, did not know what to do.

It was Jill's turn to take the initiative. She got round the back of Len, shoved her bunch of flowers into the surprised Ben's hand, still holding her plate in his other hand, and almost frogmarched Len into the house. So they proceeded, Ben leading the way down the hall with flowers in one hand and the plate of unappetising cold food in the other. Len followed, looking more and more sheepish, pushed even more by Jill. Meg and Leighton had continued eating. Meg tried to make conversation between mouthfuls, but it was hard work, not because Leighton did not want to talk but because he wanted to finish his meal and get back to the footie.

"Why are Jill and Ben so long? What is keeping them?"

The same thoughts were going through Leighton's mind, but he did not want to express them. Embarrassment hung heavy in the air.

"Sit down next to Meg," invited Jill as Ben pushed a chair beneath the confused and puzzled Len, still holding the other flowers in his left hand.

Looks were exchanged!

'Here's a pretty mess,' thought Ben, a Gilbert and Sullivan fan, and trying to defuse the situation he asked loudly, "Who would like a drink?"

"A stiff whisky," responded Meg before anyone had a chance to say anything.

"And you, Len?"

"Er, I'll have the same."

"You don't do spirits," interrupted Meg.

"I do now," replied Len, "and these, Meg, are for you."

Len was relieved to have at last unloaded the other bunch of flowers. If Meg had been embarrassed before, she was now in a state of such discomfort and even harboured thoughts of leaving, but decided to stay to finish her meal and the glass of whisky now standing before her.

"And you, Leighton?"

"Just a small beer, Uncle." He felt he should stick to 'Uncle' in Meg's presence.

"Jill?"

"Oh, just an orange juice."

Eventually all five were seated, some finishing their food, some just starting. Conversation was rather stilted. Ben saw there was little headway in the situation thawing, so in between mouthfuls he simply speculated as to what might happen in Len and Meg's home. He had more than detected a 'wait till I get you home' look on Meg's face. Len's feelings were 'I wonder where all this is going to end,' but lost really in the enjoyment of Jill's excellent cuisine he did not hesitate when Jill asked, "Anyone for seconds?"

Leighton, always hungry, quickly accepted, even prepared to forgo footie for just a while.

Ben declined a second helping, but thought, 'Is this what hospitality is all about?' Here were five disparate people, of whom only two jelled together, he and Jill, and even their bond was sometimes looser than it should be.

"Nice lad?" offered Len as Leighton, forgetting there was a lovely apple pie waiting to be devoured, made his excuses and left to watch the match. Len was now in recovery mode. "I used to think all black teenagers were loud and noisy, but he seems quiet and reflective - quite the opposite of what I imagined. How come you never mentioned him when you were teaching, Meg?"

"You were never much interested in my career, were you?"

"No, not really. You always insisted work was work and should never intrude on our domestic life."

"Well, some jobs, such as those of farmers and church ministers, have work as part and parcel of family life. Not that I know many of either. Come to think of it, I don't know any!"

Apple pie being served up, the company began to relax a little.

"I'll take some in to Leighton," said Ben, always looking for a pretext to catch up on the score.

With that he disappeared, not forgetting to take his own bowl with him. The remaining trio looked at each other, but Len and Meg's glances were somewhat circumspect.

"I think we must be going," said Meg. "Thank you for a lovely evening. The story about Ben's sock was very amusing – worth using in a book."

'You want to write another,' thought Len, moving towards their coats and not forgetting the bunch of flowers.

Just then the phone rang and Jill, relieved to get out of the situation, with a hurried "Goodbye" said, "Let yourselves out" and reached for the receiver.

"Hello, Isla here" came the quick reply.

"I'm ringing to say that I have a funny feeling I need to pray for you. I know Leighton has been with you."

Jill, tired as she was, always thought it strange about other people's premonitions, especially someone as young as Isla. Christians who claimed, without much evidence, "The Lord has told me" were a bit low on her priority list.

Isla continued: "I know it is late, but something tells me all is not quite right in your household."

If it had been anyone else, Jill would have quietly, or perhaps not so quietly, exploded, but Isla was different. She was Ben's niece and a delightful girl, to boot.

"Is Leighton still with you?"

"Yes. He and Ben are watching footie. I gather there is a penalty shoot-out, whatever that is. I hear lots of shouts from the lounge from time to time. OK, let me recap on the evening," and as briefly as she could make it she recounted all that had happened during their time together with Meg and Len.

"How interesting!" was Isla's response. "I only know about Meg from what Leighton has told me. I sometimes see them in the paper shop and she seems a very unhappy person." (She was on the point of saying "miserable old git", but stopped herself in time.) "OK, I've got the picture. I think I can pray a bit more intelligently. Our group meet from 10.30 to midnight every Friday evening. Goodnight, Jill. God bless. Sleep well. Must go." And with that she hung up.

'Help, help,' thought Jill. 'Our domestic life is going to be common knowledge. The church will know as well as the rest of the street. Meg and Len will hear about it and I'll never be able to look them in the eyes again!'

Her speculating was interrupted by loud shouts as Ben and Leighton emerged.

"We won 7–6 on the shoot-out!" they exclaimed, and gave each other a hug.

Jill stood by as a mere spectator. To her a shoot-out sounded a very dangerous happening, but boys will be boys. 'We females have more important things to think about and do than twenty-two grown men kicking a ball around.'

"Must be going," said Leighton as he wandered towards the front door.

"Isla rang," said Jill.

"Did she want to speak to me?"

"No, not exactly."

"What did she want?" He was intrigued why his adoptive sister should ring at this time of night.

"Oh, she had a premonition that she should pray for us."

"She gets them all the time," he responded, which was not strictly true, but that was how he saw it. "She has this slightly odd group that meets on Friday nights. A bit weird, I think, but Isla will probably end up becoming a nun or a vicar. I don't know which is worse." And with that he offered a polite "Goodnight" and "Thanks so much" and was gone.

"What an evening!" cried Jill.

"What an evening!" agreed Ben, thinking of the night's footie.

Not too far away another couple, Meg and Len, also reflected on the past few hours. Conversation was rather strained, but easier than it had been in recent months.

"What a nice hospitable couple Ben and Jill are. What makes them tick?" said Meg.

"Don't really know" was all that a sleepy Len could reply. "Goodnight, Meg." And with some effort he kissed her goodnight.

Meg was totally taken by surprise at this first real physical contact for years.

"Goodnight," she muttered. "Do you know something?"

"What?" Len was ready for sleep.

"I've lost my bra."

"'Spect it's behind the radiator" was all Len could add.

AM-DRAM

"You are looking so very beautiful tonight, my darling, certain to steal the heart of many a young man at the ball."

Francine looked in the mirror as she made another 'final' adjustment to her hair, and saw Nicholai standing behind her.

"Why are you looking like that?" Her reflection hid a half-smile which she took some delight in, mixed with curiosity.

"Oh, I am so proud of you," he quietly replied. "Countess Francine - who would have thought it? Why, we have only been married a year and your beauty is the talk of the whole town, if not the whole country."

"Oh, darling, you are so kind. I want you to put your arms around me and whisper you love me."

"Certainly, my dear." His mid-European accent and heavy perfume seemed to grow stronger.

"But what is that in your hand? I dare not turn round to see."

"Just a poker, my love. I intend to strike you a dozen times, one for each lover you have taken in the past twelve months. This one is for—"

He raised the metal bar and was about to bring it down on her head when the director shouted, "OK, we'll leave it there."

Gregory, standing in the wings, was aghast. At

seventeen he could not believe adults could behave in such a way. His drama teacher had encouraged him to join the Artley Players in order to get at least some experience of acting to help his studies in dramatic art. His parents thought it odd for him to study like this. He had struggled with his outside exams, but had made the sixth form, just. English literature and writing about drama would not form much of a base for getting a career, but they were the subjects he enjoyed. He also discovered that Beccy, her mother and father were also into am-dram.

His Uncle Dennis, who lived nearby and came round every Saturday, chiefly to watch *Final Score* and then demand a cup of tea and supper, disapproved of 'performing arts'. He snorted, "Whatever next? Going on to do a degree in it, I guess." (It was more of a statement than a question.) "They will be offering degrees in subjects like firelighting or eating habits in Borneo or some other rubbish. Wasn't like it in my day. Left school with a couple of O levels, I did. All that fancy education - where does it get you?"

"Perhaps Greg will be a famous actor one day. I can just see his name in lights in the West End - Gregory Penfold," said his mother.

"Some chance!" replied Dennis, whose only excursion into the world of culture was to attend the annual pantomime by the Artley Players, but of late he had somewhat tired of it, especially when the front-of-house manager had asked him to laugh a little less enthusiastically.

"But it's funny," retorted Dennis.

"But not as funny as you seem to think," responded the manager, adding that other members of the audience had complained.

Greg's mother had given up on her brother's rather bombastic ways. 'Poor Dennis,' she thought. Elsa had left him and gone back to her native Austria after only two years of marriage. His rather mundane clerical job had shrivelled away with the advance of the computer age and he was left with nothing much to do. He had no hobbies to speak of and the only clubs he joined, such as Scrabble, had asked him to leave after only a couple of sessions. When invited to volunteer for the 'Meals on Wheels' delivery service he remarked that 'I don't really do people' and, whispering under his breath, 'They are all scroungers, and anyway why can't their families look after them?'

Greg's father did see one or two redeeming features in his brother-in-law, but he had to admit they were hard to find.

For his part, Dennis had reluctantly agreed to come to see the play. The director had agreed to Greg having a very small part and to understudy one of the minor characters.

"Is it funny?" asked Dennis, who was rather ambivalent about attending.

Greg had obtained three complimentary tickets so his family could observe his first attempts on the stage.

"No, it's not a laugh a minute," replied Greg.

"*Blood on the Bedroom Carpet* doesn't sound hilarious to me, but OK, I'll be there."

The Artley Players had been in existence for a long while and their productions were always eagerly anticipated in the village. In fact, they could point to at least three generations having taken part at some point and more than one marriage, but sadly a couple of productions had to be just shelved because of extramarital affairs among the cast – situations which caused producers and directors more than a headache, especially when it involved Harriet's husband and the then leading lady.

When the news zoomed round the village the response from Dennis was typical: "What do you expect?" Nevertheless, despite the cancellations, he eagerly awaited the next production. "I know it's part of your schoolwork project, but don't you get involved, and besides I don't know why you want to be an actor. No one in our family - and I should know - has ever been one. Spending your days pretending to be someone else - it ain't natural, that's my opinion."

Greg's parents were, of course, much more supportive.

"If that's what the lad wants, OK. At seventeen he has plenty of time to change his mind. He needs a boost to his self-confidence and this could just be it. His academic achievements to date are not too much and he has little interest in sport."

Greg's mother was more sympathetic. In her wildest dreams she envisaged him as a star in the West End, and this was only the start.

The first evening of the production duly arrived. The audience filled the hall, with only a few complaining about the hardness of the seats, saying the hall committee should have replaced them with more comfortable seating. Gentle music filled the air and a sense of anticipation was experienced in the audience. The music quietened to a whisper; the curtains moved very slowly and out into the spotlight stepped Greg dressed in a nineteenth-century costume.

"Ladies and gentlemen," - his voice was full of confidence, his back ramrod-straight - "I present to you *Blood on the Bedroom Carpet.*"

The spotlight moved away to the bedroom scene.

"I knew it - our boy has the lead in the play. Our shy, slow-learning Greg is going to be famous." Greg's mum could barely control herself, but just managed to suppress herself - even more so when Dennis gave her a nudge in the ribs, as he knew what his sister was like.

The play continued around the conflicts and intrigues of two rival families in some mid-European city; one family had known considerable wealth but was now poor.

'A play in two acts very suitable for amateur

productions' was the publicity blurb. There had been considerable debate in the committee as to whether they should do it.

"The title might put people off coming, but it might pull them," said Jenny, who usually had the largest say.

So it was agreed. Rehearsals were set up to a strict timetable.

"I understand young Greg wants to join us. Don't see why – his family has never been part of the Artley Players, and his Uncle Dennis spends much of his time criticising all that we do."

"Nevertheless, let him come!" decided Jenny, who had been briefed by Greg's drama teacher as to what she might expect.

Very few in the company thought much of the play.

"Who is this Will Spear? Did he write anything else?" was a typical response.

"Load of rubbish. Count me out," said Dave.

Eventually enough people were persuaded to take parts, though one or two who usually took some of the leads decided it was time to turn their hands to lighting, programme selling and making interval tea, coffee and so on.

At the end of the performance the applause was restrained rather than enthusiastic.

Dennis made the comment "That prompt girl had the best part, but she could be heard at the back of the hall. How many times did she have to repeat herself, especially when that count fellow forgot his lines?"

Greg soon changed and met his family.

His mother's face glowed. "My boy, my boy," she cooed. "The play was awful, but the cast coped with it well – but I think you were wonderful."

And then she enveloped him in her ample bosom. It was the sort of embrace that any teenager would have hated, let alone a shy seventeen-year-old male.

Beccy, who also only had a minor part, and whose

presence Greg had almost forgotten, came up and said, "Well done."

This almost knocked the ground from under his feet. To get his mother's effusive embrace was one thing, but Beccy's commendation was another! He couldn't wait to get back to school and share his triumph, however small, with others, pursuing a potential drama career, or at least an A level in performing arts.

As they prepared to leave the hall, Dennis, as usual, had to have the last word: "Only twelve words, a risible amount, that's all," he uttered, "and you are making him out to be a new David Tennant or something!"

His words fell on deaf ears.

"What do you think, Beccy?" Greg plucked up courage to ask for what he thought was a more objective opinion.

"Well, as you know, I was backstage most of the time, but I thought you looked real handsome and before long you will get a proper part."

"Thank you. I will do – I will get on the stage, er, er . . ." he stuttered, whilst she looked at him sympathetically. "I wonder if I could come round to your house, and I could bring some scripts and we could read through them."

Beccy, who was hoping for something a little more romantic, sounded quite enthusiastic.

"Yes, that will be nice."

But just then Greg's parents and Uncle Dennis decided it was time for home as it was getting late.

Blood on the Bedroom Carpet was due to run for three nights with a matinee, mainly for senior citizens, on the Saturday afternoon. It was just as well there were only four performances, as the audience on the Friday night was less than half that on the previous evening.

Comments flew around the cast. "Who decided we should do this awful play?" and so on, and, as is the nature of things, people looked around for someone to blame.

Then Meredith, who played the part of the Count, dropped a bombshell. "That's it. I've had enough. You can stuff your awful rubbish. I, for one, will be watching TV tomorrow. You will have to find someone else."

Now, as with many organisations, the Artley Players relied on trust, goodwill and large doses of understanding to help produce the productions.

"We will have to cancel!" exclaimed the director as Meredith stormed out of the door leaving his costume behind but his face still covered in make-up.

"What about the old folks tomorrow afternoon, let alone the supper evening?" The director looked at the grim faces of the cast. A couple of the girls were in tears. The situation looked hopeless, or worse than hopeless.

Luke the treasurer piped up. "We will lose a lot of money and the club's finances are in dire straits as it is!"

The mood of the group lightened a fraction, but only a fraction, as various ideas were floated!

"What about old Art? I'm sure he would do it. He played the lead for us for many years."

"Don't be stupid. He's well past it and now very deaf," said someone else. Perhaps someone could read it."

"Wouldn't be the same."

"I know I never liked that Meredith, always fancied himself as a ladies' man, but the play *must* go on."

All agreed that the performances would continue, but they could not agree how. It was getting very late, but there appeared no way of solving the dilemma other than someone dressing in the Count's costume and reading the part.

"What about Greg? Could he not do it?" It was Beccy who piped up, and a dozen pairs of eyes turned on him.

He was tired and knew that his parents were waiting for him outside, wondering why the delay, having seen Meredith rush out and drive away in a hurry still in his make-up.

Greg stood speechless, which is not what an actor is

supposed to be, but stuttered, "Me! Me?"

"Go on, you can do it." Beccy was now at her most persuasive.

Silence for several seconds, then Greg said, "OK, I'll give it a try."

A mixture of relief and delight swept through the group.

Beccy came up close to Greg and said quietly, "I know you can do it."

Greg, feeling a mixture of apprehension and pleasure, said, "I'll do it for you, Beccy."

"Hold on, Greg, you will be doing it for the players and, not least, the old folks and those who have paid for the supper evening."

The director found a script and gave it to Greg. In fact, the part of the Count was not all that long since, after the opening scene, he was arrested and thrown into prison and then did not appear again till later in the play.

'Gone 11 p.m.,' the director thought. 'Well, we have nothing to lose.'

"Mum, Dad," called Greg as he ran out into the car park, where his parents still waited, wondering what was happening.

Uncle Dennis had, of course, tried to avoid coming as it was his pub night.

"Mum, I've got the part!"

"What part, dear?"

"Why, the Count. Meredith said he couldn't take any more, and there was no one else to do it. Isn't it wonderful?"

Greg's father was less than excited, but his mother was over the moon.

"Can you learn the words in time?"

"I will, if it means staying up all night."

"No need for that,"responded his father as they drove home.

Nevertheless Greg put the script beside his bed and

woke a couple of times in the night to go through his lines.

His mother, in the bedroom next to his, thought she imagined, in her drowsy state, words being uttered in a heavy mid-European accent.

News soon got round the village. The shoppers on the Saturday bus were full of it. "Young Greg taking Meredith's part. I never did like him. Doesn't need to act," said Maisie, "pompous on stage as well as off it. I can't wait to be there this afternoon."

Word had even got to the next village, and the 'Silver Tots' cancelled the Saturday bingo session to come.

Greg tried out his lines in front of his mother, who, of course, could see little or no fault in her son. The proceedings were interrupted by a ring on the doorbell.

"Who can that be?" she wondered, thinking that, by chance, it might be some West End producer or even the BBC.

"Go on, Mum – answer it" was Greg's response.

The door was opened and there stood Beccy.

"Come in, come in, child" was his mother's greeting.

(The young but sophisticated Beccy could not cope with being called 'child'. She was a grown-up woman – well, almost. Nevertheless she accepted the invitation, but declined a coffee and met with Greg, whose eyes shone with delight.)

"Just came to wish you well this afternoon. Sorry I can't be there. As for all the wrinklies, my gran was invited but says she's not old enough yet. Anyway, I'm off to watch Jack play rugby, but I hope to be there tonight, if I get back in time." With that she gave him the lightest peck on the cheek, whispered "God bless" and was out of the door almost before Greg's mother could open it.

The latter's imagination knew no bounds, stretching to not only Greg's name in lights, but Beccy's as well. However, her dreaming did not exactly get as far as planning a wedding, but the potential of Beccy being a daughter-in-law was not far from her thoughts.

"Mum," enquired Greg thoughtfully, "what did she mean, 'God bless'?"

"Oh, it's nothing - some people say it all the time. It's like 'good luck'. It doesn't mean all that much. We don't believe in God in this household. If He is around He doesn't bother us much. Go and ask Uncle Dennis. He's got a lot less time for God than we have, and that's not much!"

Greg was in a real pickle; he felt very nervous about his part in the play as well as confused about Beccy. Did she have a rugby-playing boyfriend, so that his chances with her were somewhat slight? Nevertheless the words 'God bless' would not go away. Greg's mother had gone to quite a bit of trouble to prepare his favourite meal of steak pie and chips, but Greg could eat little.

"Uncle Dennis will scoff it when he comes for *Final Score*."

However, Uncle Dennis had other plans.

Well before time, a queue had formed outside the village hall. The vicar, who lived in the next village and who had put his Sunday preparations on hold, found himself trying to calm the excited group.

The hall manager looked over the queue and spotted half a dozen teenage girls. "You can't be pensioners," he shouted, trying to make himself heard. "This show is for the OAPs. Come to keep Gran company, have you?"

The girls sniggered and giggled. "Eh, yes," said the boldest one, not very convincingly.

"Come to see young Greg make a fool of himself?"

"No," said another, "we think he is very brave to take on the part at short notice."

"Oh, all right." The hall manager was all for a bit of peace. "You'll have to stand at the back and no twittering or giggling. This is a serious production and we don't want it messed up by you lot. You'll have to pay full price. I gather money is lost on this OAPs' afternoon."

This caused great consternation among the girls, who

were soon on their mobile phones either ringing or texting their parents to get the necessary funds.

"But, Mum, you said," pleaded one girl.

The queue shortened and was moving forward when the coach party from the next village arrived. Despite most of them wanting the toilet and a few grumbling about missing bingo they were soon ushered inside.

Minutes later a harassed man in his forties said, "Here you are, girls - enough cash for you all to enjoy the show." And with that he drove off as speedily as he had arrived.

Greg and his mother had sneaked past the queue and escaped the teenagers, round the back to the dismal dressing room where the wardrobe mistress was waiting.

"You are just about the same size as Meredith. Try it all on. I'm sure it will fit you."

Indeed it did, much to his mother's delight.

Next was the make-up, which Greg thought was odd, but nevertheless he submitted to the pot and brushes of Vera, who had done the job for the company for many a year. Eventually he emerged and his mother nearly swooned.

"My darling boy, you look every inch the Count."

"Thank you, Mother. Remember this is meant to be a very mid-European play."

So the curtain rose on the matinee performance with the opening scene in the bedroom.

Greg began: "You are looking so very beautiful tonight, my darling, certain to steal the heart of many a young man at the ball." Greg had the words and accent off to perfection. He had practised on the cat several times that morning (the cat was not impressed).

So the opening scene proceeded and, even if Greg's cat, Floss, had been disdainful, the elderly audience lapped it up, especially when half of Greg's moustache fell off. He did not notice, but others did, and Vera cursed the type of glue she had used to fix it. Enough for those in the front row to wonder if it was part of the play.

Greg continued with the words "I am so proud of you." He had opted for a Germanic accent instead of a French one.

So the first act continued until the Count, who is later accused and imprisoned, had raised the poker following his denunciation of the lovers Francine had taken in the past twelve months.

"This one is for—"

With that the curtains closed rapidly; a crash and an ear-piercing scream were heard. Francine, played by Hayley, was not too good at screams, so it was left to Vera, who had never fancied acting, but enjoyed this moment of glory.

The audience loved it, but one or two were puzzled. Why was it not funnier, as the only comic moment was Greg losing part of his moustache? Was it a comedy? It wasn't billed as such. The only information the programme had given was that it was '*Blood on the Bedroom Carpet*: a Victorian melodrama in three acts with six scenes'.

The curtains opened to reveal the same scene; this time with copious false blood swimming around the floor (Bert in props had ordered twice the amount needed 'just in case', he said.) Greg, with a new moustache firmly fixed in place, sat, as the Count, on an ornate bedroom chair, staring at the floor with a bloodstained poker in his right hand. A section of the audience could see Francine's lifeless body half off the stage. Hayley, who played Francine, wasn't too good at playing dead bodies - come to that, she wasn't too good at playing live ones - but there was no one else who had the looks and the build to play the part, brief though it was.

Enter Inspector Morsi.

"Ho ho, vot 'ave we 'ere? Looks a straightforward case to me, don't you agree, Sergeant?" But before the Sergeant (played by Eddie, the local bookmaker) could reply the Inspector uttered, "Count Nicholai, hime charging you with the wilful murder of Countess Francine. Have you anything to say?"

Greg, who had really got into the part, merely said, "Nope," a word which he had practised hard for the past eighteen hours.

Just then a comment was heard from Vera: "Mind where you are stepping - we don't want all that blood walked over the place. Once it's in the carpet it's so hard to get rid of it."

They were bit puzzled - why so much blood? But then they took it in their stride.

Greg's mum interrupted: "No, not my boy," but no one really noticed.

Handcuffs were produced and employed; then the Sergeant marched the Count off to prison. The play continued for another hour, through prison and court scenes, where the Count pleaded not guilty to murder as the curtain came down for the interval.

The discussion over tea and biscuits was "Of course he's guilty. He had the poker in his hand." There was no one anywhere prepared to find him innocent, despite his 'not guilty' plea.

Greg stood in the dock. The make-up girls had gone to town to give him an ashen face. His mother, in the front row, could not believe that it was her son being tried for murder. She lived every second of it, while Greg's father folded his arms and thought what a lousy play it was and, of course, apart from Greg, what a rotten cast too!

As the second act continued, the prosecution opened its case with forensic evidence being presented. The shortage of cast members meant that only a couple of witnesses were called who vouchsafed that the Count was a wicked, horrible man, who deserved to hang for this terrible crime.

"No he doesn't," cried out Greg's mum, much to the disapproving looks of those sitting close at hand.

The boy playing the Judge (Damien) had been chosen

not because of his acting skills, which were minimal at the best of times, but because he was the oldest member of the cast and the director felt he had to give him a part.

"Is there any case for the defence?"

At this point Greg could not believe his eyes, for up stepped Beccy, suitably dressed as an East European lawyer.

"Yes, your honour, I wish to present the case for the defence." So with an eloquence beyond her years she outlined her case. The fact that the Countess had died could not be denied, and she *appeared* to have lost a great deal of blood (though not nearly as much as the props department had spilled on the floor). Warming to her subject (Greg was now very impressed) the lawyer showed that the Countess had slipped and fatally hit her head on the dressing table and in so doing had knocked over a bottle of red paint, which covered the bedroom floor.

Damien, the Judge, commented, "Yes, all very well, but how did the poker get into the hand of the accused?"

"Oh, that is easy: he had picked it up intending to stoke the fire, when it slipped and landed in what the prosecution call blood."

The Judge looked round the courtroom (it was a country where juries did not exist), then thought for a moment. "I find the accused not guilty."

With that the court exploded as did the audience, and – especially Greg's mum – went wild. Greg and Beccy hugged each other as if it were real.

"How did you get the part? I thought old Tony Hewins was the defence counsel."

"No, he is down with the flu, so I got a call late this morning and I didn't want to tell you. They offered me a script to read, but I just made it up as I went along."

"Wow!" was all Greg could utter.

Time was moving along. Beccy went home, telling her family all that had happened. Greg's parents collected him and they all went home, where a grumpy and despondent Uncle Dennis sat watching *Final Score*.

"Lost again, lost again," he muttered, totally ignoring the trio who had just entered and their triumphant exclamations about the play.

A hurried supper was marred only by Dennis's truculence, and soon they were on their way back.

Again the hall was packed, and the news had spread like wildfire that two seventeen-year-olds had taken over parts at short notice and that the senior citizens went home enraptured by the play. Soon there was a queue for entry, one or two wondering if Greg's false moustache was going to fall off again.

Those who had bought tickets for the supper tucked in with relish since the bar had been opened some time earlier. Quite a few somehow also managed to be fed, despite not having paid. Nevertheless there was plenty for all, and after the tables and chairs were packed away the audience settled down to enjoy the play.

Greg was just making final adjustments to his costume when in walked Meredith and declared, "I am playing the part after all. Can't let a mere whippersnapper like you take over."

"Oh, help!" cried Vera.

Greg was struck dumb, and the director was nowhere to be found. Greg slumped down in his chair.

"Come on, young lad, get that costume off. I want to look the part."

Just then the door opened and in walked not the director, but Uncle Dennis.

"Just come to wish you well, lad. Eh, heck, who is this?"

His eyes met Meredith full on, who said, "I don't know who you are, or what you are doing here, but I am playing the part, and I've told Greg he can go."

That was enough for Dennis. The tiny dressing room was warm enough already, but now, with three bodies in it, was very overheated. In an instant Dennis had grabbed Meredith by the collar and had frogmarched him outside, notwithstanding Meredith had half changed, with his trousers around his knees. The ladies came out of the female changing rooms, amazed at what they had heard and saw. Once outside, Dennis gave Meredith a mighty punch on the mouth.

"How dare you try to usurp my nephew's part."

Meredith sank to his knees; all his bluster and flamboyance had evaporated. He felt his mouth and realised blood was oozing from his lip.

"I – I . . ." was all he could utter.

Quite quickly some people at the end of the queue realised what was happening and went to his aid. Dennis disappeared into the darkness. One or two wondered if this could possibly be part of the play. One whizz-kid wondered if the play could be rewritten as *Blood on the Bitumen* rather than *Blood on the Bedroom Carpet*. Meredith's wife was found in the audience and was taken to him.

"What have you been doing? I can't trust you to be on your own for a second. Here, let me wipe your lips. I'm taking you home." And off they went leaving two empty seats, which were soon filled.

Dennis, feeling rather smug, slipped into the hall by a side door. He had known, since he was a kid, how to get in without paying. He found a seat, next to Greg's dad, who had heard, first-hand, from Greg about Beccy' s impromptu performance, and looked round to see if he could spot her family. Many of the audience appeared to be from Beccy and Greg's sixth form. Quite a few of them had evaded payment for the meal, but had spent quite a bit at the bar (now closed).

The curtains slowly opened, deliberately slowly, as more than once during rehearsals Darren, aged twelve, had pulled too hard and they had come off their runners. Darren was reprimanded and told he would get the sack if he did it again, but he knew that was impossible as there was no one else to do it.

The audience looked in wonder as Greg, dressed as the Count, prepared to utter his well-learnt lines.

He was interrupted by his schoolmates shouting, "Go for it, Greg" and "Sock it to her" and so on, with a few of the girls giving a scream or two.

Eventually a sonorous voice offstage requested the audience to calm down and enjoy the play.

"Darling, you are looking very beautiful tonight."

With all the incidents beforehand, let alone Uncle Dennis's eviction of Meredith, Greg wondered if he could still remember his lines. He made a light touch on his top lip to make sure all was securely in place. He thought, 'I'm doing this for Beccy and also for Mum and Dad, Uncle Dennis and Floss the cat.

So the play proceeded to the interval, when the bar opened again.

"Watching this gives me a real thirst" was one local comment.

Some of the teenagers made the most of the opportunity.

When Beccy came on the stage, robed this time in wig and gown - somewhat strangely as the play was set somewhere outside Britain - the teenage lads, fuelled a little by alcohol, whistled and shouted, "Go, Beccy, go." So much so that the confident Beccy had to pause a moment before she could continue.

The play concluded with rapturous curtain calls, with Beccy and Greg summoned to the front of the cast. The director and also the chairman of the parish council made speeches - the latter was somewhat overlong explaining how the council loved to support community groups - and everyone, especially most of the teenagers, went home happy. One or two wondered if the Artley Players could choose something better next time. All, of course, except Meredith, who sat at home wondering how he had got in this mess! His wife only had a modicum of sympathy for him and refused to take him to A & E.

"You'll be OK in the morning. Take a couple of paracetamols and you will be fine."

Beccy and Greg (when he could get away from his mother's gaze) said goodnight.

"Greg, I wonder . . ."

Greg was on mental tiptoe wondering what would come next.

Beccy continued: "My mum and dad thought it would be nice if you would come and eat with us. Would Thursday be OK, about six?"

"Lovely" was all Greg could reply.

He was on cloud nine. He had thought possibly of McDonald's or KFC, but this was wonderful.

When he told his parents, his mother was in rapture. Not only was he the star of the play, but he had this lovely girlfriend. In her fantasy world she was almost going shopping for the wedding outfit.

Her husband, phlegmatic as ever, merely said, "Calm down, dear. It's nice for Greg to be invited, but let's leave it at that. He won't need a chaperone."

Thursday was a day when Beccy and Greg had a couple of free periods and they met briefly, an event not unnoticed by her giggly friends.

"OK for this evening?"

"Yes, what do I wear?"

"Come as you like, but not in school uniform."

Greg went round to his local garage, and bought some flowers for Beccy's mum. Greg's mum had suggested he did this, pressing a £10 note into his hands. On the spur of the moment Greg got two bunches, one for his hostess and one for Beccy. The table was laid and Greg was surprised to find he would be sitting at a table, which he had not done since the days when each week he went to his late gran, who always decreed that was where they ate.

She said, "Can't stand those TV dinners."

Beccy's mum, who looked very prim and tidy, invited him to sit down; she enquired about his studies and his interest in the stage. Conversation flowed easily, interrupted only by the appearance of Beccy in a very attractive green-and-gold dress.

Beccy's mum (Kate) explained she was mostly vegetarian but was happy to cook meat for others.

"Is a pork chop OK?"

"Yes please," was all Greg could respond, thinking that his mother's efforts at family catering would have resulted in something grossly underdone or burnt black, neither of which was edible.

Beccy's father said, "We say grace in this household and hold hands together."

Greg had never met this before, but he liked the idea of holding Beccy's hand and the squeeze she gave him afterwards.

Peter explained they were sorry to have missed the play, but were delighted to hear how well it had gone, not least because of last-minute stand-ins. "I should explain, and it was naughty of Beccy not to say so [Greg could not countenance the idea of Beccy being naughty even for a second] that we belong to an organisation called Midnight Angels."

Greg' s jaw dropped so much that for a moment he forgot to eat.

"It's a Christian group that goes into the town every Saturday and Sunday to help young people who go clubbing, and often drink too much alcohol. We have been doing it for four years, ever since we felt Beccy could stay on her own for an evening. Safety is the watchword. Mind you, we often get into some funny situations, but I won't go into that now or your food will get cold."

Greg, apart from his stage triumphs, enjoyed himself enormously. Beccy, who usually had a lot to say, just smiled at him demurely. She was proud of her parents for what they did, especially as they both had demanding and responsible jobs. Greg's thoughts were in a whirlwind. He loved the food, especially the home-made orange cheesecake. 'What do these people believe?' His dad and Uncle Dennis had warned him to keep clear of religious nutters, as they called them, but these people were normal. Oh yes, Beccy's mum was vegetarian, but that is quite common these days.

After the meal, Peter enquired what Greg would like to do? Greg thought it was great to be asked.

"I'm afraid we haven't got a telly these days as the last one broke down and we have not replaced it. We usually read or play games like Scrabble or Monopoly."

'What a strange family!' thought Greg. 'Can't wait to get home and tell my mum and dad, as they have the telly on all the time.'

"Actually I think I had better get home as I have some homework to do for tomorrow. Something about the Globe Theatre in Shakespeare's time and as it is now. You know there is a school trip to London to see it."

"Yes, we know. Beccy wants to go on it too. I'll get the car," offered Peter.

"Thank you for such a lovely meal," responded Greg, adding cheekily, "I hope I can come again," knowing he dare not invite any of them, let alone Beccy, to his home.

"I'll see you to the door. You were wonderful," said Beccy.

"So were you," Greg replied as she gave him the lightest kiss on the cheek.

Back home, his mother was all agog to know how he got on and what was the food like, what were Beccy's parents like, what were the curtains made of . . . ? And so on and so on.

They are a bit different from us. They are Christians. They go to church, including Beccy, and they are involved in late-night street work in town. Midnight Angels, they call themselves.

"I told you, religious nutters. You wait till Uncle

Dennis hears about this. He will give Beccy's dad one, just like he did Meredith in the car park last Saturday."

"Dad!"

For the first time for quite a while Greg felt he could stand up to his father, not least because all the negative remarks were coming from behind a tabloid newspaper whilst reality TV blared out from the corner.

His girlfriend's father's honour was at stake, if not that of Beccy herself.

"We'll do well to keep clear, son, that's all I'm saying, and don't get asking that girl round here."

"Don't worry, I won't."

With that he stormed off to his room, all thoughts of homework forgotten as he threw himself on his bed. At seventeen he was too big to cry, but his feelings were at rock bottom. He'd had such a lovely time with Beccy's family and that feather-like kiss had sealed the evening, and now to come home to this! After lying there for what seemed ages, but was only twenty minutes, a knock on the door disrupted his tangled thoughts.

"Who is it?" he shouted.

"It's Mum. Can I come in?"

"Yes, if you want to."

His mother could not believe what she saw. The room was spick and span – the only disturbance was that Greg had lain on the bed. For over two years Greg had told his parents that this was his room and they were not to invade his space.

"Mum, why is Dad so rude?"

"He's rude to me sometimes, dear. Come and give your mum a big hug."

Greg needed no further requests and they hugged each other for quite a while.

Eventually Greg said, "I have some homework to do for tomorrow. It's comparing Shakespeare's Globe Theatre then and the modern one on the South Bank."

"Look, son, forget it for a while."

"Well, it is only preliminary notes. The real write-up is after the visit next week."

Mum's last words were, "Well, try and get to sleep."

Mrs Williamson was indeed understanding when Greg explained the situation next morning. All the other students had prepared their five-minute presentations, and Mrs Williamson thanked them all and outlined the details for the coach trip next week.

The day duly arrived and Greg, ever hopeful, was expecting to sit next to Beccy all the way there and all the way back, but she sat with her pals, giggling on the back seat for most of the outward journey. Mrs Williamson had arranged for the party to see behind the scenes and, indeed, two of the minor members of the cast were able to spend time with the group all asking questions, which came thick and fast.

'Very unlike the Artley Players in our village hall,' thought Greg. 'The contrast could not be greater.'

After their packed lunches, they settled down for *The Tempest,* wishing it was *Romeo and Juliet*. Greg, of course, wanted to play Romeo to Beccy's Juliet.

Afterwards, back on the bus, Mrs Williamson reminded them all that the project presentations would have to be in on Friday. On the way back the back seat had been commandeered by five noisy lads and the girls had to sit elsewhere.

"Can I come and sit with you?" Beccy was her most charming self.

Greg's spirits rose sky-high and he did his best to ignore the raucous shouts from the back. "Watch it, Beccy, that Greg's a crafty one," etc.

They got down to discussing all they had seen and heard.

"Wasn't the chap who played Prospero great?" was Beccy's opening gambit.

Mrs Williamson realised that on these trips a certain

amount of pairing off took place, but did her best to keep an eye on the group.

"Did you enjoy the play?" Beccy continued.

"Yes and no" was all Greg could reply, not believing his luck that this lovely girl was sitting next to him for the journey home.

The conversation did not exactly fizzle out, but Beccy found herself snuggling up to Greg in a way she had never done before. Greg's mind also wandered off, not least to his visit to her parents' last week. He had often wondered why he was an only child, but had never dared ask. On the rare occasions he had visited his parents' bedroom he had noticed lots of photos of a pair of toddlers about two and a half years old as well as numerous ones of himself as a baby and as a child.

"What are you thinking about, Greg?" a dreamy voice murmured in his ear.

"Only wondering why I'm an only child. Are you one too?"

"Yes, I am. I had twin brothers, a couple of years older than me, but they were killed in a terrible car accident when I was only five."

"Oh, I am so sorry," Greg slowly replied. "Did your parents take it badly?"

"Yes, they did. At first there was a lot of crying, and sometimes shouting. I guess Mum and Dad blamed each other. Then they discovered a real faith in God and ever so slowly things began to change, and now in Midnight Angels they have a real outlet for their faith."

Greg remained silent. He thought, 'Her parents might be called "religious nutters", but not my Beccy.' He felt very much that Beccy was his, and now they had something in common, in that each of them was an only child.

It was a very weary group of sixth formers who staggered off the coach. One or two of the braver lads had smuggled cans of lager on board, but had managed to keep the consumption quiet. Mrs Williamson and other members of staff had their suspicions, but they too were tired and wanted to get home.

"Did you enjoy the play?"

Greg's mum was full of curiosity. No one in her family had ever had an interest in the arts before; it had never been encouraged in her childhood. Greg's father took a different stance, especially when he discovered a couple of blond hairs on Greg's school jacket.

"I don't think you 'ave been on some fancy coach trip to London; I bet you 'ave been skiving off round the pub with that snooty tart, what's-'er-name. Beccy, Rebecca, that's a fancy name."

"Stop it, Dad. I've got project work to do – I'm off to my room."

The drama group assembled on Friday under Mrs Williamson's tutorial gaze and each student gave their presentation about the old and the new Globe Theatre. Some concentrated on the history of the old building, pointing out that it must have been almost rural in its setting and alluding to the flowering of the dramatic arts in the Elizabethan era. Others commented on the present renaissance of interest in Shakespeare. Mrs Williamson's comments were full of encouragement and she felt that Beccy's contribution was the best. However, her assessments were kept private until the end-of-term reports.

"Beccy, I would like to come and talk to your parents," said Greg as they waited for the school bus.

Beccy was very curious to know why, but Greg would not let on.

"Come round tonight about eight o'clock, OK?"

Beccy's parents were rather puzzled, wondering if it was something to do with their beautiful daughter.

"Mr and Mrs Simpson," began Greg hesitantly, "I

would like to join Midnight Angels."

"Well, Greg, that is wonderful. We are always looking for new recruits, but there are two big hurdles," replied Beccy's dad.

"First is that you are not old enough!" It was Beccy's mum who spoke.

"I'm eighteen in a couple of months' time. I'll be a man then." Greg drew himself up to his full height, which was not too high.

"We could put you down for the next training session."

"Training?" queried Greg, feeling somewhat threatened. "I don't need training to help with teenagers out late on the street."

"I'm afraid you do, but we will see what can be done."

"And the second?" Greg was puzzled.

"Well, I will put it gently," said Mrs Simpson. "It is that you are not yet a Christian."

Greg was lost for words. "I just don't get it. You mean I have to go to church and accept all that religious stuff. You don't need to have religion to do those things."

"That's true, Greg." Beccy's father spoke. "But we do it because we feel God is calling us to do it. Here is a leaflet about Midnight Angels. You might like to take it and read it and we will pray about it."

So Greg wandered home. He didn't even have a chance to say goodnight to Beccy. Puzzled, troubled and confused, he even thought of talking to his parents, but knew that would not work.

Greg's eighteenth birthday came and went with a bang. His parents, not wishing to risk his mum's cooking, hired caterers. Even Uncle Dennis put in an appearance to wish his nephew well. Sadly for Greg, Beccy did not come. She had gone to something called Soul Survivor. Greg thought it odd when she should have been at his party.

Years later, the nearby town presented its annual community awards. It had been a lavish dinner.

"And our final award tonight goes to Midnight Angels for all their work, late at night, with youngsters on the street. And here to receive it is our very own budding actor, and Midnight Angels' deputy director, Greg Penfold."

Greg made a generous acceptance speech, thanking many, many people who were involved, and stating quite emphatically that it was his faith in Christ that had made all the difference.

As Greg said a fond goodnight to his fiancée, Beccy, he uttered the immortal words "You are looking so very beautiful tonight, my darling," to which she replied, "Greg, what is that in your hand behind your back? It's not a poker, is it?"

"No, only the community award we won tonight!"

THE DANUBE CRUISE

David, or Davie as he liked to be called, and Dyllis had been married forty years. Friends, family and neighbours congratulated them.

"How shall we celebrate?"

Davie had no idea. Indeed, the thought of celebrating anything was rather foreign to him.

Dyl, as she liked to be called, replied with a grunt as she could not understand why people made such a fuss. Her friend Carol, if indeed she could be called a friend, seemed to celebrate everything, even her divorce from Harold after some fifteen years of wedlock, or deadlock.

"Go," she said, pointing to all the large ads for cruises in a national paper. "Go and enjoy yourself. I bet Davie would go with me now I'm free!"

"No, not if he was paying," Dyl replied.

Nevertheless, Dyl did pop into the travel agents when Davie wasn't looking and came back armed with brochures. The word 'celebration' occurred in more than a few of them. She looked them over with some disdain, not least when confronted with the costs. Before Davie could find them she put them into a plastic bag and hid them in a wardrobe.

A fortnight later after another silent meal: "Well?" he uttered.

"Well what?" Dyl was never very voluble even at the best of times.

"About our anniversary, silly."

"Don't call me silly" was the stilted retort.

"I want to know what you think; otherwise it will be off to Skeggy for a week as always."

The idea of a week in Skeggy in September, a holiday no different from normal, did in fact prompt Dyl to utter, "I was thinking about a cruise."

"A cruise!" Davie was flabbergasted. "A cruise!" he nearly exploded. He supposed for a change of scenery Bournemouth or Margate might be an option, but this was way out of his atmosphere.

"My friend Carol has been on one. She says they are great!"

"Your so-called friend Carol has got more money than sense. Probably she got a lot from her divorce settlement."

"A lot more than I'll get from you if that should happen to us, but it won't!" was Dyl's response, though any observer would have thought it was said with little conviction.

It was now February and the actual anniversary was still many months away. Conversation was limited at the best of times, but the subject did crop up once or twice but no more and concluded with the usual put-downs, which rarely pierced their thick skins. However, one day when he was looking for a better pair of trousers to wear he spied the large plastic bag in the wardrobe and before long he emptied it out on the bed – her bed, since they had long ceased to have a double one.

He could not believe his eyes! Colourful, exotic brochures, sea cruises, river cruises, bulb-field cruises, cruises around the British Isles, to Egypt, to the Far East, to America and so on.

"What is she plotting now? A surprise maybe for us both or with someone else? Now, that would be a surprise. Shall I put them away and pretend I have not seen them or leave them here and see how she reacts?" He pondered his options for several minutes and decided to leave them on her bed.

Dyl came back from her afternoon bridge class, grumbled at Davie, went upstairs to change and was confronted by her bed covered in brochures. She was just about to explode when the phone rang.

"Dyllis here." She always made sure that anyone ringing would know who it was even if it was a wrong number or somebody trying to sell something.

"Carol here. Did you get the booklets about cruises? I bet Davie was surprised when he saw them."

"Yes, he must have been," replied Dyl meekly.

"And what did he say?" And before Dyl could reply she added, "Have you signed up yet?"

Carol was in many ways the opposite of Dyl - very talkative and at times very unable to listen.

"He didn't say anything!" was Dyl's truthful reply, adding, "Or if he did it was not in my hearing."

"Go on, coax him just this once. You will never get another ruby wedding anniversary."

"I might" was Dyl's comment. "I just might!"

"Who was that on the phone?" The words came over the sports pages. "Not your friend Carol again? She is always ringing up, usually about something trivial. Can talk the hind leg off a giraffe that woman can."

"It's *donkey*!"

"Donkey? I'm sure giraffe. Well, I meant it - giraffes have longer legs than donkeys, stupid!"

So it continued. Dyllis and her husband had endured more guerrilla conflict which did sometimes revert to an armed truce.

Spring came and Davie continued at the drawing office at the local factory where he had worked for many years.

"Going on your usual holiday to Skeggy in September, then?" Stephen was the only person Davie felt anywhere close to at work, and not particularly close at that.

"Well, yes and no!"

"What do you mean, yes and no? You go there every year, come back and say how bracing it was."

"I know, but Dyl is talking about a cruise."

"A cruise!" Stephen could not believe his ears. "You on a cruise? You must be joking." At this point Stephen recognised he had gone a bit too far. "I'm sorry, Davie, but you seem rather conservative for some reason."

"We have a special anniversary coming up and it might, just might, be a way to celebrate."

"Good for you, mate."

Davie was just about to add that he had seen the dozens of brochures that had been hidden in the wardrobe and spread them all on the bed and Dyl had not produced them, merely packed them up again and this time hidden them where Davie could not possibly find them.

And so it continued, both of them wanting and not wanting to talk about it.

At work Stephen was desperate to know more of Davie's plans – or non-plans, as they looked like turning into.

"Why not have a knees-up in the pub? I could propose a toast and give a little speech."

'A long one if I know you,' thought Davie, 'especially when you get some ale inside you.'

"No way," replied Davie. "She would not even consider it."

The days and weeks went by, when by chance (or was it?) Carol met Davie outside the paper shop where he went on Saturday mornings for the *Racing Herald* and a quick visit to the betting shop.

"Made a decision on a cruise yet?"

Davie looked at her in surprise. "Er, no, not exactly."

"What do you mean, not exactly? I know Dyl was getting some brochures, but that was weeks ago. You must have made your mind up by now?" Carol, who wasn't exactly man-hungry but felt she was as on fire as she had ever been, suddenly blurted out (words which passers-by were not supposed to hear), "If she won't go, I will."

Davie hastened to retreat into the nearest shop, which happened to be a Chinese takeaway, only it was closed. He had somewhere admired Carol from a distance, especially the way she had stood up to her bullying husband over so many years.

"It will be single cabins, of course."

"With Dyl and I it will be single cabins anyway."

This conversation, if it could be called that, now attracted a small audience, positioning themselves within earshot but surveying the menu in the window of the Chinese takeaway.

"These two, are they married or what?"

There was no clear answer.

Davie hastily made his excuses and, with his paper tucked under his arm, hurried his way home.

"Get it booked, Davie, or we will be too late!" was Carol's parting shot. (She was getting good at parting shots, especially in public.)

'What does she mean? If anyone is coming on this cruise it is going to be Dyl and me.'

Carol was not quite so easily put off and still harboured thoughts of such a trip even if it meant going with someone as dull as Davie. Single cabins might be a problem, but with a little female ingenuity that could be easily overcome, especially as many of these cruises offered free drink.

Carol's suggestion was just the spur Davie was looking for.

"I saw all those brochures, dear."

'Dear' was a word he rarely, if ever, used.

"Oh, yes!" But Dyl did add, "What did you make of them?"

"Expensive" was Davie's retort. "No wonder they can produce such colourful contents the amount they charge! All the same, I think we can afford it."

So with mutual reluctance they spent an evening going through them all. Eventually the pile of rejects was all there was to see, except for one for a company called STRE. STRE, it was discovered, stood for Single Travellers' Excursion and prided itself on offering exclusive travel to single people over fifty. 'You may be on your own, but you are never alone on a STRE cruise,' said the blurb. 'However, we do have a couple of double cabins.'

Before she knew it Dyl was back at the travel agent booking a cruise on the Danube in September.

"Got something to celebrate, have we?" enquired the curious agent, looking at Dyl's wedding ring. "We only have single cabins on this trip."

"That's OK. We can cope with that," replied Dyl, getting her credit card out for the deposit.

'Strange,' thought the agent: 'married but single cabins – perhaps he is not her husband.'

Such thoughts must abound in the travel industry, but of course they are not allowed to express them.

Three days later a large envelope thumped its way on to the doormat. In large letters it said, 'THANK YOU FOR CHOOSING A STRE CRUISE.'

"Now all the neighbourhood will know. You bet some of them can gossip!"

This wasn't really true, but Dyl was the sort of person who often thought the worst of people until proved otherwise.

Dyl did pop into the travel agent one more time to check insurance, etc.

"You were lucky – they were the last cabins left. Pity they are at the stern – it can get a bit bumpy on the Danube."

At this Dyl felt her heart drop an inch or two, but it had all been booked. Davie had somehow reluctantly agreed to pay for it and cancellation at this late stage would mean losing most of their deposit payments.

However, the day arrived and the taxi appeared on the

dot and they were whisked to the airport. A long delay at the check-in did nothing to improve their demeanour, but eventually after two flights and a long coach journey they checked in to their ship and were taken to their cabins. They had never seen such luxury. The reception and the comfort of their surroundings took their breath away.

Departing to their respective accommodation, in adjoining cabins, they prepared for the cocktail reception before dinner. Emerging at almost the same time, Davie was astounded at Dyl – she was positively glowing in a long evening dress. Was this the woman whom he had married but who for as many years as he could remember had held him in some sort of lofty contempt? He said nothing. She, for her part, thought he looked smarter than he had done for some time, but she held her tongue – something she found difficult to do!

Then with the help of a little alcohol they engaged in conversation with other people at the meal table, but others soon noticed they did not talk to each other overmuch. Indeed, one observant diner thought they must be brother and sister.

After the meal they joined others in the lounge for a briefing session on the safety drill, etc., as the ship set sail. They even relaxed a little more as the entertainment progressed.

Soon, all too soon, it was time for bed, progressing to their respective cabins without a word said. Both were exhausted by the travel. Davie plucked up courage to knock on her door. He put his head round the corner.

"Just going to say goodnight, Dyl. Aren't you going to give me a kiss?" It was more an order than a request.

"All right" was the grudging reply.

He had barely stepped forward into her room when there was a terrible grinding noise, lights went out and the Captain came on the intercom.

"I am sorry – we have had to stop. Ladies and gentlemen, please stay in your cabins. The emergency lighting will come on and we will restore power shortly. There is no need for alarm."

Dyl's hand shot out in the darkness and grabbed hold of Davie. He was taken aback. This had not happened for years. They both found comfort in each other.

"Don't be alarmed."

'But I am alarmed,' thought Dyl. 'Here I am in the dark on a strange ship holding hands with my husband, whom I have lost touch with over many, many years. What on earth is going to happen next?'

Eventually the emergency lights did come on, but only in the corridor. Voices were raised, mostly saying, "What is happening?"or "Are we sinking?" An intemperate voice was heard to utter, "I knew I should have never got on board." And so on.

But before very long a member of the crew came and reassured everyone: "Please make your way slowly to the bar, where there are free drinks."

"Free drinks, hey!" Davie's face lit up in the dark, only to be aware of Dyl's wilting stare, something because of the gloom Davie could not see too clearly. Surprisingly, they found themselves still holding hands as they slowly and gingerly picked their way along the half-lit passageway to the lounge. Dyl did not really approve of being in public in her nightclothes and dressing gown, but as the other passengers were similarly dressed she did not really mind. One or two, however, had got ready for bed and had hurriedly dressed again in the dark, which was quite obvious to the casual observer. So it was a motley group that made its way cautiously to the lounge, where several members of staff were on hand to comfort the more nervous and elderly passengers.

The PA system came on again: "Ladies and gentlemen, just to inform you that all is under control. We have had to anchor in midstream. After you have enjoyed our free hospitality, a member of the crew will escort you back to your cabin. If you need a torch, George at the bar has some. A diver will inspect the hull in the morning and the generator will be repaired; by breakfast time things should be back to normal. Goodnight, sleep well."

'Sleep well! How can I sleep?' thought Dyl. 'Here we are in midstream tied up to goodness knows what. I've seen the commercial traffic on the river - how long before one of the petrol tankers hits us?'

Similar thoughts fluttered around most of the other passengers' minds, though most were too tired to utter them coherently.

Davie certainly felt very odd. He rarely felt anything. 'Cold fish' was Dyl's usual gossipy comment to Carol. Still holding hands and guided by the efficient torch, they stood outside their respective cabins.

"Now I'll give you that kiss."

Dyl felt his warm embrace - something which she never thought would happen ever again.

"So she is not your sister after all!" cried a passing man after too much of the company's hospitality.

"You never know these days!" replied another as a queue formed in the half-light of the corridor, much to the amusement of the member of the crew shepherding the remaining clients back to their accommodation.

"Goodnight, Dyl."

"Goodnight, Davie."

It was as if the years had fled by and they were back to the days when they had first met. Eventually they separated while the few remaining passengers tried to get past them in the gloom.

Someone shone a torch in their faces as they parted, with the remark, "It's surprising what happens in the dark on a cruise!"

Before too long everyone settled down. Dyl looked at her illuminated clock, which said 1.05 a.m., and reminisced on her lovely encounter with Davie. Could this be the man she had been married to all these years and for most of which had never really made anything in the slightest way of a sexual advance?

A dreamless sleep ensued, and before they knew it they woke to bright sunshine flooding through the windows.

'I wonder what Davie is thinking about last night,' wondered Dyl as she made herself a cup of early morning tea.

In the next-door cabin Davie was thinking about the nocturnal events. 'What is she pondering about all that has happened?'

Their musings, and indeed the semi-wakefulness of all the other passengers, were interrupted by the Captain on the intercom: "Good morning, ladies and gentlemen. I trust you managed to get a little sleep despite the disturbances of the early hours. It appears we hit some underwater object, and until we investigate further we cannot move. We plan to offer you a free tour of the city, but it will mean being ferried to the embankment. During the morning the river authorities will engage a diver and investigate. Could I suggest you assemble in the lounge, where Frederica will take the names of those going ashore? Should you wish to stay on the ship, please avail yourself of free drinks at the bar; and Denise, our entertainer, will organise some games for you to enjoy. Once again, our apologies for the interruption to your holiday."

"Apologies be blowed!" grumbled Robert. "I lost a good night's sleep because of their poor navigation!"

Others looked askance, knowing really it wasn't the crew's fault.

As usual Davie and Dyl ate their buffet breakfast in complete silence. They didn't even glance at each other's choices. Of course the other diners noticed their body language. Some who occupied adjacent cabins continued to think they must be brother and sister; few thought they were married to each other. One or two even thought they were married to someone else.

"What are you going to do?" It was Davie who posed the question.

"I'm going on the trip, of course. What is in your mind?"

The conversation, if that is what it was, was carried on as they progressed back along the corridor.

"I'm staying here and after a few drinks I'll give them the benefit of my wisdom and knowledge."

"Suit yourself" was all Dyl could reply.

At 9.30 a.m. the vast majority of the passengers lined up in the lounge and gave their names to the courier.

In no time, it seemed, a ferry had been organised and the passengers in groups of eight or so made their way down the gangplank. A few elderly passengers were wary of such an expedition and had stayed either in their cabins or adjourned to the library. Dyl, although very physically able, had always had a fear of heights and before going down the steps she hovered at the top, but soon found encouragement to descend in the shape of a handsome young officer.

'Why can't Davie be like him?' she asked herself. 'Obviously not in his looks or age, but in his attentiveness and smile.' She recalled that she could not remember the last time she had seen Davie smile - or herself, for that matter.

Eventually, when all the party had been ferried to the embankment, heads were counted, then the urgently ordered buses took some eighty per cent of the passengers around the city on their unexpected tour. The buzz of the conversation was intense. They asked dozens of questions, such as "What really happened?" and "How long is the ship going to have to stop?" and so on, most of which the city tour guide (who had been expecting a day off) couldn't possibly answer. The cruise director, who had got on the second coach, also struggled to reply. Dyl spotted an empty seat, since most were occupied by couples, and looked out of the window to the river and the cruise ship moored in midstream.

'What a strange situation,' she thought. She was disrupted in her musings by finding a large man sitting next to her. 'Oh no!' she thought. 'Not Alan, so early on!' Many had labelled him the ship's bore. 'Not him.'

They exchanged pleasantries, but were interrupted by the tour guide explaining where they were going and what they were likely to see. The coach moved off and Dyl half turned herself towards the window, trying to ignore her fellow passenger.

"Of course I remember this place when I was a lad."

Alan was a peculiar type of person - someone who not only thought he knew everything, but talked as though he had been everywhere and had met almost everyone who was anybody. Bores come in all shapes and sizes and Alan came in the large category, both physically and in his ego. Dyl let him drone on.

"Of course," - 'Of course' was his favourite starting point - "this place has changed. I remember—"

He was cut short by the PA and Hanna, the tour guide, pointing out the city market hall, "built in the eighteenth century and at one time the largest in Europe".

"Where was I?" Alan was off again.

'How can I get out of this?' Dyl was desperate. She remembered that the coach indeed had a loo at the back, so with considerable upheaval she made her way there. Alan, whose monologue had been cut short, was annoyed that he had to move to let her out, and she could hear him grumbling in her wake. Once inside, she sat down and thought, 'A long unhappy marriage, a chaotic cruise and now this bloke sat next to me for a couple of hours or maybe more!' She was on the verge of crying when she remembered other people might want to use the facilities, so without further ado she evacuated herself and rejoined Alan.

He hardly noticed her return as he was in full flight with the young couple in front. "Of course . . ." he intoned.

Alas, he couldn't see their faces. They let him prattle on, but they had more than a smirk on their visages.

However, soon it was time for the first stop: a tour of the cathedral. Dyl was relieved to alight and the younger couple even more so. They were more interested in each other than what the tour guide had to say, and even less in what Alan had to offer.

Dyl began to be at least a little thankful for Davie. 'At least he isn't boring. He is nothing really. I much prefer him to Alan. I wonder if Alan is lonely – most men like that are really.'

Meanwhile, back at the ship, Davie was watching operations. There seemed dozens of boat police and river authorities, pollution control, a commercial diving team and various other official-looking bodies. After about half an hour, when progress seemed well under way, he left them to it, realising he had no expertise in such matters. 'In fact,' he thought, 'I have no expertise in anything, but least of all in relating to other human beings. I know – I'll go along to the library. It will be quiet there and I can browse the bookshelves to my heart's content, at least until Dyl comes back.'

The library was situated at the bow of the vessel, and as he closed the door behind him he was aware of some dozen people sitting in a circle. They were very quiet and Davie thought it must be some kind of seance.

At his entry a smartly dressed slim-built woman in her fifties got up and said brightly, "Hello. Have you come to join us?"

Davie looked at her and realised she was very good-looking and he was at a loss for words.

"I – I don't think so," he stammered. "I've just come in to browse the shelves," he added weakly, realising that the last thing he wanted was to get involved in some kind of hocus-pocus.

The woman introduced herself as Natasha and explained that four of the group were friends from a church called Woodstyle, in the Forest of Dean. She said they were concerned about the situation and had decided to meet to pray together, and the library seemed the best place.

To their surprise, word had got around at breakfast and several others had joined them – strangers, but with a lot in common. Davie had never heard of Woodstyle and was only vaguely aware of the Forest of Dean. He (wrongly) supposed it was in South Wales.

"We are just going for coffee. Would you like to join us?"

Davie felt very flattered by the invitation, especially coming from such an attractive woman.

He hesitated, but then decided. "No – no, thanks," he muttered. "My wife has gone on the excursion and I thought I would do some study on the River Danube since we shall be on it for a week." And he added, "Or in it if the ship sinks!"

"Of course it won't sink!" replied Ray, who was obviously something to do with the group. "We have been praying about it and it looks a pretty river-worthy ship to me!"

Davie was not quite so convinced, but he let it go and thought to himself, 'These people are very odd – but very friendly, which I like.' With that he let them go with broad smiles on their faces, something he found hard to replicate.

The library was much larger than he expected. It had three alcoves laden with books – many in German, which Davie could not understand. However, he did find a section on rivers and found copious volumes on the Danube, Rhine, Moselle, Douro, Elbe, Seine and Rhone – in fact, all the great European rivers.

'Why not the Thames and the Severn?' he thought. 'They are great rivers, are they not?'

He settled down with a sizeable book on the Danube. It was quiet. The others, including Dyl, wouldn't be back for ages. He read on. Suddenly he was aware of other voices coming from the next alcove, which was more than a recess, more of a cubicle.

He could hear a woman's voice speaking very quietly. Curiosity overcame him. He shifted his position and managed to move a couple of volumes at head height so that he could hear better and possibly have a squint into the next alcove.

"Funny we should meet up again like this after all these years."

The man's voice was steady and strong. Davie could not see who it was, but it was someone well spoken and he guessed they were both in their fifties. The woman had her back to him, but he could smell her distinctive perfume.

"Alan used to be a bore, but he has got worse over the years. The children have all but disowned him - not that he notices. He is so involved with himself and his interests."

"Forget him for a moment. Come here," the man suggested.

Davie could not believe his eyes and ears. Here in this holy of holies were a couple in an illicit assignment right within his hearing and almost in his sight. He was at a loss to know what to do. Cough, speak out loud or what? In the end curiosity made him keep silent.

"And what happened to you, Charlie?"

Charlie gave a brief résumé of the last twenty-five years of his life, how he had been very happily married with four lovely children, including twins, how all were now grown-up, how he had been managing director of a heating and ventilating company, but Janet, his wife, had succumbed to cancer six months ago and they had already booked this trip to celebrate their silver wedding. He said he had wanted to cancel it as he felt awkward in company as a single man.

'A little bit like me,' thought Davie, 'only I'm not single, though much of the time I wish I was!'

There was a short silence when Davie was aware of a more intimate relationship taking place.

At last he plucked up courage and as quietly as he could closed the gap in the books and coughed audibly.

"Oh, oh!" The woman became somewhat distraught. "I - I - we'd better go. There is someone in the next bay."

The man interrupted her thoughts. "Let's go separately. I'll go to the toilet and remove the lipstick and you can go and tidy your hair. Shall we meet in the lounge after lunch or where?"

Davie was fascinated by it all. He had never been party to such events before. He heard it all, but saw nothing.

"Yes, OK, but don't give a hint of our meeting like this, promise?"

"Yes, I promise," said the man, giving her a quick kiss. "Don't you want to be with Alan?"

"Oh, well, he will be asleep for a couple of hours. When he is not boring the pants off people he is usually snoring his head off. Until then."

With that she disappeared out of the door. Davie could now breathe, but found he could not concentrate on his study of the ancient river several feet below him.

A bustle on the deck above indicated a lot of activity. The PA crackled to life. It was the Captain announcing that the underwater divers had managed to free the ship from the obstruction and after a thorough inspection had declared that the ship was free to resume its journey. A sound of faint cheering echoed around the lower decks. The Captain continued, saying that they would manoeuvre along to the quayside where the excursionists would soon be waiting to come on board.

"Had a good morning?" Davie's question was really more perfunctory than a genuine enquiry.

"Yes and no. Yes, as the buildings were very interesting, but the man I sat next to in the coach - what a bore! I wish he had sat next to someone else or not gone at all!"

Davie became a lot more attentive. "What was he really like? Will you introduce him at lunch?"

"Not if I can help it! I don't want you to be subjected to all I have had this morning. Some people get verbal diarrhoea, and he seems to get it all the time!"

It was Davie's turn. "I had an interesting time in the library observing some sort of illicit assignation. The couple involved had no idea I was in the adjacent cubicle and I heard a lot of what was going on. I couldn't see the guy very well, except I guess he was past middle age, and I only saw the back of her very trim figure."

'Trust you to notice that,' thought Dyl.

Davie continued: "But her husband's name was Alan!"

"Oh, no, not the man I had to sit next to on the coach?"

"The very same one, I guess," responded Davie. "Come on, we shall be late for lunch."

They were indeed a little overdue and had to join the queue for the buffet. Davie was quite surprised – they had actually had some sort of communication. After all these years a sort of thaw had taken place, albeit the conversation was about other people.

With plates piled with delicious food, they looked around for vacant places and, much to their surprise and no little annoyance, at least on Dyl's part, the only place was with Alan and his wife, who were obviously eating in some sort of monastic silence.

"Hello," he said. "You sat next to me on the coach. I enjoyed our conversation."

'Conversation, be blowed,' thought Dyl. 'It was just one-way; I didn't get a chance to say anything much.'

"This is Lucy," he uttered with his mouth half full of salad. "I call her Luce. Don't you know, I am married to a loose woman," he intoned so that adjacent diners could clearly hear.

Lucy blushed and was about to leave the dining room, but felt that it would admit defeat.

"True words are often spoken in jest," mumbled Davie indistinctly.

"What? What's that?" Alan had only half heard.

"I said, was the trip of interest?"

That was enough to spark Alan into full flow. Food

only partially eaten, he aired his complete repertoire of knowledge about the Hapsburg dynasty, about their vast number of children, about the architecture, about the Austro-Hungarian Empire and so on.

The cruise director sitting nearby thought, 'Here we go again! If this chap would only get his facts right he could take over as commentator!'

Not surprisingly, Davie and Dyl did not feel the need for desserts and got up to leave.

"Hang on a moment, I haven't told you about the bridges on the Danube - very interesting!" But his words tailed off as he was left with just more than embarrassed Lucy. "Some people!" he expostulated to a rapidly emptying dining room. "She was all right on the coach trip - listened to every word, she did - but him, he is positively rude!"

"I'll just go for a quiet lie-down" was all Lucy could mumble as she left Alan to resume his now almost cold meal.

Back in their separate cabins, Dyl thought, 'At least Davie is not as bad as Alan. He doesn't say much, which is better than someone who cannot stop.'

Davie thought, 'That Lucy is a lovely lass!' Then the penny dropped. 'Wasn't she the woman who had the meeting with her lover in the library alcove? Blimey!' he thought. 'Some people get all the luck!'

So the cruise continued with various overnight stops and visits before sailing overnight to Budapest. The previous evening at the cocktail party Davie and Dyl deliberately arrived late so as to avoid Alan, but when they got there he was nowhere to be seen - nor his wife, Lucy. They enjoyed polite conversation based mainly on how much they had enjoyed the trip.

One man with a military bearing and a moustache to go with it exclaimed, "Too much bloomin' culture - coming out of my ears, it was!"

His demure wife whispered in those same ears, "Do be

quiet, dear. Isn't that what we came for?"

The post-dinner entertainment went on long into the night, by which time Dyl had long gone back to her cabin. She reflected on the holiday and asked herself, "Have I enjoyed it?" Then after a long thought she concluded she had. Few people other than the staff knew they had separate cabins; most concluded that it was because they had booked so late, not because they had wanted to be apart.

Buffet breakfast was suddenly interrupted by Alan storming in, shouting, "Where's Lucy? Has anybody seen my Lucy?" With the emphasis on 'my'.

Diners stood back aghast. Some stood up, but feeling helpless sat down again. The serving team, experienced as they were, had never encountered anything like this before.

Sanjay, the manager, attempted to calm Alan. "Mr Heperstall, it is all right. Please calm down. There is probably a simple explanation."

Alan continued: "All she said early in the morning was 'I must go to the library. There is something I want to look at before we leave.' I simply grunted, 'OK, Luce,' and went back to sleep again."

Sanjay bleeped the Captain, who was barely awake.

After a moment he spoke on the PA system: "Ladies and gentlemen, at the moment we have a minor crisis on board. Please resume your breakfast whilst we search the ship for Mrs Heperstall. There is nothing to worry about. If you have vacated your cabins, please go to the lounge or the library."

"Library!" shouted Alan clearly. "That is where she was heading. Perhaps she is hiding under a pile of books! I'll let her stew."

"Calm down, mate." It was the military man again. "I've seen it all before. Why, when I was in Iraq one of our corporals went AWOL and we found him in one of the villages we were patrolling. What happened to the woman I don't know – probably dealt with by the village elders, I dare say. Not so keen on adultery as we are, what, what? And Corporal Standish did not last much longer in the army, I can tell you."

The PA came on again. "We are arranging a search of the ship. Please contact Helena in the lounge so she can account for everyone else. The bar is open – please avail yourself of a free drink."

"Make mine a double whisky," shouted Alan.

"Me too!" shouted the military man.

Davie and Dyl joined the queue to register in the lounge whilst every member of the crew was summoned to join the search. They, along with many others, did not know really what to do.

Helena was sitting at her desk, checking people off, when Heather came up to her and said in an agitated whisper, "Heather Chivers. Has my cousin, Charlie, checked in?"

"No, I'm afraid he hasn't. Perhaps you can find him?"

Heather began her search, asking each member of the crew, "Have you seen my cousin, Charlie Chivers? He looks like this." She quickly produced a photo from her handbag.

The PA came on again. "I am afraid I have to report that Mr Charlie Chivers is also absent. Please stay calm. I have contacted the Hungarian police, who will be coming aboard shortly. They will probably want to interview everyone including the crew. I am sorry, but some of you will miss your flights home. We will of course make different arrangements. Please keep calm."

Dyl thought, 'I wish I could keep calm,' forgetting of course the wonderful scenery, the excellent food, the helpful staff and the joyful entertainment.'

"What shall we do, Davie?"

He thought for a moment, then uttered, "Well, we have let them know that we are here; let's go to the library and I will show you where I sat and heard the amorous conversation."

On their way they met an anxious-looking captain escorted by what seemed to be a senior police officer.

"Excuse me," interrupted Davie. "I think I can help." And he went into great detail about all he had heard in the library the previous day.

"That might explain that they are together, but where are they?"

The officer looked puzzled as well as anxious.

"We are just about to have a short discussion in my office to plan the next moves. Can you join us there in, say, half an hour?"

Davie agreed, though he knew it might be cutting it a little fine for their flight if ever they were allowed off the ship.

The library was as silent as usual, except for a small group situated in the corner.

"Hello," said Natasha, smiling. It was the same slim-built good-looking lady he had met before.

Davie felt he had to introduce Dyl. "This is my wife, Dyllis. Everybody calls her Dyl."

"Would you like to join us?"

"Why, what are you doing? Not praying, are you?" There was a certain amount of indignation in Dyl's voice. "I don't agree with such nonsense."

At this Davie interrupted. "I have just come to show Dyl where I overheard the conversation between – er, what were their names?"

"I think he was Charlie and she was Lucy!"

"Oh, I have seen Charlie. He was in the swimming pool on his own yesterday. He looked so sad!" replied Natasha.

"Well, he seems to have brightened up a bit after meeting Lucy," responded Davie.

Natasha suggested they join the group.

"Oh, no, I have a meeting with the Captain and police. I must get back straight away."

The scheduled meeting wasn't for another twenty

minutes, but it was a chance for him to make his exit, leaving Dyl stranded. She didn't know what to do, fly or cry. Natasha was one of those very rare people with extra insight into people. She sensed Dyl's discomfort, not only at the present moment but in her relationship with Davie. Natasha did not want to pry, but suggested again she could join the group.

'What me?' thought Dyl and perused the alternatives: stay in her cabin and mope or stay here. Natasha's perspicuity paid off and Dyl ever so hesitantly crossed the room to join the group. Natasha introduced each one, who greeted her with a smile and a "Hi." Dyl's attitude began to melt just a little and she perched herself on the edge of a chair. The other members, and there were seven in all, whilst lacking Natasha's insightfulness and God-given counselling skills, guessed that Dyl was not really a person who was at ease with herself.

Natasha explained to the group that Dyl's husband had overheard a none too subtle conversation in this library, and the missing couple were Lucy and Charlie.

"Isn't that the Lucy who is married to Alan? I met them the first day. I am sorry I have avoided them ever since. I know it isn't very Christian, but he is very boring," uttered a shamefaced Claudia. "I don't know how Lucy puts up with him. However, she seems to have found some sort of solace in the shape of Charlie!"

Natasha was getting a tiny bit frustrated as the object was to meet to pray, not discuss.

Jack, Claudia's husband, said, "I have met Charlie. We sat together at the quiz night - nice chap, but very much on his own."

Dyl's eyes grew even wider. Here were a group of people who could talk about people with a love for others who were relative strangers but without a hint of gossip. Without one exception, all the groups she had ever met were different: they would prattle about others in a way which was rarely loving or kind.

Heads, except Dyl's, were lowered and the group prayed. Dyl's eyes grew wider. It was indeed a jaw-dropping moment. There was a good deal of 'Thank You, Lord', as well as intercession for Lucy and Charlie. One or two, especially Claudia, prayed for Alan and forgiveness for herself in her treatment of him.

Natasha whispered to Dyl, "Is there anything you want to pray for, Dyl?"

"Not really" came the hushed reply.

After about quarter of an hour the group began to break up. Then all of a sudden Dyl burst out, "OK, God, if You are around, which I doubt, can You do something about Davie and me?"

Having overcome the initial shock, a couple, including Natasha, gathered round Dyl, who was now shouting and tearful.

"We have been married all these years and I can't remember when he last kissed me, let alone anything else! Oh, yes, the other night when the ship hit an object and I was scared he did hold my hand, but that was the first time for ages." She carried on in the same low tone, but soon realised she wasn't so much praying as slagging off God and unloading the whole situation before a God she didn't really believe existed. In effect she was unburdening herself to anyone who was prepared to listen just a little.

Someone in the cabin above heard the noise below, but couldn't quite make it out. He thought that it was just a bit of end-of-cruise high jinks and took no further action.

Outburst finished, Dyl collapsed into Natasha's arms with even more tears.

"Have you been crying?" Davie was (for him) quite understanding as they joined the queue for a delayed lunch.

The PA system sprang to life with the Captain announcing that the problem had been happily resolved and that following lunch the first departure would be at two o'clock.

"Praise the Lord," uttered Natasha under her breath.

And in the dining room sat Charlie with Wayne, Danny and Barclay, enjoying a drink, while at the end of the room were Alan and Lucy. Alan was, for him, unusually quiet and Lucy had little to say.

Davie was indeed quite solicitous. He explained that the couple had been found and that with little persuasion they had made their separate ways back to the ship. His meeting with the Captain and the police chief was cancelled at the last minute, much to his relief.

After lunch, as they packed, Davie enquired of Dyl what went on in the library. "Did you join that odd group of religious nutters?"

"No, not exactly."

"Either you did or you didn't?" Davie's tone was quite moderate for him.

"I did say something," admitted Dyl.

"Can I ask what? I thought you didn't believe in God."

"Well, I do and I don't!" replied Dyl. "After this morning I think I do."

"Go on," was all Davie could utter.

"I just shouted at God so loudly that others in adjoining cabins may have heard. That lovely lady, Natasha, was very, very kind and the others in the group really cared. They all seemed very different, especially from someone like Alan. Alan, I guess, has changed. It may be only passing, but he seemed so quiet at lunch. One or two people thought he was ill – just a state of shock, I guess."

"What did this shouting entail exactly?"

"Well, I told Him all about us."

"Doesn't He know already?" Davie interjected.

"Yes, but think: if He exists [she added hurriedly] He wants us to tell Him ourselves."

"So if this group heard it it must be all over the ship by now, let alone some of the prying members of the cabin staff."

"On the contrary, I think I can trust them to keep quiet.

They didn't say as much, but their demeanour was quietly confidential."

Luggage was dispatched to the airport. It was time for goodbyes.

Dyl was again in tears as she hugged an equally tearful Natasha. Davie wasn't far from it too. Natasha had detected a considerable shift in attitudes and realised God had indeed been at work.

A sombre, shamefaced Alan followed Lucy down the gangplank. "Sorry I was such a bore this trip. I guess I'll have to change if I want to keep you, Lucy."

Charlie meanwhile was saying goodbye to Francine, whom he had only just met. Francine had spent the entire trip alone, with a cabin next to Davie's and Dyl's. Now she was exchanging addresses and phone numbers with Charlie.

"He may have gone off with that Lucy and caused all sorts of confusion on board, but I feel I could forgive him; but let's just see."

With lots of kisses and hugs, various groups boarded their coaches to the airport.

The flight home was fairly uneventful. Very few of Dyl and Davie's party were on the aircraft. For the first time ever they found themselves in real conversation about all that happened and even trying to guess what the future might involve. For quite a while they even held hands and each was engaged in recapturing the days of courtship and marriage so many years ago.

Tired and weary, they eventually got home – a home which was quite large, having been previously a police station on the edge of the village, purchased because Dyl had inherited a sizeable sum of money early on in their married life. She had ideas of bringing up a family in such a home as well as entertaining people. Such ideas soon faded and marriage became rather humdrum. Davie was never one for flair and imagination, but they stuck at it simply because they didn't really see any alternative. Their contemporaries wondered why there were no children, and after producing their own became more and more distant; so they eventually began to live in a marital no-man's-land, which both of them somehow accepted.

The taxi deposited them and their cases at the front door, and after paying the fare Davie realised that there was a small parcel and a bunch of flowers on the doorstep.

An accompanying note said, 'To Davie, enjoy a drink on us, as friends come close to God. Natasha.'

Dyl was positively ecstatic over the flowers – something she had not received for years and years. Her note read, 'To Dyl, from Natasha and your friends. "And He will come close to you."'

Without wondering how Natasha had got hold of their address, their attention was drawn to the fact that a large white van had appeared. Two men got out, then one of them enquired as to the right address and they began unloading what turned out to be a double bed. Davie and Dyl could not believe their eyes.

"Where has this come from?"

Davie owned up as he waited to sign the dispatch note.

Dyl waited in suspense as Carol drew up in her motor home.

"Hi, Davie and Dyl. I've got a surprise for you. Look in the back: it's a double bed for you both. I have no use for it now."

"One for each of us?" cried Davie.

The men were kind enough to carry the beds upstairs. Dyl and Davie collapsed in each other's arms, laughing so much that their neighbours wondered what all the noise was about.

'Perhaps God does answer prayers after all,' thought Dyl.

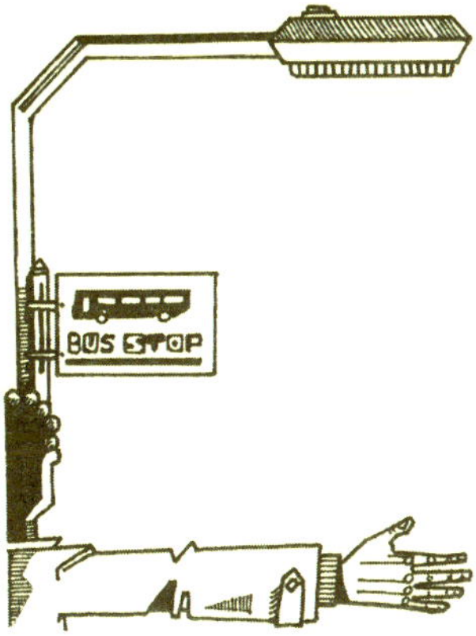

EDIE'S NEW BUS PASS

"New bus pass, is it?" enquired Ada as they waited in the biting wind at her stop, trying to get what shelter they could amongst the other would-be passengers, most of whom appeared grumpy, especially as the No. 31 appeared to be late.

"I've been waiting twenty minutes," said a disgruntled voice at the back.

"Me too," said another.

"Go on, Edie," persisted Ada, wanting as much to pass the time as to see Edie's mugshot. "That's incredible," she cried so loudly that half of the would-be passengers appeared to forget the cold and crowded round to look.

"If I may say, you look years younger! Where did you get it done? Did you go to one of those photo booths? I never did trust them. I had to get a passport done once and it seemed as if I was sitting in a public loo – a very public one!"

Edie responded, "My grandson did it for me. He is supposed to be studying photography, but I can't understand why he wants a degree in that. You can apparently get a degree in anything these days. I expect they will have one for tea making next!"

"Or waiting for buses," cried a frustrated voice at the back.

Nevertheless the No. 31 did arrive in the end and the

passengers clambered on board. The driver looked at the new pass as Edie tried to zap it on the scanner, but nothing happened. The driver, a good-humoured chap, looked slightly puzzled, and the queue waiting behind began to express their feelings.

"No good," said the driver, "you'll have to pay."

"But I'm eighty-two," replied Edie.

"Sorry, love," replied the driver.

Now, one thing Edie disliked was being called 'love', even if she used the expression herself from time to time.

"I've no cash," she cried.

"OK, Edie, here's the money," said Ada, and before long they were seated on the lower deck all the other passengers were on board.

"Funny that," said Edie after they had drawn breath.

"Funny that," replied Ada. She had a habit of repeating other people's comments after them.

Edie appreciated her kindness, but ignored her. 'Why, why?' she thought. Was her new pass invalid? What explanation was possible? Wrong photo? Wrong number? She did, however, get the chance to quiz the driver when they got to the bus station.

"Sorry, love." It was those words again. "You will 'ave to go back to the council."

"The council," mumbled Edie.

She was someone who always had a love-hate relationship with authority. On the one hand she relied on the pension she received as her husband had had a good job with his local council. On the whole she found officials very unhelpful when it came to filling in potholes in her road.

"Not like in my Edmund's day," she would shout. "He would have men out here damn quick sharp and no mistake."

The urban council official at the receiving end of Edie's jibe seemed unmoved and gave the standard reply of "It's a matter of priorities, madam."

"Priorities indeed!"

Edie's snort was even louder as she slammed the phone down. But it had all started quite some time ago when her problems and joys became enlarged when a stranger knocked on her door.

Latif appeared on Edie and Edmund's doorstep late one night, a teenager, perhaps fourteen or fifteen, dressed in ragged clothes and obviously hungry.

Edmund, with little thought, said, "Come in. Can I give you something to eat?"

Edie, ever the cautious one, nevertheless provided the stranger with some of her delicious casserole and enquired a great deal about his home and where he had come from and so on.

The young lad was somewhat wary of such generous hospitality. For weeks he had scraped and starved, eating thrown-away food and sleeping in bus shelters, cadging money where he could, yet he could not believe such open-hearted generosity. Yes, he had kept clear of the law, but only just! And in fact he had become suicidal. Yet here it seemed was the complete opposite of all his previous experiences.

"Where are you staying tonight?" Edie was always persistent in her enquiries.

"Oh, my mate lets me sleep on his lounge floor."

"Is that really true?" Edie was not only persistent, but perceptive.

"No, it's not." The lad broke down in tears with half a glance at Edmund.

She responded: "Why, you can sleep here at least for tonight – you can have Wayne's room."

Wayne, their only son, had been killed in a motorcycle accident, just after getting engaged a few years ago. His fiancée, Charlotte, had kept in touch for quite some time after, but now had married and had children of her own, so contact had become a good deal more infrequent.

Edie said, "Why, we don't even know your name?"

"It's Latif," he stuttered through his teeth. "Can I have a shower, please?"

"Certainly."

Edmund, though affected with arthritis, managed to usher their guest to the bathroom. "Let me show you to your room."

Latif needed no second asking, and soon he was ready for his new bed.

Sleep well, son" were Edmund's final words.

'Son?' thought Latif.

"Tell us your story over breakfast."

Edmund had taken early retirement from the council where he had worked for over thirty years. The pension was more than adequate and they had bought a nice bungalow on the outskirts of their village, with a pretty view down the valley.

"It's just what we want," Edie said to her friends. "I have persuaded Ed that the new room can be exactly the same, with all Wayne's things in it."

And all Wayne's things were certainly in it. As Latif looked around, his tired eyes surveyed the scene. Even Wayne's football boots were there, with the mud still caked on them, as well as Wayne's cricket bat, the ball he had taken six wickets with for the village team and so on. Latif had heard of the word 'shrine' before - indeed, in his native country every crossroad was, it seemed, littered with them. It was all very strange. Did Wayne live here? Where was he now?

Latif slept so soundly, but at 8.30 he was woken by a knock at the door.

"Would you like a cup of tea, Latif?"

A cup of tea! In bed! Had he died and gone to heaven?

"Look, we have found some of Wayne's clothes - we think they might fit you. Come to breakfast when you are ready."

Breakfast was indeed a lengthy meal as Latif told

virtually his life story and Edmund and Edie shared more than a little of theirs.

"Well, I must be on my way."

"No, not before we have read the Bible and prayed with you."

Latif thought to himself, 'Well, these people are so kind. But are they some sort of religious cranks?' But he acquiesced somewhat reluctantly.

"No, Latif, you are not going yet."

Edie was determined that this young lad was not going back on the streets again.

"I'll ring Father Reilly and ask what can be done."

'So this couple are religious idiots after all!' He had heard about such people and became very, very wary.

Father Reilly called round within the hour. He was an energetic young man who took his calling to the ministry very seriously, but he had never had a situation like this before.

"The lad needs to pick up with continuing his education and there are signs that Latif is a quick, bright boy. All I suggest is you ring the surgery and get him medically checked out. I'll contact my friend Monica at social services, but from my limited experience I don't want them to be closely involved just yet. I'll be in touch to find out what family he has really got and where they are.

Things moved quickly, and slowly after that Latif began to feel he was at home. The secondary school head actually came to visit. This was indeed a strange situation. Room could be found in year eight, but she suggested on a temporary basis and, just for the first instance, two full mornings only, with Edmund dropping him off and picking him up at lunchtime. Latif was quizzed at length about his family and background. He became quite cautious, but eventually divulged that his father was Estonian and had left a couple of years ago; then his mother, with six other siblings to look after, had more than suggested Latif took to the road.

"You are old enough to look after yourself; come back when you have made your fortune."

"What is your surname?"

"Why do you want to know?"

The questions came thick and fast – so much so that Latif simply clammed up.

"Where indeed do you come from?" Monica, the social worker, persisted.

Redditch, or was it Redhill or Redcar? I forget where now," Latif uttered.

Latif's mother, for her part, said little to anyone about Latif's quick departure. When the school and others eventually enquired she misled them with a remark that Latif had to go to live with his father in Estonia. Somehow that seemed to satisfy the officials. They already had a heavy workload and this explanation, which could not be verified, seemed to satisfy them.

Back home at Edmund and Edie's Latif settled into a regular routine. Social workers came and went, committees met and eventually Edie and Edmund received a letter saying it was recommended that Latif should go and live in a local children's home. Edmund and Edie were dumbstruck. The letter continued that in two and a half years' time Latif would be eighteen – old enough to make up his own mind. Then followed all sorts of legal jargon, eventually concluding that at their age Edie and Edmund were too old to look after a teenager.

Edie was in floods of tears. "What are we to do?" she cried.

Edmund put his arm around her and said, "Has anybody really asked Latif what he wants?"

"Well, well, all sorts of people have quizzed him about his past, his surname, etc., but as far as I can see nobody has asked him about his future. Yes, they have been very kind—"

Just then the door opened and Latif stood there. He flung his arms around Edie.

"Why, what's wrong?" He nearly said 'Mum', but stopped himself just in time. He espied the letter, grasped it and hurriedly scanned it. "This is awful," he shouted. "I am stopping here. I am fifteen and a half and I can make up my own mind. If I can't be adopted by you, I can adopt you!"

After things had calmed down, they made a drink.

There was a knock at the door and Melissa arrived. Melissa was a vibrant lady, the sort who never takes no for an answer, and this had extended to almost every area of her life. She was the daughter of Edie's best friend, Brenda, who in recent years had experienced a remarkable change in her life. Melissa looked at Edie's tear-stained face. She had met Latif several times and drew her conclusions very, very quickly.

"Look, you know I am a secretary to Craig Wilson, our MP. Leave it to me. I'll see what I can do. Before I go, let me pray for you and Latif."

Edie was a little shocked. Praying in her church tended to be formal and centred on the Mass. Individuals praying to God were not discouraged, but at the same time there was little teaching on prayer itself. Edie readily acquiesced as Melissa implored the Lord to sort out the situation, adding that God must have sent Latif here and that they loved him very much. With that she swept out of the door.

All sorts of events happened in the next week or so. Phone calls and emails flew around with great rapidity. Various official people came and went and after much discussion it was agreed that Latif could stay where he was for the time being, but the question of his adoption was very much put on hold.

It looked like just a bundle of clothes lying in the corner

of the alleyway. Passers-by scarcely gave it a thought. Litter was a common sight in some streets. Latif just about noticed it in the half-light as he walked home from school on a winter's evening. He had barely gone ten yards past when he wondered what it was.

"Who could have left such a big pile of clothes in such a heap?" he said to his teenage friend Mick. He said, "I'll tell Ed and Edie when I get home."

But something made him stop and turn round, and at that point he saw it move and an arm stretch out. He stood still. He had had plenty of advice to keep clear of strangers, but this was different. After what seemed ages, a male figure appeared, dark, swarthy, perhaps fifteen or sixteen, thin and dishevelled, yawning through lack of sleep. Latif and Mick walked a few steps back. They were now between two street lights and it was difficult to make out exactly who the stranger was.

Latif plucked up courage. "Hello," he nervously said.

The figure nodded his head and said nothing beyond a mumbled grunt.

Latif went a bit nearer and boldly stated that he was Latif and this was his friend Mick, and stretched out his hand.

The figure began to stare, pulled his tatty blanket around him and shouted in a language (if it was a language) so that passers-by, including some of Latif's fellow pupils, wondered what was happening.

Mr Medland, Latif's geography teacher, was also passing and tried to help. He spoke to the stranger in French and, indeed, his limited German, but all he got was a shake of the head or grunts or a shout.

"I'll call the police," he responded as he got out his mobile phone.

"Please don't do that, sir. I was a stranger, a bit like him, not so long ago," cried Latif.

"Well, what shall we do?" was the response.

Latif noticed the response referred to 'we'. He had a growing respect in the school, which extended beyond his classmates and included the staff, not least Mr Medland.

"I don't know," he replied as they faced the thin, emaciated figure.

"He's hungry, sir."

"I can see that," replied Mr Medland, beginning to think he was going to be late home. Normally a placid character, it was a situation he had never had to face before.

"Sir, can't I take him home?" asked Latif.

Mr Medland ignored that and still thought ringing the police was the best option.

"What is your name?" The gentle teacher spoke very slowly and distinctly.

"Nappi" was the hushed response.

'At least we are getting somewhere!' thought Mr Medland.

"He's lonely and abandoned." Latif was in his persuasive mode.

So with considerable struggle and trying to hold their noses they encouraged Nappi to gather up what possessions he had (and they were not much), and with an arm around each shoulder they struggled towards Latif's home.

"Drugs or drink, I guess," muttered one passer-by.

"Latif, what are you doing? Has your friend had an accident?" It was two teenage girl classmates of Latif, who had only recently taken a shine to their newish fellow pupil.

Mr Medland replied, "No, he's not had an accident; he's not a drunk. We are just taking him round the corner to Latif's home to give him some food and to warm him up."

"We will come too," said the pair, anxious to find out where Latif lived as much as anything else.

Karen rang home on her mobile, explaining to her mother that they were going to be late and not to worry as there was nothing wrong.

Edie opened the door to the strange sextet and urgently called Edmund from behind his crossword.

"What is it now?" he grumpily responded.

He could hardly believe his eyes, and he was even more startled when Edie invited them all in. Mr Medland explained the situation, saying that it was really a police matter, but as the strange lad was obviously hungry and cold, he had been encouraged by Latif as a temporary measure to bring him here.

Edie was soon handing round hot cups of soup. The two girls by some sleight of hand found themselves positioned either side of Latif, a situation which he found quite flattering.

Wide-eyed but visibly brightening up, Nappi looked around him and thought, 'Who are these people who are so kind? And these two girls in school uniform, do they live here as well? What is this place? And who are the older couple and the younger one who helped me here?"

Edie decided it was time she took charge. "Look, Mr Medland, I expect your wife is waiting for you."

"Indeed she is. It is our wedding anniversary and we have planned to go out for a meal tonight."

"Off you go - don't keep her waiting."

"Thank you," the teacher replied. "Here's my number. Let me know what happens. Goodnight, all."

And with that Edmund let him out, thinking, 'That is one less. Now, how can I get rid of these two girls? Haven't they got homes to go to? That poor young man might be homeless, but they are not.'

However, Karen and Sara had no such intention. They were busily engaged in conversation with Latif, recognising that he had a similar background to the figure stretched out on the floor fast asleep and full of soup.

Edmund and Edie found themselves involved in a conversation that they had experienced before. Certainly it was a dilemma not of their own making, but how to resolve this was the real problem.

"That is two young men we seem to have acquired.

When is the third one coming? Edie, you always say things come in threes."

"This is no time for light-heartedness" was Edie's response. "I'll ring Ada – she will know what to do."

Ada was Edie's best friend at church. She always appeared to have an air of supreme confidence and always (or nearly always) had a solution to most things.

"Ada Tomkins here. I am sorry I cannot take your call at the moment, but if it is urgent please try my mobile number."

"Ada, it is very urgent. I'll try your mobile" was all Edie could mutter, scrabbling through all sorts of odd bits of paper to find the elusive number.

All to no avail – Ada's mobile number was unobtainable. Edmund and Edie looked at each other in a way they had not looked for years. A tear came to his eyes.

"I don't need to say about having only Wayne, how we blamed each other for years – quite wrongly, it seems – but now we have got two. Well, almost two."

Suddenly Nappi woke up. "Where am I? Who are you? What are you doing? Help!" he shouted. It all sounded like a very rough Russian dialect which both Edie and Edmund did not understand.

Still sitting on the floor, Edie put her arms around him and said softly, "It's OK, Nappi – we are your friends."

Nappi heard the word 'OK' and knew he was indeed in safe hands.

Meanwhile the two girls did not know what to make of it all. Sara's mobile kept ringing, but for once in her life she ignored it.

"It's only Mum and Dad wanting to know what is happening."

But it wasn't. It was various friends who had heard or half heard about them going off with Latif and co. and wanted to be in on the action.

Edmund and Edie's phone rang.

"Ada here. Tell us your story and I'll see what I can do to help."

So Edie, as briefly as she could, told her what had happened.

"OK, OK, I'll get in touch with social services and the police. I have a good friend who can speak excellent Russian, but she won't be free until tomorrow." With that she put the phone down.

Edie's head was in a whirl. What had she let herself in for? Things were beginning to get out of control. It was one thing to give a homeless teenager food, a shower and clean clothes, but now they were having to involve the whole vast army of the authorities to help solve the problem. Edmund had mixed views on involving various statutory bodies when Latif arrived; now it seemed the situation was about to repeat itself.

Ada was the first to arrive.

"OK, I get the problem: you have another homeless teenager on your hands. He has invaded your space." (This was a phrase she frequently used, especially in regard to her husband.)

"No, it's not like that at all." It was Edmund's turn to speak. He was never overfond of Ada. This bossy women was in fact his *bête noire*. He explained in exact detail what had happened.

"Do you want him to stay?" Ada was nothing if not blunt.

"Well, yes and no – I don't know" was all Edie could mumble.

Just then a loud knock on the door announced the arrival of the police. Edmund was quick to answer. The officer and his PCSO following behind were nothing but polite.

"Excuse me, sir."

Edmund was flattered to be called 'sir'.

"Can we come in?"

The house was now very crowded: four young people,

Ada, Edmund and Edie and two officers of the law. And then came another ring on the bell – it was Sara's mother.

"Is my daughter here?" She was almost at screaming pitch. Then, catching sight of the police officers, she cried, "Is she in trouble? What's she done?"

"Come in," an almost breathless Edie cried.

Sara had got to a point in her life where obeying her parents was now an option, but at this point she spilled her side of the story. The police officers held their breath and felt frustrated in their task.

"Does this qualify as a domestic?" PCSO Willis, who was very new to the job, wanted to know what, if anything, her role was in the proceedings.

Sergeant Dennis cleared his throat and motioned to Nappi to come forward. In the crowded room this was difficult.

"Who are you?"

Nappi looked blank – a vagueness that may have been deliberate or just the result of fear of the 'long arm of the law'. For months he had been trying to avoid the police forces in several different countries; now he felt cornered and he shrank back in horror.

"Who are you?" Sergeant Dennis began to feel his frustration level beginning to rise and he did not like it.

Ada, however, not one to hold back, said in her schoolgirl French, "Who are you?"

"Nappi," the lad replied.

"Where do you come from?" Again Ada stepped in.

Nappi shook his head and half mumbled a reply which sounded like Don-something.

'It won't be Doncaster – I don't think he is English.' However, she kept her thoughts to herself.

The rambling incoherent interrogation continued.

"Why are you here?" Sergeant Dennis spaced the words out as if Nappi was deaf.

Ada gave it more of her best French: "Why are you here?"

Again nobody could make sense of Nappi's reply. Both officers were perplexed. The Sergeant called the station to seek advice. In the meantime the PCSO stepped forward and, with her superior's approval, indicated that Nappi should turn out his pockets. Automatically Nappi did so, since he had had to do this more times than he could remember. His pockets produced very little except what was probably a faded photo of his parents, a couple of euro coins, a tattered handkerchief and an old bus pass. There were certainly no drugs. With some reluctance the PCSO started a body search as she had recently been trained to do.

Sara looked on and wondered if she could do this, but the thought quickly vanished.

"Nothing, Sarge."

The Sergeant's phone rang and he quickly answered it. It was his superintendent calling for them to return as a large fire had broken out and every available officer was needed to control the large crowd watching the blaze.

"Look, I've got some details, but you had better come down to the station - say nine o'clock tomorrow morning. Case of an illegal immigrant," I think.

And with that they left. The others remained stunned. Fancy a fire breaking out at Bywell. I guess it must be arson, judging by the way those two officers sped off.

"It will be a disaster!" exclaimed Ada.

So thought Sara, Karen and Sara's mother, who simply said, "I expect you have homework to do."

So with scarcely a backward glance they exited, but not before Sara noticed a wink from Latif.

Edie, Edmund, Latif and Nappi looked at each other with a mixture of embarrassment and amusement.

"I'll put the kettle on," said Edie.

"I want something stronger than that!" exclaimed Edmund, moving to the sideboard, where the whisky was stored away from visiting eyes.

As the officers got in their car the PCSO said, "You

never know, Sarge, what he might have hidden - a knife maybe."

But Sergeant Dennis wasn't listening at all. He was saying, "Yes, Super; no, Super," to his boss on the phone. He was just about to give another of these replies when the phone died.

Then, addressing the young PCSO, he said in his best sergeant's voice, "You go back to that lot and find out what you can. I'll arrange for someone to pick you up." With that he was gone.

The PCSO recorded the contents of Nappi's pockets in her notebook. She was intrigued by the old senior citizen's bus pass. It was in very poor condition. The photo was rather faded and the pass was at least two years out of date.

"Where did you get this from?" PCSO Fay Willis felt she had good authority to ask now that her sergeant had left.

Nappi looked blank. Ada did her best, saying she would translate, but to no avail. There was a degree of embarrassment all round whilst Nappi, glad to be in the warm, just stared ahead. The PCSO put the various items on the table, and recorded that they were in the possession of Nappi with the necessary time and date.

"Might be needed in evidence later."

"What evidence?" shouted Edmund, who had largely been a spectator at the proceedings, but was on his second glass of whisky. "Well, if he is charged with being an illegal immigrant they need vital proof." Edmund was having none of this. "What do you mean - a tattered handkerchief, two euro coins, his parents' photo and an out-of-date bus pass, which somebody probably dropped and this lad picked it up thinking it might be useful. Look at him."

The whole assembly, including Latif, turned their gaze towards Nappi, who indeed looked a mess.

"He's lonely, afraid and unable to communicate. What are we going to do?"

Ideas were not forthcoming, but the local hostel was mentioned.

Edie simply said, "I'll go and make another cup of tea."

Latif was the only one to express any enthusiasm, with a defiant, "I want him to stay here. Please, please let him stay."

"That's not in your hands," said PCSO Fay Willis. "If he is proved to be an illegal immigrant he will have to be deported."

"But he speaks Russian," Latif responded. "He cannot be illegal – they are our neighbours and friends."

"Doesn't work that way, son. All sorts of people speak Russian who should not be here." But the officer stopped short of giving the lad a lecture on immigration law as she recognised that she knew very little about it.

As the evening wore on, a real feeling of frustration seemed to be creeping in. The only person who seemed to respond positively was Nappi, who felt warm and accepted.

The word got around that the Jenkinson family were in some sort of trouble.

"I knew they shouldn't have given a home to that young lad," muttered old Mr Baynes from across the road, but he didn't bother to call.

Father Reilly did call round, but felt rather helpless in the situation. He tried his bad Russian with Nappi, but didn't get very far. Had Nappi run away from home because his father was violent? And had he smuggled himself on a ferry to Dover and hitch-hiked his way across England? Perhaps a friendly British driver had given him a lift or he had hidden himself at the back of the lorry and escaped detection, living off odd bits of food and what he could find at the backs of restaurants until he had ended up looking like the bundle of clothes when Latif found him.

He had proffered the fact that he was named Nappi after Napoleon, who was a great hero of his father. After that about all he ever said was his oft-repeated name.

"Thank you, Father" was all Edmund could say, and with that the priest departed, having other more pressing calls to make.

Edie exclaimed, "What a day! I think it is time for bed. You show Nappi how to use the shower and I'll fetch the camp bed from the garage and look out a change of clothes. Nappi can sleep in Latif's room. I'll just pop the news on TV."

From the news she discovered to her horror about a continental lorry driver, one Joe Parkins, who had been arrested for smuggling illegal immigrants into the country. Could that be the driver that transported Nappi across the Channel?

So somehow they all settled down to sleep, but to Edie sleep would not come. She tossed and turned. Edmund, beside her, grumbled and told her to shut up.

"Ed, I am worried that if that is true, housing Nappi could be a crime and we could be arrested for homing an illegal immigrant. We could be imprisoned." She cried out so loud that Latif was aware of it in the next room. She got out of bed and began pacing around.

"Come back here!" exclaimed Edmund. It was more of a command than a request.

At that moment Edie knocked a book from off her dressing table. It was a Bible, given to her by her late mother. It had rarely been read. It opened at Psalm 127 v. 2: 'He gives sleep to those He loves.'

'Obviously He doesn't love me,' thought Edie, in her bemused state, never thinking to ask, 'Why doesn't He love me?' or 'If I love Him will I get my sleep back?'

Her nocturnal meandering thoughts were halted by Edmund grumpily asking, "Edie [he rarely addressed her as Edie], why are you poncing about now? What did you knock over? Come on back to bed."

"OK, but let me go and have a wee."

"All right" was the mumbled reply.

Back in bed Edie did not answer Edmund regarding what she had knocked over, only saying, "Ed, you can give me a cuddle," and nothing more.

From that point on they both slept very well - so much so that Edie felt better than she had done for weeks. Somehow she felt the mess they had landed in would soon be sorted out and it was all under some sort of control. But whose control? The police? The social services? Her neighbours and friends or even the school?

The next day dawned bright. Latif got ready for school.

"Mum," he called out - he had stopped calling her Edie - "why can't Nappi come to school with me?"

"Don't be ridiculous," shouted Edmund. "For one thing he cannot speak English; two, he has to find somewhere to live; and three, the police want to interview him."

"Why can't he live with us?"

It was the first time Latif had ever raised his voice. The logic of a fifteen-and-a-half-year-old did not really meet the understandable world of someone five times his age. On hearing the raised voices, Nappi appeared. His quizzical face expressed two things: (a) he was hungry, and (b) what was all the commotion about? He guessed it involved him, but hadn't a clue what it meant.

"Nappi, come and have some breakfast."

On hearing his name he came down the stairs and rushed to the table piled high with cereals and fruit. He couldn't wait to get started, whilst the other three looked on in amazement at his lack of table manners.

"Latif, go or you will be late for school - hurry."

Reluctantly Latif disappeared to catch the school bus.

A ring came on the doorbell, and Nicky introduced herself along with her colleague, Fran, from the local social services. Nappi found himself confronted by two pleasant women, one of whom spoke excellent Russian. Nappi, with his rough accent, understood her pretty well.

Questions came thick and fast - Full name? Date of birth? Parents' names? Place of birth? How did you get here? And so on and so on. Edie stood back amazed. Nappi, who had said so little in the past twelve hours, was now able to spell out quite clearly what had happened to him.

Nicky, having heard the translations from Fran, responded by asking through Fran for Nappi to stay in the room whilst they went into the dining room to discuss the matter. Edmund was now rather frustrated with the whole business, Edie was feeling confused and the two social workers were puzzled as to what the next move should be. Nappi was left with some comic picture books to look at, feeling not too pleased that his future was being discussed without him being present.

"As I see it," began Nicky, "we have two options. One is to send him to Sparfield Immigration Centre, which as you know is forty miles from here, or we could find a place for him in a local children's home. There are really no other options. There followed a series of frantic phone calls to all sorts of authorities, all of which were very sympathetic but could offer little help.

Nicky felt so helpless as she reviewed the situation. "Nappi is from Donabisk. He's a foreign citizen. At fifteen and a half he is classed as a child. He has no home and no prospects. There's little if any chance of him being reunited with his family, even if they could be traced. He has only his ragged clothes, two euro coins and someone else's bus pass," Nicky expostulated. "I really don't know what to do!"

Edmund interjected, "I don't really understand you social workers. You claim to have all the answers, so why oh why can't you sort it out?"

"We are not infallible, sir."

(Edmund was delighted to be addressed as 'sir'.)

"We are often the ones people turn to as a last resort, very often when problems seem unsolvable, as this one does. I have to take him to the police station soon."

"He could continue to stay with us." It was Edie's turn to interrupt the flow. "He spent last night in Latif's room. Latif found him – he is his friend."

Nappi opened his big olive eyes. He understood the word 'friend' and for the first time hoped something positive might happen.

Edmund responded: "No, he can't continue to stay here!"

"Look," said Nicky, "we could perhaps give you a grant to cover clothing, board and lodging for the next two weeks while we make urgent enquiries as to Nappi's background and home life. If you would like to come to my office, say at 10 a.m. tomorrow, I will have £200 worth of vouchers for you to use." And with that Nicky and Fran swept out of the door on to another urgent case.

"And the Son of Man had nowhere to lay His head," mumbled Edie.

"What is that?" Edmund was still mildly in his bombastic mode.

"I said—" again mumbled Edie.

"I know what you said!" Edmund felt his anger rising. "Have you gone even more religious?"

Even after a hearty breakfast Nappi was still hungry. He could not wait for dinner and tore into the first thing he saw. The others realised he had not learnt to use cutlery, or if he had he had forgotten. Edie tried to explain about knives and forks; she also hesitated when she was about to say grace.

Edmund looked at her.

"Go on," they said almost in unison, say, 'Thank You.'"

"Well, I don't know. I don't want to embarrass our new-found friend. Look, he has already grabbed a chicken leg and looks as though he wants to get hold of the potatoes. What are we letting ourselves in for?"

"Jesus didn't have knives and forks to eat with. What's so different?"

"Oh, all right," responded Edie. "Thank You, Lord, for bringing Nappi here. Thank You for all the food. Keep us mindful of the needs of others."

Nappi at the mention of his name wondered what this strange ritual was all about, but it didn't stop him grabbing a hot potato. With a loud shout – "Oh! Oh!" – he promptly dropped it on the floor. He dived down and scooped it up with both hands. Fighting for food had been commonplace in his young existence. Natalia, a girl he met on a train, had showed him how to get chocolate bars out of the back of a machine, but that only lasted a day or so. As he had explained to Fran, waste scraps from the backs of cafés and restaurants were his usual diet, except for the occasional hamburger he did not pay for. This was indeed different.

During the meal Nappi eventually mastered a knife and fork, but preferred to use a spoon. Edmund got out a dusty Russian dictionary and an old phrase book they had acquired second-hand some thirty years ago. Out dropped two photos.

"Cor! Look at that," he cried. "You on the beach at St-Tropez."

"Give it here at once."

But before they could be passed over, one dropped in the casserole. Nappi's eyes lit up. Was this the woman who was sheltering him? She didn't look like it now! But in a flash Edie retrieved the snaps and covered her embarrassment, as well as the photos, with a dishcloth. The meal proceeded with a number of fluctuating emotions but was interrupted by the phone.

Edmund said, "I'll get it." He'd been hoping that his mate Graham might call; but no, it was Nigel, Edie's rather interfering brother.

"In a bit of bother, are we?" was Nigel's querying statement. "Thought I'd give you a ring to see if I can help."

'How does he know?' thought Edie.

But Nigel had a nose for almost anything. Critics might describe him as a busybody, but that would be an understatement.

"Look, I'll come round and help."

"No, thank you," Edmund replied as he rapidly put the phone down.

"Everything OK?" responded Edie as he resumed his place at the meal table, avoiding the three pairs of eyes which were upon him.

"Not really" was all he could mutter.

Edie was thinking more about the distress caused by the photos than her brother's interfering ways. So slowly, very slowly, she finished her lunch.

Later the early evening news was on TV, but nobody paid it much attention.

Suddenly Nappi jumped to his feet: "I know that man – he's a neighbour where I live," he shouted in his Russian dialect.

Edmund managed to glean that there had been protests in favour of independence in Donabisk, but it was a small item squeezed in at the end of the programme. It took a while since Nappi had to write it down and Edmund had to translate it with the aid of his ancient dictionary and phrase book.

Eventually he turned to Edie and exclaimed, "If Nappi knows the guy should we get in touch with the Russian authorities?"

"I expect Nicky, from social services, has done that" was all Edie could comment.

After supper the two lads disappeared into Latif's room, where Latif introduced his new friend to computer games.

Later, as they settled down to what they expected to be a sleepless night, Edie whispered in Edmund's ear, "You know I read a text in the Bible last night where it says God gives sleep to those He loves. Do you think it's true?"

"Don't know and don't care" was all she got from her curmudgeonly husband.

"Tomorrow I'll go and talk to Julie up the road."

"You'll do no such thing," said Edmund rapidly sitting up in bed and speaking so loudly that the boys in the next room woke up and wondered what was wrong. "It's all right finding a verse in that old tatty Bible – you can read it if you want to – but don't get involved with that Julie and Max. I'm told they go to church every Sunday."

With that he fell back on to the pillows and they both turned to sleep, but sleep didn't come!

Next day, Saturday, after breakfast Edmund went to catch the coach as Rangers had an away game.

A knock came at the door. It was Greeta and her friend Sara.

"Hello," said Edie.

But before she could say much else, Greeta exclaimed, "My dad is having a barbecue! Would the two boys like to come?"

"Come in and ask them yourselves" was all Edie could say.

The quartet found themselves crammed into Latif's bedroom, where they found the boys engrossed in their electronic games. However, Nappi knew the word 'barbecue' and before long they were on their way.

Nappi indeed found it delightful as all the females he had ever encountered up until now had been poor and miserable and often scathing or in fear of approaching him. These girls were different.

Before long Edie found herself on her own. 'I'll take the chance and go and see Julie and Max,' she thought. 'Nobody will know I've been.'

Julie and Max were indeed at home.

"Hello, Edie. Come on in. What can we do for you? Would you like a cup of tea or coffee?"

Edie had hardly put her foot in the door, but she knew the

welcome was real because this couple seemed so genuine. Edie, tremulously clutching a mug of hot coffee, soon poured her heart out, telling the whole story, correcting in her hosts' minds what they had heard or half heard on the street. Julie and Max felt a little guilty for not offering help earlier.

The conversation just flowed almost entirely from Edie with just the occasional gentle question from Max. Two more cups of coffee later, and after more than one bout of tears, Edie decided it was time to go, though in fact she had no real reason to leave. As she was about to disappear she described her sleepless nights and how she had knocked over an ancient Bible, which had opened at 'He gives sleep to those He loves.' "What does it mean?" she asked.

Julie explained what it meant, adding bravely, "Edie, you are beloved. We love you and, more importantly, God loves you. I wonder if you can accept that?"

"I don't know" was Edie's timid response. "I go to Mass from time to time. Father Reilly has been a great help in these difficult times. He is a busy man and we owe him a great debt, but I feel there is something missing in my life."

"Let's pray for Edie, Ed and the boys," said Julie.

'This is odd, very odd,' thought Edie as two pairs of arms enveloped her.

Afterwards the embarrassed visitor heard, "I guess the gap in your life should be filled with Jesus."

Edie made her way home very slowly, pondering the idea that the gap in her life could be filled by Jesus. Could it?

"I hope we weren't too heavy on her," said Max. "I don't consider myself in any way an evangelist, but I felt it right to say what I did. Heavens, is that the time? Dana and her children will be here soon."

Julie replied, "Perhaps soon we can all have lunch together and we can share a little of these incredible events."

Back home Edie made herself a sandwich, and as the

sun had come out she daringly opened a bottle of wine and went and lay on the lounger in the garden.

Edmund came back from the match jubilant, for his team had won. He looked through the window and saw Edie asleep in the garden and witnessed both the old Bible on her lap and the half-opened bottle of wine.

"How dare she!" was his first response. "She doesn't drink. She will sleep it off."

Half an hour or so later Edmund deemed it was time to make contact and went into the garden, and to his horror he found his wife dead, with a wine glass in one hand and a Bible in the other.

A lot then happened - ambulance, paramedics, doctors and a hospital admission.

Breathless and excited, the boys had the news broken to them as they reached home. Howls of pain echoed through the house.

Max and Julie, having spent a lovely time with their daughter and grandchildren, felt it right to enquire what had happened and, on being told, they shared with Edmund that they must have been the last persons to see Edie alive.

It was indeed sleepless nights for the trio, but echoing in Edmund's ears was the invitation to join Max and Julie at their church. "You can bring the boys too" were the last words he had heard.

So very early next morning, being Sunday, he plucked up courage to knock on Max and Julie's door.

"The boys and I would like to take up your offer."

Eventually they all crammed into Max's car and set off, getting to church just in time. Edmund thought it odd that it was held in a school. 'I like proper churches with organs, choirs and things,' he thought, but he could not back out now, especially as the two boys were delighted to see Greeta and Sara, their new barbeque girlfriends, who were in the music group.

Max and Julie made sure the trio came back to lunch,

though it was difficult to drag the boys back from the attentiveness of their new female friends.

Edmund had been surprised by the prayers and tears of strangers. Over lunch Max and Julie recounted the conversation of the previous day. Edmund, now having eaten his first real meal for some time, sat entranced. But eventually they all wandered back home, wondering what the future held for each one of them.

At the inquest the verdict was death by natural causes. The funeral in the local Catholic church was indeed a solemn affair, but was highlighted by Max and Julie's story relating something of their last moments with Edie. As he turned to go out of the church behind the coffin, Edmund wondered who all the strangers were and realised that they were people from Max and Julie's church.

Edmund started sorting things out, slowly at first. Julie came to deal with Edie's clothes and jewellery. Max took Edmund down to the pub a couple of times.

Fran and Nicky came from social services and said they had a place for Nappi at a care home, to which he responded, now in quite hesitant English, "This is my home. I don't want to go anywhere else."

The social workers knew that he was almost sixteen and they realised they had little power to force him away from a family where he was beginning to feel loved and wanted.

So, despite their devastating loss of Edie, the trio settled down. Nappi was allowed to go to school, albeit temporarily. This social services case confused them, and Nicky and Fran didn't know what to do.

Weeks later there was a ring on the doorbell and a well-dressed couple stood there, but before they could say a word Nappi rushed past and shouted in Russian, "Mama and Papa," and threw himself into their arms. Bewildered and confused, Edmund invited them all in. Nappi found himself translating for his parents, explaining all his adventures and relating how Edie, Edmund and Latif had been so kind.

Events after that took their own course fairly rapidly. Nappi prepared to go home to Russia. Social services and the school were informed of the outcome.

"You had better keep these," Edmund said, producing the two euro coins and an odd green piece of plastic Nappi had with him when he arrived several weeks ago."

"No, you keep them – they will remind you of me."

So Edmund stuck them on the mantelpiece and thought nothing more about them.

There were tearful goodbyes and they were gone. "Come and see me in Russia" were Nappi's last words as he bade his friends farewell.

Then, years later, Edmund in his widowed life moved to a new bungalow and started going to worship with the help of Max and Julie.

Three great events marked these years: his baptism, Latif and Greeta's wedding and the eventual birth of his granddaughter, who was named Edie in honour of her grandmother.

One day after Sunday worship he got into conversation with Rona, a short, dumpy woman in her late fifties, with a radiant smile. She was very different from Edie and had never married. They shared a cup of coffee together, then another, and before long almost everyone else had left.

Almost without thinking he said, "Look, let's stop in the café and have some lunch."

In no time they shared each other's life stories.

"Oh, mine is very dull compared to yours!" exclaimed Rona.

It was nearly three o'clock and the owner of the café wanted to close, so they said their goodbyes.

"Look, come over to my place for lunch, say on Tuesday," was Rona's parting request.

"OK, love to."

"It's on the bus route."

"I'll be there for 12.30," replied Edmund.

He made his way home, thinking, 'My life seems to be going in some wonderful directions.'

However, the pairing-up hadn't gone unnoticed by Max and Julie, who gave a wry smile and a wink to each other.

Tuesday came and Edmund duly left the house with Rona's instructions in his pocket and a small bunch of flowers from his garden. He searched for his bus pass, but couldn't find it until he remembered it was behind the clock.

The bus was coming down the road and a breathless Edmund just made it and produced what he thought was his bus pass.

"Can't take that, mate," responded the driver. "It's out of date and you are not a woman."

Other would-be passengers were getting frustrated behind him as he fumbled for the money, paid and sat down.

'Fine start to a new romance,' thought Edmund as he clutched at the ancient green card, which he knew had belonged to Edie. 'So for years each of us had the other one's bus pass. How strange is that!'

NO SEX PLEASE, WE'RE CHRISTIANS

(With acknowledgements to the long-running farce *No Sex Please, We're British,* co-authored by the late Tony Marriott.)

"Jeremy, what are you writing?" enquired Judith. "You seem so secretive about it. I thought you had given up journalism a year ago!"

She tiptoed to look over his shoulder and exclaimed, "*No Sex Please, We're Christians*! Why on earth are you writing that? Perhaps the 'no sex' is for the future, but you are not a Christian – how can you pen such rubbish?"

"Jeffrey, our neighbour across the road, has asked me. He said he had been commissioned to pen it for a magazine, 2,000 to 3,000 words for *Rad Evang Magazine*."

"What on earth is that?"

"It's a Christian magazine," he replied. "Jeffrey recommended that since we haven't been married long we might have something to contribute."

Judith for once was dumbstruck.

Their wedded life had an interesting beginning.

After Jeremy had left his job at the local newspaper he had tried to find other work, but his age seemed to be against him somehow. He settled into a routine which involved going down to the local park at 9.30 a.m. each day. The snack van opened at 9 a.m. He ordered tea and three buns, the same every day, which the proprietor thought slightly odd, but it was not his business to enquire. Come rain or shine, snow or howling gales, Jeremy always took his refreshments to his favourite seat and broke up the two remaining buns to feed his feathered friends. He longed for human company, but these birds would do for now. Before long he had a robin eating out of his hand. He even imagined the birds would be there waiting for him each day. Chaffinches were his favourite and a pair of them became quite tame.

Every day it was the same routine. After his winged friends' breakfast he sat back to reflect on his life, sometimes under an umbrella, sometimes enjoying the sunshine. Even snow did not deter him. In such a climate the café owner sometimes had Jeremy as his sole customer for the day. Then he noticed a short woman of about fifty passing by, but paid little attention to her or her dog. Each day they saw each other, but never as much as said hello, let alone made any eye contact.

Then one day the young Sealyham dived for a piece of cake which the birds had somehow missed under his seat.

"Monty, Monty, behave yourself. I'm terribly sorry!" exclaimed the woman. "He is not allowed anything like that at home."

"I had better not give him some tomorrow when I come!" exclaimed Jeremy. "I'll get some dog biscuits instead."

"Please don't trouble yourself," replied the woman, and with that she walked off, half dragging Monty with her.

For the next week or so Jeremy stuck to his usual routine, but the woman had decided to change her walk to avoid this strange man who seemed so lonely. But one day, Monty, maybe with his recent memory of cake, decided which way they should go and there was Jeremy sitting in his usual seat.

"Hello." Their greetings, uttered at the same time, caused them both a certain amount of embarrassment and they smiled.

"Sorry I didn't buy any dog biscuits," uttered Jeremy.

"I did," she said. "For a few days I decided not to come

here any more in case you tempted Monty with cake."

Before he knew it, she had sat down beside him. She introduced herself as Judith and said that she had been widowed for two years, that her husband had been a dentist and that she had been a marriage guidance councillor.

Jeremy said little about himself, except that he had been a journalist, that he had retired recently and that he had no family to speak of.

"Yes, Jeremy, I know the name as I get the *Sunford Chronicle* each week. I saw that you had left after thirty-five years. Now I can put a face to the name. I'm delighted to meet you." Feeling she had now somehow overstayed her welcome, she added, "Come on, Monty, let's give you a run around the common."

And so it continued. Jeremy visited the café, ordered his usual three buns, took them to his seat, fed the birds and, to his surprise, waited eagerly for Judith and Monty to arrive. Each day Judith stopped a little longer and became keen to know about Jeremy and the world of the printed media. He was ever more keen to find out more about Judith using skills he had absorbed over many a year in the world of the local press.

Jeremy plucked up courage and said, "I could do with another one of these. Would you like to join me? All this talking is thirsty work."

Jeremy, in spite of having a female editor, had always found it difficult to relate to the opposite sex. As a young reporter he had been sent on assignments, such as interviewing the families, and sometimes widows, of the victims of road accidents or industrial calamities. Usually he managed to get a colleague to go with him, but just occasionally he was left on his own in female company, from which he did his best to extract himself as soon as possible. Work went on like this until he acquired a more secure position. If the truth be known, he preferred his own company rather than any companionship, either male or female.

"See you tomorrow!" were Judith's parting words. "Come on, Monty."

'I very much hope so,' thought Jeremy.

So apart from a couple of weeks when she went to see her far-flung family it became an established pattern. The café proprietor became curious: who were these two who consumed his beverages? He jumped to the obvious conclusion that they must be having an affair, but they looked too old for that. As yet he had not seen any sign of affection – not even a peck on the cheek, let alone holding hands!

So spring fell into summer. Their routine was the same and fortunately, as they saw it, no one they knew had interrupted their daily tête-à-tête.

Then one day, not without hesitation, Judith asked, "Would you like to come to supper one evening?"

Jeremy was taken aback. "Well, it is kind of you to ask, but I need to think about it."

There was something attractive about Judith, but also something strange. He could never work out why she never came to the park on Sundays. Surely Monty needed walking every day of the week, not just on six of them!

It was Monday morning.

"Hello, Jeremy. How are you today?"

"OK" came the non-committal reply.

Judith, with all her counselling experience, guessed that wasn't really true, but did not enquire any further. It was exactly a year since he had been retired, so it was not a day to celebrate.

"Well, have you decided?"

"Decided what?" Jeremy was almost abrupt, but hurriedly added, "Yes, I would love to come. Is Friday OK?"

"Lovely!" was Judith's response, and with that she walked off with Monty.

'Strange,' thought Jeremy. 'I only know she is a widow

called Judith and I don't know where she lives!' However, within the next couple of meetings he discovered she lived at 56 Damian Court, a ground-floor flat not far from his home.

Friday duly arrived, and after their usual meeting and bird feeding they parted with "See you tonight. Goodbye for now."

Jeremy was in a real quandary. What should he wear? There was his suit if he could still get into it. He decided on a blazer and smart trousers. He had rarely been invited out to dinner in the past. Someone once said to him that journalists never make friends, only enemies, and he had found that to be true. Yet here was this attractive woman inviting him to her home.

'What's the catch?' he wondered and his mind even went to 'Is there a story here? Perhaps I could sell it to the *Sunford Chronicle*!' Such thoughts did not stay with him for long. He contemplated for some while what to take and decided on both flowers and a bottle of wine.

At 7 p.m. he duly rang her doorbell, and there was Judith looking incredible in a pink-and-white dress. Her hair, which he had noticed over several weeks, was perfect. Monty, who by now treated Jeremy as a real friend, was joyous in his greeting.

"Come in, please." Judith's welcome was as big as her smile. "Roses and Rioja – my favourites!" exclaimed Judith.

Jeremy's eyes grew large. He had seen the inside of many a home in his journalistic career, but this took some beating! However, his professionalism clicked into place and he merely congratulated Judith on her lovely abode.

The meal proceeded at a leisurely pace. They were rather shy in each other's company, but Jeremy the more so since this was a strange experience for him.

After the meal they both sank into the sofa and Jeremy, using skills he had acquired over many years, began to quiz her about her background.

She talked about her childhood without siblings, how she had been a marriage guidance councillor, and how she had met and married Trevor, who was a dentist. After a gentle courtship they married in an Anglican church – neither believed very much, but it seemed the right thing to do. Judith's mother was very keen that everything should look right. She even telephoned the rector more than once about the arrangements, especially the flowers. Trevor and Judith enjoyed the intense marriage preparation that the church offered and were surprised by the middle-aged couple who led the session relating to sex.

"Men are like gas stoves, the heat goes out quite quickly, but women are like electric ones and lose their heat more slowly."

So here was Judith, a potential young bride who was absorbing things which she thought she knew but in very different ways – not least when Adam and Carole pointed out that Christian teaching about sex wasn't just about procreation and should be fun! However, it was quite a shock to learn that Adam and Carole's stance was that sex outside the marriage bond did not fit into God's plan.

'Why bring God into it at all?' thought Trevor, but he ruefully concluded that they had to have their 'God slot'.

Long before that Judith and Trevor realised they were in love and within a couple of weeks had moved in together. Judith's parents did not approve, but not for any Christian reasons.

"We didn't do that in our time," Judith's mother said, "but that's what young people do nowadays. Perhaps they will get to know each other better before the wedding."

Judith felt a certain guilt about sex before marriage, but could not put her finger on the reason why. Most of her contemporaries did it, so it must be all right.

Trevor did not care much one way or another. He had slept with a few girls in the past, but Judith was different.

Yes, she was just as passionate in bed as he was, and even more so one hot summer's night on the local common. However, he did notice a certain lack of inner calm, which he put down to pre-wedding nerves, even though the big day was several weeks away.

So one Saturday morning before a trip to the supermarket, Judith quietly said, "Trevor, I've been thinking."

"Um," Trevor grunted from behind the sports page.

"I've been thinking. . . ." She paused for a long while then simply said, "You know that couple at the marriage preparation session?"

"You mean Adam and Carole?"

"Yes. Were they right about this Christian thing about sex?"

"Maybe!" Trevor would not be drawn from behind his paper.

"I think we should go and see them!"

At this Trevor was forced to come and face her. "All right, but I can't see why."

So later on Judith rang the rector to get Adam and Carole's phone number. Contact was made and Adam was delighted that someone had responded to their input into the church's marriage preparation. Most couples were indifferent to what they had to say and quite a few were indeed hostile to it all. Trevor was neither. He just wanted to go along with Judith. Adam and Carole welcomed them into their home, settled over a cup of coffee, gave them a little of their background and explained why they were involved in the church's marriage preparation and so on.

"In view of what you said the other Sunday evening, I feel somewhat guilty about living together before we are married." Judith found it difficult to get the words out.

"Well, I don't!" retorted Trevor.

After further gentle words of explanation, Adam enquired as to what they were going to do about it.

"Nothing!" Trevor felt himself trapped. "It's what everybody does!"

"Everybody?" enquired Judith.

"Well, doesn't everybody?" Trevor retracted.

"Look, we would like to make you an offer," said Adam. "When is the wedding?"

"Five weeks' time." Trevor and Judith were at least agreed on that issue.

"What offer?" remarked Trevor, still in his sullen mood.

"Well, if one of you would like to come and live with us for that time, I am sure God will honour that."

'What a load of nonsense!' thought Trevor without exactly expressing it.

Carole, who had been listening quietly to the debate, now joined in. "I hear that you, Trevor, haven't got a home to go back to, whereas Judith could go back to the flat."

"Of course I have a home to go to. It's the flat Judith and I are renting – at least until we buy a home of our own. I am not impressed by your interfering ways," expostulated Trevor.

Judith, however, was warming to the caring, loving attitude of Carole and Adam. She could see that there was something different about them which she had never met before. Of course she had been shocked when Carole had boldly stated that most people married for lust, not love, which made her try to think about her relationship with Trevor.

She could see Trevor was agitated and, trying to soothe him down, whispered, "Darling, why don't you try it, say, just for a week? I'll cook you a nice meal each evening, but you can sleep here."

A long pause ensued and eventually Trevor grumpily agreed. "What do you want me to pay?"

"Nothing," said Adam. "Just treat our home as yours. Both the children are away at university, so you can choose which bedroom you would like."

So Trevor and Judith drove back to the flat and he packed his clothes in a suitcase ready to move in with Carole and Adam.

"Come here, Judith." And before long they were in each other's arms.

"Let's go to bed now," whispered Judith, "just one more time."

"No," said Trevor. "Carole and Adam will be expecting me."

So with considerable reluctance he settled into Wayne's bedroom, admired the wallpaper, TV, etc., and perused his choice of books. To his horror he saw not one Bible but two.

'How can anyone read such ancient rubbish?' he thought.

However, his musings were interrupted by Carole calling upstairs, "Would you like a cup of tea, Trevor?"

"Yes, OK."

"Or something stronger?" It was Adam calling from the lounge.

"A beer would do nicely!" was Trevor's response as he came down the stairs.

'This is nice. Why are these people so kind? There must be some catch in it.'

"What do you want to do tomorrow? Obviously you will be seeing Judith!"

"Oh, I keep goal for the Red Lion – it's just a pub team. We don't win many medals, so the lads blame me most of the time."

Adam was just about to ask how many clean sheets Trevor had had this season when he switched tactics and said, "I guess Judith will come and watch you?"

"She usually does, but she finds it boring; she prefers to go shopping with her mum. I can't tell you how long they were buying the wedding dress, and now Judith talks about changing it!"

Sunday dawned bright and clear. Trevor collected his kit from the flat and Carole and Adam prepared to go to worship at their local church.

Trevor met the lads at the changing rooms in the park. Trevor's manager, if that is the best description of him, stood fuming as two of the team had failed to turn up. Others were hardly in the best state to play as they had been celebrating Gary's birthday the night before.

"Where were you last night, Trev? Getting into marriage practice with that gorgeous bird of yours?" It was as much a question as a statement.

"As a matter of fact, I have moved out!"

"Moved out? You are up almost at the altar, lad!" interrupted George.

But before Trevor could add any more the groundsman unlocked the changing rooms and the boys charged in.

"Well, that is history." Judith had told enough of her life. "Cancer is a terrible thing - Trevor found it difficult to come to terms with it. I managed to have time off work to nurse him, but in the end he went to St Agatha's Hospice. They were wonderful - indeed, the church as a whole gave us terrific support. The pub football team were OK up to a point, but could not really cope with the fact that they were losing their old goalie. Well, that's my life, or much of it. As to children, we both desperately wanted them, but the demands of being a marriage counsellor and Trevor's sudden illness put a stop to that."

Jeremy had listened with care and patience to Judith's long story and he knew for the very first time he was in love. It was very, very strange. Judith for her part was fascinating. She had many lovely memories of Trevor and had decided very firmly she did not want to be involved emotionally with another man.

Her aged mother had consoled her with "You will soon find someone else. You are an attractive woman, Judith. Don't bury yourself in your career." But she had stopped short of saying, "You will soon forget Trevor."

However, all Judith's resolve was soon melting away. Her many friends both inside the church and outside, at the gym and at work, said, "Why don't you find another guy?"

Her closest friends at church even started praying along the lines of "Lord, you know Judith – please provide another man for her." They kept their prayers to themselves, but that didn't stop other people's curiosity as to her future.

She did get asked out by Malcolm, a careers advisor. They enjoyed each other's company and she even went as far as meeting his children, but the fact that he had been divorced twice made her hesitate and the relationship cooled after a few months.

Then came the walk in the park and meeting Jeremy.

"You look different!" It was Adam and Carole's joint response as Judith came round for one of her regular supper dates. "Who is the fellow? We can see something has inspired you, you look so radiant."

"Well, it's nothing," was Judith's embarrassed response.

"Look, Judith, we have been friends now at least twenty years; we have had some pretty dark times together."

"Well . . ." Judith could hardly get the words out. Here was this confident woman – some would say overconfident – struggling to speak with her closest friends. "I – I think I'm in love."

"Well, who is it?" Surprise and delight were the order of the day.

The meal was delayed as Judith recounted her meeting Jeremy.

"But is he a Christian?" It was Carole's concerned response.

"I don't really know!" was Judith's reply. "I haven't really quizzed him about spiritual matters. He knows I go to church each Sunday. He goes to the park to feed the birds, as he does each day, same time, same place. I don't really understand it – he must be quite lonely."

"Don't get involved with him just because he is lonely."

"I don't agree." It was Adam, gesticulating with his fork. "The Bible teaches that marriage is about compassion as well as procreation."

"Who said anything about marriage?" Judith was now on the defensive.

A ring on the doorbell interrupted both what was now an animated discussion as well as the meal. It was Gabrielle, the new pastoral assistant at the church.

"Hope I'm not interrupting anything?"

"You are!" Adam breathed through his teeth.

"Come on in. Can we offer you something to eat?"

"No, thank you. I've already eaten."

"A glass of wine?"

"Well, just a drop of fruit juice – I'm driving home."

"I just want to introduce myself, as it's important to get to know as many of our congregation as soon as possible."

'I bet that vicar sent you,' thought Adam, but he smiled and said, "How nice to see you. I trust you are settling in well?"

"Oh, yes, indeed," gushed Gabrielle. "I have managed to get to know quite a few folks already." ('Folks' was one of her favourite words for people.) "I went to see Jeremy – you know, the retired journalist. He's quite lonely, I guess, but perhaps he's not going to be lonely in the future! Oh dear – I shouldn't have said that." She blushed.

Judith, however, had gone to the loo, so she had not heard what was uttered.

"Perhaps you know something we don't know?" responded Carole.

"I think I should be going. By the way, it's Gabbie – they shortened it to that at college. My friends suspect I have the gift of the gab!"

'Too true!' thought Adam, but again thought it wise not to express such sentiments.

So Gabbie left a little more hurriedly than when she arrived. "Bye for now," she said as she made for the door.

"Gabbie, you haven't touched your fruit juice!" uttered Carole.

"Leave it until next time," she called out as she left.

'Perhaps there will not be a next time,' thought Adam.

"Now, where were we, Carole?" he asked as Judith reappeared. "Our meal is now half cold – let's get on with it. What were we discussing?"

"You were discussing whether I should marry Jeremy!" responded Judith. "Adam and Carole, you are my best friends in the church, and you have been a wonderful support over many years, especially when Trevor was dying and ever since. I love you dearly, but I haven't decided to marry Jeremy and he hasn't asked me so it really isn't any business of yours." And then she continued at some length. Adam and Carole were silenced – especially when Judith hit the table with her dessert spoon. "Perhaps I should be going," she said, and burst into tears.

She began to get up from the table.

"No, don't go." It was Adam. "We will talk about other things."

And with somewhat forced interest he enquired how things were at her work, and Carole asked about Monty the dog. However, there was something of an unreal atmosphere and, despite their long-standing relationship, each party felt somewhat uneasy, almost the whole evening.

"Thank you again for such a lovely time. There is one thing you can do for me."

"Such as?" enquired Carole.

"It's just that I don't want any gossip spread about Jeremy and myself. You know how people talk."

'Especially in the church,' thought Adam.

"Bye for now. Oh, by the way, who was it that came when I was in the loo? I could hear a woman's voice, but not what was being said."

But before Adam or Carole could respond she had gone. Carole and Adam looked at each other.

"Time for washing-up!" said Adam.

"No, leave it until the morning," responded Carole. And with the slightest glint in her eyes, she said, "It's time for bed."

Judith was of course much involved with pastoral care in her church. Her experience and skill set meant she was much in demand. Simon, her minister, relied on her heavily. Judith in turn pressed him to preach about people's needs – of course the need for salvation, repentance and forgiveness featured high on the agenda. She eventually plucked up courage to email him as to why he had never given sermons on debt or even on sex. Much to Judith's frustration he took a long time to reply.

Yes, he recalled that he had preached on relationships and the debt that was owed to God, but he said he could never preach on sex. 'There are those in the congregation that would not approve and some might even walk out.' However, he said he might reconsider it if Judith spoke – perhaps not a sermon as such, but a sharing meeting where church members were encouraged to talk about their faith and their work.

Judith duly thanked Simon and replied rather haughtily that the minister's task was to preach the whole of Scripture, not just part of it.

Simon did not seem offended, but after consideration decided not to reply.

'Obviously, a case of "No sex please, we're Christians",' thought Judith.

Judith and Jeremy began to see a lot of each other. They found so much to talk about and were very easy in each other's company. They chatted about their careers, how they had interesting jobs which involved people a great deal. In time Judith plucked up courage to ask Jeremy where he stood regarding the Christian life. Jeremy for once was at a loss for words.

"No one has ever asked that of me before. Yes, I believe there is a God and He is looking after me, but I don't feel the need to go to church. Yes, I prayed when my sister and my mother died, and I did pick up a leaflet called 'Is Your Life in a Mess' but I binned it. Judith, I respect you and the way you live your life. Unlike some so-called Christians, there is not an ounce of hypocrisy in you." And he blurted out, "I not only admire and respect you; I'm falling in love with you. Will you kiss me?"

'Oh dear,' thought Judith as she responded enthusiastically with Jeremy's arms around her.

However, many members of Judith's church were very aware of the situation and the minister, Simon, was very keen that splits should not occur. However, when presented with a petition by ten members asking for a church meeting to discuss the subject, he could not resist any longer. However, he did ring Judith, whom he knew to be a much loved member. They discussed the matter at length, and he was surprised that she seemed to take it in her stride, though she privately thought she could end up the victim of a certain type of witch hunt. The church members agreed to meet together to pray about it, and Judith was very happy not to be present.

The meeting in the church hall was in the end poorly attended. Of the original ten who requested it, only seven turned up; another three came, but they were the sort that attended everything! Adam and Carole were not there, but Gabbie was! Simon opened the meeting with prayer and read from the Scriptures.

Tom, who was in his eighties, a retired town planner and later a local councillor, had instigated the petition. He opened the debate by saying, "The Bible says men and women should not be unequally yoked, as I understand, Mr Chairman." He often reverted to his town councillor mode. "As I understand it, Judith is planning to marry the former journalist, Jeremy. We know all about him through his articles in the *Sunford Chronicle*."

This was too much for Gabbie. "Look," she said, "I know I haven't been here for very long, but I think – in fact, I know – that Judith's life is her own private matter. In fact, although I have had reason to chat to her a great deal lately she hasn't ever mentioned that she might marry Jeremy. It's a possibility given their friendliness, but marriage is not an option – at least, not yet."

"It's all right for some people to spout," said Jim. "I was divorced before I married Kathleen. Yes, we are both Christians, but does that make us unequally yoked?"

Simon listened to them and other contributions both for and against, and finally offered his own contribution. "I note the signatories of the petition are almost all men, except one. I note that most church members have chosen to stay away, not because there is footie on TV, but presumably because they feel it is Judith's private business. I have to say that in a way I too am unequally yoked, since Irene is disabled. It hasn't prevented her having two lovely children, but we are not equal in the accepted sense. Yes, she loves the Lord, but we are not the same physically."

Jim offered the proposal that there should be a vote, a suggestion that was quietly turned down by Simon. Jim, not to be outdone, suggested that every church member be required to register their approval.

"What on earth do you mean?" cried Gabbie.

"I expect you to speak up for her – but after all, her job is not one most Christians would approve of." The voice was from Aziz, who being new to the church wondered what the meeting was all about. "Is that what Christians do? I thought I had left Islam for something better!"

Simon, using all his tact, said he could not agree to a questionnaire being put to the whole church, so after twenty minutes the meeting closed with prayers, while a small rump of disgruntled members were talking in a huddle in the corner. Simon was quickly on the phone to ring Judith and he told her the outcome of the meeting.

"Fine," said Judith. "I understand. I will continue to pray about it. Goodnight."

Things seemed to move quite swiftly after that.

"What are we waiting for?" was Judith's somewhat impatient response to Jeremy when they next met up.

"I don't know!" was their joint response, and before they knew it they were sitting in Simon's study fixing the date and time for the big day. They found themselves being booked in for the intense marriage preparation groups. 'I don't really fancy this,' was the uppermost thought in both their minds. 'Sitting with all those young people! Why, some of them might be teenagers.'

Judith reminded Jeremy that many years ago she had taken part in such groups with Trevor, and they reluctantly agreed to attend. Simon, who had got to know the situation well, gently explained that there was a spiritual side to marriage and that Jesus was sometimes referred to as a 'bridegroom'. Judith listened intently, but Jeremy only listened with one ear, as it were, and much of what was said went over his head. He kept asking himself what had he let himself in for? For him marriage and religion, especially the Christian religion, were in two different compartments and had nothing really to do with each other. Well, they would be getting married in church as that was what Judith wanted and it was a much nicer atmosphere than in a registry office or even a hotel.

The day duly arrived and both Jeremy and Judith felt very nervous. Jeremy had very few family guests whilst Judith seemed to have invited all sorts of cousins and distant relatives. The church was very full. The music group had practised for a couple of weeks.

"I'll leave the order of service to you, Ju – you know about such things."

Indeed, to the casual observer it seemed as if Jeremy was something of a minor participant in the proceedings.

The reception and the honeymoon were also left to

Judith's imagination and skills. Everyone wanted to be present – well, nearly everyone, except those who had in the church meeting opposed the match.

Simon preached a brilliant sermon on marriage and the Christian life, but sadly most of it went over Jeremy's head. Nerves and a certain lack of interest no doubt played their part, but worst of all was Jeremy's desire to get it all over with. In his career as a junior reporter he had covered a number of weddings. The one that stuck in his mind most clearly was that of Micky Dempter, the notorious gangster, who married his moll at an outdoor ceremony at his ten-acre mansion. Jeremy remembered it because some of Micky's heavy mob tried to confiscate his notebook and his photographer friend Mark had his camera smashed. Those days were long past and now, at sixty, it was his turn.

He had thought about marriage, but had dismissed it from time to time. Which wife would cope with his lifestyle – being called upon for a news story at any time, day or night, as well as coping with the usual daytime role? The *Sunford Chronicle*, he thought, always wanted its pound of flesh, and he was no exception. But that was in the past.

Finding a best man had been difficult. Judith had suggested Patsy, her friend, as a 'best woman', but he settled on Danny, who had succeeded him when he retired. Danny, he knew, was a changed man. There were difficulties with his wheelchair, but with the help of Peter, the verger, they were soon overcome.

Service over, the reception was held in the church hall, now transformed into a 'palace'. Jeremy had long given up the idea of any kind of flamboyance and so left it to Judith.

It all went by in a whirlwind and before long they were at the airport checking in with their luggage.

"I've booked us into a nice small hotel on the front at Antibes."

"OK, fine by me," was Jeremy's response.

It was really fine because he had never been abroad before and he disliked seaside holidays, having had to endure them as a child. He thought to himself, 'If this is what married life is all about, so be it.'

After an exhausting flight and exquisite dinner they retired to their room. Jeremy was disappointed to find there were single beds. They were so tired that they collapsed in sleep. They did have a quiet cuddle and a kiss. Jeremy was disappointed as he did expect something more on their wedding night.

The next morning Judith was up first and into the hotel pool before breakfast. Jeremy enjoyed a lie-in despite the warm sunshine streaming through the windows. Jeremy's idea of breakfast was a traditional one, so he was slightly taken aback when confronted with croissants and coffee instead of his usual porridge. He did pluck up courage to ask Judith what they could do today, their first full day of married life. He was hoping for a tour of an art gallery or two. Judith announced firmly that it was indeed a day for the beach, but first, she stated firmly, "We must read the Bible together."

"Count me out on this one, Ju! I think I had my share of religion yesterday. I'm going to look for a newspaper – I'm sure I noticed one round the corner. I am sure in a town as swish as this someone sells British newspapers."

"Look, I'll meet you at the top of the steps. I've booked a parasol and sunbeds. It's number forty-four, in case you miss me."

But miss her he did. Judith had given him a few euros and he soon found a news stand. He could not believe the price, but before long he was sitting on a seat enjoying the news and the hot sunshine. After half an hour or so he walked down the steps, took off his new sandals and gingerly walked along the beach. He could not believe his eyes – almost all the women were topless. He had never seen a such sight before. And when he got to number forty-four he saw that Judith had exposed her breasts as well. He was speechless with astonishment. He had married Aphrodite after all!

She said, "I will never let you see me naked, not until . . ." Her voice trailed off.

'But,' thought Jeremy, 'this is halfway there.'

So it continued, with Jeremy consenting to paddle, even up to his waist, while Judith, belying her years, swam in the warm turquoise waters.

On the last night there was a terrific thunderstorm and in the early hours Jeremy found Judith's comforting presence in his bed, albeit Judith had wrapped herself in her dressing gown.

"Jeremy, I'm so frightened," she whispered.

At last, Jeremy could feel at least a little useful, and he wrapped himself around his new wife. However, he thought to himself, 'What's the good of all this Bible reading and praying when this violent storm is raging outside?' However, such thoughts soon evaporated.

All he could remember after that was Judith singing very softly, "All through the storm your love was . . ." But she trailed off as she fell sound asleep again in his arms.

This was all some months ago. Jeremy was enjoying married life – well, most of it. Judith had her church work and clinic. She enjoyed meeting her friends. They seemed very different (well, most of them) from those he knew in the newspaper business, which was so 'cut and thrust'. Judith seemed to cope with everything.

He had taken to walking in a big way, sometimes going with Monty to the park to feed the birds. The café owner noticed he was now an infrequent visitor and eventually asked him why.

"Got married," was Jeremy's non-committal reply.

"What, to that dishy lady with the dog?"

"Yes, sir." Jeremy was all smiles. "And this is our dog."

The café owner bent over the counter and smiled. "And so it is! So it is," he repeated. "Here, have these buns on me. That's what I call romance!"

But Jeremy was stuck. Judith noticed his anxiety and even a sleepless night or two.

"Why don't you pop over to Jeffrey and say you can't really write that story?"

"Oh, no, that would be copping out."

But nevertheless he found Jeffrey at home. He produced a draft of his script and asked for Jeffrey's comments.

Jeffrey guessed there was something more than an experienced journalist struggling with an unlikely script.

"Things all right between you and Ju?"

"I feel boxed in. I am very much in love with Ju, but it comes down to this – she won't have sex with me unless I become a Christian."

It was now Jeffrey's turn to be shocked. He had never heard anything like this before. Yes, he had taken a risk in asking Jeremy to write the article, which he, Jeffrey, obviously wanted to edit. He assumed Jeremy was a Christian. Yes, he had heard some talk of a very few people boycotting the wedding and of a meeting being called about it all, but as he belonged to another church he had dismissed it as 'churchy' gossip. Jeffrey prayerfully assembled what he thought were his counselling skills. The problem was as much his as Jeremy's, and so he offered to relieve Jeremy of his task.

"Oh, no!" cried Jeremy. "I enjoy doing it – words, words, words, words have been my life. It's just I feel I'm not getting anywhere. Yes, I believe in God, but He doesn't seem to believe in me!"

Jeffrey, to his surprise, was again lost for words. It was a situation he had never experienced before. Suddenly he had a brainwave. "Look, here's a copy of the Bible. It's called 'The Message'."

"Oh, we have got one of these!" exclaimed Jeremy. "Ju

reads it every day." Nevertheless he took it.

"Try reading the Song of Songs from page 1182."

With that Jeremy left and smuggled the book home.

"Jeremy, darling, what are you reading?"

"Oh, nothing really. It's just a book that Jeffrey lent me to help with his article!"

Nevertheless, when Jeremy had gone to the loo she had a surprise when she saw he was reading 'The Message', and what is more it was open at the Song of Songs. She had always accepted that the Bible was the word of God, but in her thirty-plus years as a Christian she had never given more than a glance at this particular section. It had been given the title of 'not very nice'. However, she left Jeremy to it.

He read on. Here were expressions of intimacy which he had only previously seen in the tabloid press and elsewhere, not intimacy in the context of real committed love between a man and a woman. Phrases like 'I am weathered but still elegant.' Why, that's Judith to a tee! He read voraciously and got to chapter 4 and could not believe what was written. 'Your breasts are like fawns.' Better than those he saw on the French beach! He read it all through at least three times.

"Ju!" he called, he rarely raised his voice. "Come here, and quick."

Judith, who had half expected this, was soon at his side.

"Why haven't you told me this before? Why, the couple in this account - I know it's poetry - why, that could be us - well, almost!"

Judith smiled into his eyes. He was nearly at the point of tears.

"It could be," Judith responded.

'It could,' thought Jeremy.

The next day Jeffrey called round with his wife, Sandra, to say *Rad Evang Magazine* had postponed printing the article. They still wanted it, but at a later date.

"But I'm all fired up!" Jeremy was either angry - which he didn't do very often - or confused - which he did quite a bit.

"Well, get it all together and you, me, Judith, Carole and Adam, of course, can look it through together. A sort of educational conference."

"I know the score. I have had to face plenty of those in my time. Just one thing more: reading this several times, I feel [and Jeremy didn't do feelings much], I feel it's a bit like God's love for me - intense, personal, real." He hesitated as tears welled up in his eyes and he stuttered, "Would you pray for me?"

"Why, we certainly will."

But just as the group gathered round there was a ring at the door.

"I'll go!" cried Jeremy, asserting his manhood once more.

He opened the door to a delivery man.

"Please sign for this - it is addressed to your wife."

"I certainly can."

He scribbled an acceptance signature, and he rushed back to the group.

"Now, where were we?" cried Jeffrey.

"Open the present!" cried the group in unison.

Judith did so and out fell a glamorous see-through nightie.

"Wow!" everyone cried.

Judith looked at the label.

"Hold it up to the light."

Which Ju did.

"I can see right through it!" cried Jeffrey.

To which Sandra gave him one of her 'looks'.

A belated wedding present was all Jeremy could offer.

RONNIE'S NEW HOME

Ronnie was finding it hard in the care home, even though he had been there three years. He went there when Aggie died and he missed her terribly. People there were kind – well, mostly – but often patronising, especially in the morning.

"Good morning, Ronnie," they would say. "Have you been a good boy?"

By that, they meant that he hadn't peed in his bed, or done other things. In any event, he would get a clean bed and settle down for the day. The one who asked the question was also the one who brought his food. Anyway, what was good or bad about it? It happens – it's part of life. He was never a big guy, even if they did call him 'big ears', or Mr Spock, so it was easy for them to help him up, he mused. Still his hearing was OK and his sense of smell was more than adequate. He could often identify smells coming from the kitchen. The other day they had rabbit pie – ugh! He had always been a vegetarian. He remembered the garden at home with rows of lovely lettuce – Cos, Little Gem and lots of others. The carrots were nice, especially young ones once the dirt had been licked off. But that was all in the distant past. The vegetables here were all right, but they were not like the ones grown in a garden.

Just then, Ronnie noticed a door had been left open, so he thought, 'Why not have a look at the outside world?'

The care home did organise trips out, but he was never taken on one. Perhaps they thought he might wee in the coach.

Whilst he was pondering what to do, his mind went to people who had made it to the outside world. There was Dora, who had gone but she never came back again. Did that black van parked in the yard have anything to do with her disappearance? What happened to Fred, or Joyce, or Arthur? When people disappeared like that, the staff often brought in flowers. Ronnie wondered why. He loved the smell of flowers. One they brought in had a card that said, 'In mem—' But enough of these musings.

That door was open and Ronnie was going to see what was beyond it. He hadn't stood up straight for a long while, so he thought he'd try on all fours and perhaps if he went that way they wouldn't spot him!

Once outside, Ronnie sniffed the air. 'This smells great - fresh like Aggie used to smell. And the garden - oh, the garden! And I do miss the cuddles and hugs I had with Aggie, even when she got old. Here they pick me up and put me down, they pat me as if I were a dog, but they don't seem to have time for cuddles. Let's get round the corner, and past the rubbish bins - they do smell a bit - and bins that say 'Recycling'. What's that? They had cycling when I was a lad - I remember I was once nearly run down by a young man - but that too is in the past.

'Here's to freedom! Hello, there is another property here; it's a bit darker than the home, but they will never find me here. I'll call it "Ronnie's New Home". It smells a bit damp, but it'll do for a while.'

Then a voice said, "What are you doing here, Ronnie? How did you get out? Don't you know it's lunchtime and we have a special salad for you today?"

With that, Ronnie was indeed picked up, taken back into the home and put back in his hutch.

THE UMPIRE'S DISMISSAL

George had been brought up in a cricket-mad home. Everywhere there were cricket books, pads, gloves and a bat or two. He couldn't escape the fact that his father, Rigby, had once played minor counties cricket. He claimed he played only one game and it would be difficult to find his name if anyone cared to peruse the records. However, locally he was someone to be reckoned with. His stature on and off the field was not something to be ignored. Sadly, Rigby's wife lived in some sort of fear of him. No, he had never resorted to physical violence. Among his clubmates he was seen as a gentle giant, but inside the home it was a different picture. Alice had thought of leaving him many, many times. She tried to discuss it with Janine, her really one-and-only friend, but each time she seemed to get conflicting advice. She tried praying, but it didn't seem to work.

"Perhaps God is busy or not at home today. Why do I always ask when He has a day off? God has a day off all too frequently," she said to herself.

Such was the atmosphere.

Rigby had great plans for his only child, plans he enumerated at great length, at which Alice nodded and smiled (one of the few occasions when she did so). They were of course very careful to make sure George did not hear.

"I'll make sure he gets into the junior XI at school, even if I have to bribe the sports teacher."

So George was wheeled in his pram down to the club, where Alice with a degree of reluctance helped with the cricket teas. Of course he was much admired by the other women.

"Looks just like you, Alice" was the general comment, with more than one thinking, 'He doesn't look a bit like his dad.'

Alice responded with a certain pride. "Oh, Rigby has great plans for him. He hopes he will be a professional one day."

"Why, he is only three months old. How can you tell at this stage?" It was Nora, the chief tea maker, who intervened.

"Rigby says when he held his thumb when we got home from the hospital it was like holding a bat."

Nora, who was just about to reply, held her tongue. She had seen enough ambitious fathers' dreams of their children's futures fall to dust to know that this one might come to nothing.

As George grew up, on summer days Rigby could not wait to get outside to play ball with his son. But from an early age George did not seem to be interested.

"Catch it, George!" was often a forlorn cry.

George, however, was more interested in the garden, and from time to time pulled up a plant or two. 'Just to see how it is growing' was his infant thought.

"Come on, George!" His father was becoming exasperated. "Rex [the dog] can catch it better than you!"

Rex was frequently blamed for tearing up plants. He cocked his ear when his name was mentioned, but otherwise took little interest in the proceedings except when the ball was thrown in his direction.

It was the same at the seaside, where they went for a few days in summer. Even in wet Woolacombe it was Rigby who marched off to the beach in order to 'practise'.

So George grew up with the love of a caring mother, but an intolerant father. He began to make real progress academically but his interest in sport disintegrated year by year, much to his father's chagrin and dismay.

"I don't care if he gets to university as long as he makes the school team. It's not surprising he can't catch - he doesn't want to run."

And as for holding the bat, it seemed beyond George's skill. Rigby was on the point of giving up. He had had enough of George's tears and "Sorry, Dad, I can't, I just can't."

Then Rigby thought about his old mate in South Africa, Villiers du Pont. He searched the Net to no avail, and eventually found an old diary entry giving a phone number.

"The du Pont residence," said a haughty female voice. "Who is it? Who is calling?"

Rigby explained who he was and that he wanted to talk to Villiers.

"Mr du Pont is very busy right now." The voice seemed even haughtier.

"Put him through," Rigby heard in the background.

"It's Rigby here."

"Rigby who? Do I know a Rigby?"

"Rigby Sanderson."

"Oh, yes, I remember you. What can I do for you?"

Rigby explained about George and cricket and how he knew Villiers had played for Northern Province. "Perhaps you can do something on Skype, or give him a tip or two if you are coming to the UK." A note of desperation was now creeping into Rigby's voice.

"Sorry, mate, I don't really remember you and I need to go now. I have an important meeting to attend. I'll call you back."

But he never did.

George's mother's hopes for her son were much less ambitious. All she desired was that he would do well at school, maybe get to university and meet a nice girl, get married and have a couple of children. Beyond that she had no sporting dreams. All this she kept to herself. She knew it was her task (and it often was a *task*) to keep the home together, even under the demands of her husband and his increasingly thwarted dreams.

So George grew up in this tense atmosphere. He felt the demands of his father and expressed his feelings with tearful episodes in his mother's arms. Once he sobbed, "He doesn't take the slightest interest in what I do at school, except sport, which I hate. I hear he tried to bribe the sports teacher to get me in the cricket team and even booked me a place on the winter indoor nets session. Please, please don't tell him I didn't go. The library was open that evening and that is where I went. Of course he quizzed me, but I think I managed to convince him. I even banged my arm on the door to convince him that was where the ball hit me. As far as I am aware, nobody from the junior club will say anything. My mates at school will keep schtum."

At this point Rex decided he too would like a cuddle, so George poured out all his woes into the dog's hairy ears.

Rigby found himself promoted to area manager, which entailed a good deal of travelling and several nights away from home. This in some ways was a relief to Alice. George found that their relationship deepened as the years went by. However, weekends were somewhat dreaded, especially in the summer. Rigby, however, was not pleased when he was demoted to the second XI. The club chairman (a post which Rigby had several times aspired to) firmly said that if he was not available for practice midweek he could not expect to play for the first XI.

One Saturday morning as Rigby was practising his forward defence shots in front of the bathroom mirror (much to Alice's disgust) the phone rang.

"Dad, it's for you. It's Villiers!"shouted George.

Rigby plonked his well-oiled bat down on a pile of clean washing.

"Villiers, my old friend, how are you?"

"Fine. Look, I'm at London Airport. I'd like to come and meet you. Are you around this afternoon?"

"Sorry, mate, I'm playing cricket today. How about tomorrow morning?"

"Sadly, I'm tied up tomorrow. How about Monday?"

Rigby mentally checked his diary and realised he could be home that evening, and without consulting Alice he said, "OK, come for a meal - say 7 p.m.?"

"OK."

"And you can meet George."

"Fine."

"You've got our address - it is easy to find by satnav."

Rigby announced the news to Alice, who by now had found the bat on the clean washing and was not too pleased. She was even less pleased about the proposed guest. They had rarely had people for meals, and then only one or two of Rigby's clients.

"What do you serve a former Northern Province cricketer?" she asked herself. "Springbok? Buffalo? Lion chops?"

"Sorry you failed to score again, Rigby." The young somewhat arrogant second-XI captain's sympathy sounded rather hollow. "We really need the runs. Your boy is nearly old enough to play, isn't he? Won't he take up the family tradition?" This was indeed adding insult to injury.

Rigby could only respond gloomily that George hated cricket, and even under extreme paternal pressure could not catch a ball or hold a bat straight. "Let's leave it, shall we?" Rigby said as he stalked off to the changing room, but with lots of shouts of 'Howzat!' coming through the window, he knew his team were losing yet again.

Alice had married Rigby after only a brief courtship and encouraged by her parents. "He's got really good prospects, dear," and "Wish I'd married a sporting hero," her mother had said.

A grunt by her father from behind the newspaper told the room what he thought of the comment.

However, the image of the wonderful sporting hero had soon faded long before George was born and she found herself washing his socks, shirts and jockstrap, cleaning green off his flannels and whitening his boots well before each match. Rigby often remarked, "A good player is a smart player," and so Alice had to comply. She wanted to be proud of her husband, but that pride soon faded. In the early days she had been persuaded to join the tea rota, but gave up after a couple of times claiming the other ladies were rather snooty, and George's needs soon gave her good reason not to be involved.

Rigby recalled that he was pleased George was going to be born in March, when the birth date was discussed. "Won't miss any games."

"What if it's a girl?"

"It won't be, I know!" The 'know' was said with such authority that Alice wished it was a girl just to spite him. "We shall need a good leg spinner in twelve years; then I shall look forward to playing with him."

But that was all in the past.

So Villiers duly arrived and there was the usual pre-dinner chit-chat, and George came down from doing his computer homework.

"This is Mr du Pont, he used to play for Northern Province in South Africa."

"Oh, yes, we spoke on the phone."

Villiers responded, "How nice to meet you, young man."

Alice paused in her domestic responsibilities. This man was charming, polite and the opposite to all her husband had become.

"I admire all your cricket memorabilia. Isn't that a 1948 MCC v Australia scorecard? I seem to remember Bradman was out for ninety-eight. And one for his final test at the Oval, when he was out for zero. You certainly have got some stuff."

There indeed was stuff, though of course Rigby wouldn't call it that. Stuff which could not be hung on the wall was laid out very carefully on a long table in the lounge. It even included a box, as worn by Denis Compton. Rigby was very careful to label every item and gave strict instructions about dusting each one, especially Denis Compton's box.

Tired of adult conversation, George crept back upstairs.

"That was a lovely meal!" exclaimed Villiers.

"Sorry it wasn't springbok or buffalo," replied Alice.

Rigby, after a glass or two of South African red that Villiers had brought, thought he had mellowed somewhat. Indeed, he actually congratulated Alice for her cooking, though his compliments were somewhat muted.

After the meal, as they settled down for coffee, Rigby was at his most ebullient self. "Let me show you some posters. I've got pictures of our team for the last twenty years."

"Actually, I must be going. I've an important conference tomorrow. That is the main reason for my trip to the UK."

Rigby's face showed his disappointment since he arrogantly thought that Villiers' visit was to see him and, not least, to coach George.

As they said their farewells, "Look, mate," said Villiers, "I don't like handing out unsolicited advice. . . ."

Rigby and Alice wondered what was coming.

"Don't let cricket be your God; it isn't mine." And with that he left.

Rigby and Alice were somewhat gobsmacked. Alice recognised the truth behind the parting remark, but Rigby was livid.

"How dare he abuse our hospitality with remarks like

that? No way is he going to come near my boy!" The *my* was stressed.

"He's my child too," enjoined Alice, but Rigby was too angry to hear and stalked off to his study, leaving her with all the domestic tasks of clearing away.

George, who heard raised voices emanating from below, thought nothing much of it and got down to finishing his maths homework.

As Villiers left, both the visited and the visitor reflected on the strange evening. Rigby at one point could not sleep and got up and wandered around the house. Everywhere he looked, even in the loo, there were cricket reminders of matches he had played and those in which he wished he had been a participant. At 2 a.m. he had very confused thoughts, which were not helped by the large glass of whisky he had drunk. Suddenly he realised he was not alone as Alice stood behind him.

'Is this what life's all about?' The thought flashed through his befuddled brain, but he dismissed it as quickly as it came.

Alice turned to look at him. She said nothing, but put her arms gently round him. The word 'fool' was on her lips, but died before it could be uttered. Rigby had been married long enough to guess her thoughts. The successful sales manager, the one-time 'almost made it' cricketer, was now struggling to make the second XI and was not even being nominated for the all-powerful committee. Yet what hurt the most was the fact that George, his one and only son, had so little interest in the game he so loved and worshipped.

"What do you make of Villiers?"

Alice had eventually persuaded Rigby to come back to bed, where the effect of the whisky was beginning to loosen his tongue.

"OK - nice looking guy" was all Alice's response.

"Is that all?"

By this time Alice was sound asleep.

Villiers in the meantime was emailing his friends in South Africa. 'Hey, I met this cricket-mad guy, Rigby, and his faithful wife and young son who hates the game. I dropped a bombshell that cricket was his God. Don't think he liked that one, so will you pray that the idol he has made for himself will fall down and somehow, I don't know how, will be replaced by a real faith in Christ?'

The replies came back thick and fast.

'Will do, mate.'

'Game on,' said another.

'Praying hard, let us know progress.'

And so on.

The Dynamo Prayer Group was a group of sportsmen based in Cape Town who met once a month. Different sports, different Churches, but all dedicated to encouraging others in and into the Christian faith.

Rigby knew nothing of this. He busied himself in his job, and as he travelled he thought of all the hundreds of people he had met. But no encounter was like the one he had had with Villiers.

George at school received high praise for his maths homework, and at break time told his mates about Villiers' visit.

They were not impressed, but Lucy, always a bit nosey, piped up, "Oh, yes, I know about Villiers du Pont. My mother worshipped him. He was in all the adverts."

The boys spun round. "Lucy, you don't know nuffing. You are too nosey for words. Bet you have never been to South Africa!"

"Yes, I have," replied Lucy with a smirk. "My dad took us there for a holiday. I know a lot more about him than you do." And with that she stalked away with with her nose in the air.

Friday duly arrived and, with almost religious intent, all Rigby's gear came out for inspection and cleaning. During the week Alice had made sure his whites (two pairs), jockstrap, shirt and a couple of handkerchiefs were in almost pristine condition. Rigby was fastidious - almost too fastidious - in regard to his kit. He despaired when in the team especially the younger ones were scruffily dressed when they came to the ground and didn't change much when they got on the pitch. The young captain was pleased he had got eleven players and cared little how the team looked. However, Rigby as the senior player, who always thought he should be captain, stood out from the rest.

'Poor chap,' thought Evan, the wicketkeeper. 'What's the point of looking smart when you are over the hill?'

Whether by choice or by the captain's decision, Rigby now batted at number seven.

'At least some of the opposition bowlers might be a little tired when I go in!' he thought.

"Howzat!"

The cry went across the field and Rigby trudged his weary way back to the pavilion, from which he had only emerged a few minutes ago.

"That umpire needs to go to Specsavers!" was Rigby's immediate response to the LBW decision, a view which he shared with his fellow team members and anyone else within hearing range.

When the opposition batted, there were a couple of dropped catches, a fumble in the field, and a fall which resulted in a large green stain on Rigby's whites. This just about completed a rotten afternoon. The chairman of the selection committee was all too aware of Rigby's decline, but refrained from commenting as yet.

"Had a good game, Dad?"

"Don't ask, Son" was all Rigby could grumpily say as he threw his gear in the corner. "They will ask me to play for the third XI next - but there isn't a third XI."

It was Alice who now tried to console her defeated hero.

"Stuart here."

It was couple of days later when the chairman of the selection committee rang. "I'm sorry, Rigby, but we are going to have to ask you to stand down. Yes, yes, you have done well in the past, but our second XI are keen to get promotion and young Marshall Phillings has been doing well for his school."

"But he is only fourteen and I am fifty-seven" was Rigby's stuttered response.

"I'm sorry, Rigby. You can be twelfth man if you like."

"If you like?" Rigby was almost beside himself. "This is what it has come to!"

Alice's restraining hand on his elbow discouraged any expletives.

"Why not think about umpiring next year? You know Howard is standing down at the end of the season. The county run a very good training course during the winter."

"What can they teach me about cricket?" shouted Rigby, but the line had gone dead.

"You can play with me!" It was a thirteen-year-old George's logic.

"No, I don't think so" was all Rigby could utter.

Alice responded, "You could take up bowls!"

"Bowls!" Rigby exploded. "That's for old men and women."

Alice, as the more than dutiful wife, duly cleaned the green off Rigby's cricket whites and as usual laid his kit out on the spare-room bed. Rigby surveyed the scene and, before he knew it, he flew into a rage and threw the stuff across the room. It was only June and his cricket career was over.

"Stuart here. Look, Rigby, we think we may have been a bit hard on you. We are sending an email to thank you for your services to the club and, of course, refunding half your player's membership fee. By the way, I understand your boy is good at maths."

"Yes, he b— well is" was all Rigby could utter.

"If so, would he like to consider becoming a scorer? Why not bring him along tomorrow?"

"I won't, but Alice will," he replied, volunteering them both without even consulting them. Rigby was always good at volunteering other people.

To his surprise they both agreed.

"But you don't like cricket!" was Rigby's response.

However, he did sit down and with some reluctance explained what all the umpire's signals mean.

Alice duly took George to the ground and introduced him to Betty, who had been the club's scorer for more years than she could remember.

"What are you doing here, Alice?" It was Marjorie, head of the tea makers. "Are you going to join the tea rota again? And where's Rigby? And why, this is little George!"

Marjorie was always asking questions, but rarely if at all waited for an answer. Her memories of George were related to when he was a toddler and George for many years had gone to his cousin's on Saturday and Sunday afternoons - any excuse to get away from the game and, not least, his father's boasting.

"So will little George be taking his father's place in the club?"

Marjorie did not wait for an answer. One look at George's face told her she had overstepped the mark.

"Look, Marje . . ."

Marjorie hated being called Marje. As she had said many, many times, "I'm not a cheap spread!"

George drew himself to his full height (which was not very much) and declared, "I'm thirteen and a half. I don't like cricket very much, but I love figures. That is why I am here, to learn to score. As for Dad, you will have to ask him yourself as to why he is not here."

With that he stomped into the scorers' box, where he

found a place beside the comfortable Betty.

Alice and Marjorie eyed each other with a mixture of confusion and hostility.

"Rigby is not playing any more!" Alice's response was more than abrupt.

"Not playing?"

"He's been offered the job of twelfth man, so I guess when he has considered it he might come down to the club again." Alice bridled in defence of her husband, whose strengths and weaknesses she had assessed many years ago.

So George settled down to learn the art of cricket scoring, which he took to like a duck to water. He chatted to the opposition scorers in the box and was welcomed by both captains.

Dave, the home captain, commented, "Sorry your dad isn't here today!"

"Oh, he's busy" was George's excuse for his father. "Mum's around. You can talk to her if you like," he added as he settled down to his new task.

So that is how the summer panned out. Alice took George to score for the club, and before long he was travelling with the team to away matches. Rigby, after a more than angry phone call to Stuart, rejected the offer of being twelfth man and for the time being Saturdays and Sundays saw him slumping with a book in a deckchair. However, with a cheery wave goodbye for Alice and George he did trim the borders and pull out a few weeds from time to time.

Autumn soon came and although both teams had a good season Stuart did not regret dropping Rigby, whom he regarded as more than a liability in more ways than one. However, one evening he rang Rigby and after a few brief enquiries about Alice and George asked whether Rigby would consider going on the next county umpiring course in Northampton, which was six weeks away.

Rigby did not know how to respond. Again he thought, 'What can they teach me about cricket? I who have played for so many years, including playing once for a minor county team.'

"OK," he said, "tell me the dates and times and I'll get there."

"Fine," said Stuart. "The club will refund the course fees if and when you pass the exams." And with that he rang off.

The club was always desperate for new officials and Rigby, despite his irascible temper, thought he might make a decent umpire.

"Exams, exams!" he almost exploded to Alice, glad that George was out of earshot. "I haven't done exams since I was at school!"

Nevertheless the next six Tuesdays saw Rigby in the club room of the local county ground. He surveyed his fellow students with the superior look he had always held for most of his fellow human beings. Most were younger than himself, and to his horror there were young women; nevertheless he stuck it out. The presentations were very professional, and although he didn't admit it he did learn one or two things. The instructor was a kind man, but he soon weighed up Rigby and his stance. The last evening was taken up with questions and an hour-long written exam. Rigby and the two eager young women did not ask any questions and were eager to sit the exam and get home.

He looked at the exam questions and thought contemptuously, 'It's like being back at school again, only worse.'

He flew through the questions and had soon finished. He thanked the instructor and made for the exit before his fellow students had finished.

The envelope from the Umpires Association lay on the mat as Rigby came home from work. Rigby picked it up and tossed it aside, along with a couple of early Christmas cards and a good deal of junk mail.

'At least I can claim my fees back from the club,' he thought.

"Are you not going to look at your post?" enquired Alice as she too got home from her part-time job at the local florist.

Rigby ripped open the envelope, and to his horror there was a letter from Ricky Herd, the county examiner, explaining that Rigby had just failed the exam mainly by getting the LBW rule wrong. Rigby exploded so loudly that George upstairs in his bedroom could hear his father's anger.

"What! What right have they to fail me? I – I who have played cricket, loved cricket, worshipped cricket all my life! Have they to reject me now?"

Alice was close to tears. "I'll get some supper, darling." The use of the word darling was rare in this household.

"No, I don't want any supper. I'm off out."

Rigby headed for the front door in confusion and anger. No sooner had he got outside and slammed the door behind him than he realised he had left his car keys behind. Not really knowing what to do, this once supreme person hesitantly rang the doorbell. It was George who answered. He looked at his father with confusion written all over his young face. Rigby took him in his arms and sat down on the hall chair.

"Your dad ain't much good. He's a failure!"

"Oh, no, you're not!" It was George's turn to assert himself. "You're my dad and no one else's. Go and find Mum and we will cook some supper together."

'Wow!' thought Rigby. 'My sport-hating lad is becoming a man!'

So George and his dad managed to cobble some scrambled eggs and bacon together. Alice had long pulled back her tears. There was something to be proud of after all.

Her pride increased a couple of weeks later when the new company CEO called Rigby into her office.

'What now?' he wondered.

Imogen sat behind her desk. She had long steel-grey

hair and was in her mid-fifties. Her grey-green eyes followed everything and everyone around the room. Other staff did not quite know what to make of her. She was so different from her predecessor. However, she did have a winsome smile that Rigby found almost infectious.

"Rigby," – she stood up, offering her hand – "please sit down. I'm Imogen, by the way, but please don't call me Midge – I don't like it. Rigby, you have been with the company, what, nine years, and your sales records have been excellent."

Rigby wondered what was coming. He had been dismissed as an umpire even before he started; was he now to lose his job as well? This elegant woman was probably a new-broom-sweeps-clean type. He had seen enough of Scandinavian detective films to know what this kind of female was like – or so he thought.

"As you know, Wallace is retiring next month, and I would like to offer you the post of senior sales manager in his place."

Her smile was disarming. Was it the smile of a tiger about to devour its prey or was it real?

Rigby thought a moment. At fifty-seven he hadn't thought about promotion as such, but it didn't take a second or two to say, "Well, yes, thank you."

"There are a couple of forms to sign and Gloria, my secretary, will give you details of the enhanced remuneration package. There will of course be times when you will have to work late and be away from home a lot more than at present."

Rigby could not wait to ring Alice with the good news.

"I'm delighted," she responded. "What's she like, this new boss of yours?"

Rigby replied, "Icy, cool, efficient, slightly Scandinavian."

"Pretty?"

"Not really."

"What do you mean, not really?"

"Well, she is the CEO and we underlings are not supposed to notice."

"Let's go out for a meal tonight to celebrate." Alice was soon sharing in the excitement of Rigby's new role. "How about the Cricketers Arms?"

"Oh, no, not there. I'm past it as a cricketer and my umpire skills have been dismissed before I start. The Red Lion will do."

So in a quiet corner of the pub they enjoyed a meal together whilst Rigby explained his new job. Rigby had always been something of a hero to Alice (well, some of the time), an image that had been savagely tarnished recently; but now she began to get some pride in her husband.

Seven months later Rigby spent three days supervising the firm's stand at the National Exhibition Centre in Birmingham. It was tiring work. He enjoyed the hospitality and bonhomie with clients and colleagues alike, and took care to ring Alice and George each evening to catch up on the day's news.

On the last day, having congratulated himself on the orders received, he headed for home down the motorway. However, he felt it right to pop into his office to make sure his report was ready the next day.

At the end of the corridor he noticed a light shining under the door of the CEO's (rather plush) office and thought to himself, 'She is working very late.' He tentatively knocked on the door.

"Come in, Rigby," a female voice responded. "Why, Rigby, what brings you here? Please sit down."

"Oh, I just wanted to get the report on the exhibition in order for first thing Monday."

"That's OK," replied Imogen. "I was just finishing. Have you eaten?"

"Well, as a matter of fact I haven't."

"Well, why not go and get a takeaway and a bottle of

wine, and you can report verbally? I gather you got some very good orders."

Rigby returned with the Chinese takeaway and a bottle of expensive white wine (he deduced that either the CEO or the firm would be paying). He knocked on the door, boldly this time, and it opened to show that Imogen had changed into a translucent yellow shift. Rigby could hardly believe his eyes. This, he felt, was going to be more than just business reporting. He did not know what to do.

"Come over here and pour out the wine," said Imogen, producing two glasses.

Rigby duly did as he was told (after all, she was the CEO). Imogen lay back on the couch. Rigby was overawed by her loveliness.

"Come here, Rigby," she said with Scandinavian coolness.

Overwhelmed, Rigby threw off his shoes and was taking his trousers down when his mobile phone rang in his pocket.

"Rigby," – it was Alice – "George is in hospital. Where are you? Can you come at once?"

"Yes, darling, straight away."

He recovered his trousers and shoes, bade a quick goodbye to the prostrate and frustrated Imogen, and left in a hurry. The tearful Imogen poured the expensive wine down the loo and binned the rapidly cooling takeaway. Soon she was dressed in her normal working clothes. She locked the door and proceeded down the corridor some minutes after Rigby.

The security officer at the end of the corridor was more than a little surprised to see both Rigby and Imogen rush past himself, but thought little of it other than to check each office door was securely fastened.

Likewise the man on the gate did not give much thought to the two employees leaving so late – one, Rigby, dashing off at high speed, the other a little more cautiously.

Rigby managed to find a parking space at the hospital.

He found enough change to park for six hours since he had no idea what was wrong with his son. Finding his way to the children's ward, he met Alice at the door.

"He's going to be all right" were Alice's reassuring words as they found George lying in his bed.

"Daddy," uttered George. It was the one word Rigby longed to hear.

Within seconds a junior doctor appeared and said that the result of the test showed it wasn't appendicitis after all. However, he said they would keep George overnight and discharge him the next day. Alice was invited to stay for what was left of the night.

Rigby stated that he was very tired.

"So am I," said Alice grumpily.

Rigby opted to go back home. He gave his son a kiss and gave Alice a hug and a goodnight kiss.

'That's strange!' thought Alice. 'He has the odour of a Chinese takeaway and expensive perfume on his clothes!' But she put it down to the people that he had met with at the exhibition and resolved to ask about it later (but she never did).

Rigby made his way home. He cleaned his teeth, had a shower and got into bed. Although worn out by the day's events he could not sleep. The exhibition, the encounter with Imogen, George in hospital and the long lingering thought that Alice might suspect something kept him awake until the early hours.

'Is this what life is really about?' he kept asking himself, but without getting anything like an answer.

He was woken up by the phone ringing.

"Alice here, darling."

He was delighted to hear her voice, but at the same time was somewhat incoherent in his reply.

"George is fine." The excitement in Alice's voice was all too apparent. "He can come home. Can you come and collect us?"

"I certainly can."

Rigby was now fully awake, and after a hasty bowl of cereal was soon driving to the hospital.

The rest of the weekend, lazy though it was, passed in something of a whirlwind. The sun shone beautifully. George opted out of scoring, wanting to spend time with his dad (and mum). He realised, even in his teenage mind, that he had probably had a narrow escape, and the memory of the awful stabbing pains in his stomach would be with him for days to come.

Monday morning came soon enough. George went off to school with an adventurous story to tell, Alice to her part-time job and Rigby to his office, where there was a message telling him to report to the CEO at 9.30.

'I expect she wants the exhibition report,' he thought as he busied himself with minor matters. 'I don't know what else it could be.'

At 9.30 he duly knocked on the CEO's office door.

"Come in, Rigby" was the response.

Imogen was standing in front of her desk; the lounger was nowhere to be seen.

"You know Cliff Fortescue, at least by name" was her icy statement (Cliff Fortescue being of course the MD of Staybrek).

"I won't beat about the bush," said Mr Fortescue, who liked to be addressed formally. "Imogen here stayed late on Friday night, and she says you took advantage of her and attempted to rape her!"

Rigby was aghast. He opened his mouth, but little came out. Mr Fortescue continued, ignoring Rigby's attempted denials. Rigby looked at Imogen, casting his mind back to Friday, but her grey-green eyes were emotionless.

He was just about to utter, "Is this some kind of stitch-up?" But he would have interrupted Mr Fortescue in full flow.

"Look, Rigby, whatever the truth of the matter, and I believe what she says is true, it's the good of the company that's at stake. We don't want to dismiss you as such, but we will offer a generous redundancy package. If you cannot accept it we shall have no other recourse than to go to the police. We have, of course, the circumstantial evidence of the security officers to back up the fact that the two of you were in her office late at night, and the cleaner has evidence of food and drink being brought in. We are offering the usual redundancy package plus your salary and bonus to the end of the year on the condition nothing more is said."

Rigby glanced at Imogen, who remained icy-cold. 'Where are the diaphanous shift and the tempting lips?' he wondered.

Mr Fortescue continued: "You haven't got long to think about it." And, raising his voice above his five-foot-four-inch height he almost shouted, "I want an answer now!"

Rigby thought that it wasn't only a matter of the good name of the company, but his reputation in front of Alice and, not least, George. It didn't take him long to make up his mind and, looking at them both straight in the eye, he said, "OK, I will take the offer, but we agree that nothing is said and that I can go a free man. I would state here and now that that woman tried to seduce me and nothing like rape occurred. I'll clear my desk." And with that he left, slamming the door behind him.

"Where are you off to now?" It was Susie bringing his coffee in.

"Never you mind. You won't see me again!"

So with his briefcase and a few minor possessions, including photos of Alice and George, he got in the car and drove off. News of his departure flew around the office. Speculation was rife. Had he been sacked? If so, what for? And so eventually a statement appeared on the company website to the effect that Rigby had left the company by mutual consent (though if Rigby had seen it he would have disputed the 'mutual' bit).

"I bet that Imogen woman has got a lot to do with it!"

shouted Susie with more than a hint of jealousy. "As for that Fortescue bloke, we only ever see him when there is a crisis!"

So the office eventually settled down. A few days later, and much to her surprise Susie was promoted to Rigby's job.

In the meantime Rigby, full of twisted emotions, drove to his favourite spot on the river. His somewhat erratic driving was noticed by one or two other car owners and not least by a lorry driver who honked at him vigorously. Nevertheless Rigby made it the two miles to the picnic site, a spot which he, Alice and George had enjoyed many, many times in the past. His first thought was to throw himself into the river. It was beginning to be a hot day and the water looked inviting; but no, he just sat in his seat and thought and thought and thought. 'Is this what life is all about – success and failure, promotion and dismissal?'

He bought a drink and a burger bun from the adjacent sandwich bar, and he whiled away the time by taking a couple of short walks and trying to sleep.

Eventually it was time to go home, and with much more care he drove home, taking care not to pass his office en route.

"Had a good day?" was Alice's cheery opening.

"Not bad," replied Rigby, responding to her warm embrace.

And so the pretence continued each day. Rigby left at his usual time, drove around for a bit and parked by the river. The proprietor of the sandwich bar got used to seeing him and was glad to have a regular customer. He seemed to get home very much at the same time, which aroused Alice's suspicions just a little. George was delighted to see more of his father. Alice eventually plucked up courage to enquire why Rigby wasn't spending time away. Rigby replied non-committally and added that his new job required him to stay home for much of his time.

He deliberately avoided saying he'd been to the 'office' as that would have been an outright lie rather than a half-truth. As part of the pay-off he had been allowed to keep the company car.

"Didn't I see Rigby's car down by the river?" It was Winnie, a neighbour of Rigby and Alice's, at the checkout at the local supermarket. "I sometimes walk Barney along the riverbank."

"No, he would have been in his office at that time" was Alice's response.

"Must have been mistaken" was all Winnie could say.

A week or so later curiosity got the better of Winnie and she took her dog down to the river car park, and sure enough there was Rigby's car. She enquired at the sandwich bar, bought a sausage for Barney and was told the owner of the car came each day, went for long walks along the river, came back at lunchtime, bought a burger bun and then set off in the opposite direction. The owner of the sandwich bar was, of course, curious to know why his customer was smartly dressed.

"Must be lonely. Perhaps he is a widower or a bachelor. He will be back just in time to join the rush-hour traffic. I don't know why he doesn't leave earlier." Winnie described Rigby and the owner said that description fitted him very well. "Come back at around half past four and you will meet him."

Now, meeting up with Rigby was not really on Winnie's agenda. Obviously he was not with another woman, a piece of tittle-tattle she would have enjoyed, but what was he doing here day after day? Obviously he was not at work, but what was he doing? It was a real quandary. Should she tell Alice or not? She decided to keep it to herself, which given her personality she found very difficult. Perhaps Rigby was going through some emotional crisis, or perhaps he had holiday leave and had not told Alice and George. She decided to watch and wait.

Sure enough, as she looked through her window each weekday she saw Rigby's car arrive on to his drive at almost the same time. Wasn't there something the man at the sandwich bar said about him joining the rush-hour traffic? That seemed strange.

"Why have you taken to looking down the road?" It was Ralph, Winnie's husband, who often worked from home. "For the last three days I've seen you doing this. Do you fancy that Rigby bloke?"

"No, not at all. It's nothing."

"Nothing must mean something!" was Ralph's retort as he disappeared out of the room.

So the saga continued, Alice puzzled, George pleased and Winnie baffled. How long could the pretence be kept up? Rigby struggled with this as he strode along the riverbank, whatever the season (he had taken good care to keep a lot of dry clothes in the back for occasions when he did get wet).

He said to himself, "I won't confess until I have the courage to throw myself in and face Alice and George. It will have to happen sometime, but not just yet."

Alice's suspicions were further enhanced when she noticed how tanned and slim he had become! 'Perhaps he goes to the gym in his lunch hour,' she surmised, but didn't get as far as asking him.

The dilemma came to something of a resolution when Winnie rang Alice one Saturday morning. "Come round for coffee. Bring Rigby and George with you."

"George will be out with his mates. I'll try to bring Rigby, but you know how grumpy and morose he has become."

Winnie did not know this, but had suspected as much for a while.

At eleven the two women met in Winnie's lounge.

"I'll be frank with you" was Winnie's opening remark.

"Would you be anything other?" was Alice's response.

The tension was beginning to rise, broken only by

Ralph popping his head around the door and saying that he was off to the golf club and would not be back until four-ish. "Expect you have plenty to talk about" was his parting remark as he kissed Winnie goodbye.

'Too true, we have,' thought Winnie as she considered how to approach the subject. "Alice, would you say we have been good friends over the years?"

"Not really" was Alice's somewhat stony reply. "Friendly neighbours maybe, but bosom pals, certainly not. Why do you ask?"

Winnie was now resolved on a full-frontal approach and she explained how each day she had seen Rigby's car on the riverbank and confirmed that it was the same one that he drove home each weekday. "What is he up to, Alice?"

Alice, confused and tearful, could only mutter, "I don't know, I don't know." With that she downed her half-drunk cup of coffee and fled out of the house down the road to her home.

Alice was in a real quandary. It was a somewhat tense weekend. She took George to score for the cricket club – well, at least on the Saturday; on the Sunday it was raining and Rigby miserably stomped around the house and garden (something he was becoming good at).

On Monday morning she let Rigby kiss her goodbye and allowed him to go off to work. By now the deception was wearing very thin. Around 9.30 she got on her bike and followed his trail down the road. She remembered there was a side gate for the pedestrian entrance to the office block, and after dumping her bike in the hedge fumbled in her wallet and found the entrance code which Rigby had given her so she could visit him at work. She glanced left and right to see where the security guard was standing, then she checked the CCTV camera angles, dialled the code and got inside the gate. It did not surprise her that the car in Rigby's parking space was not his black Passatt, but a blue Peugeot. Even quicker than she had entered she got outside, and recovered her bike. She undid the scarf which had covered her face and cycled home, musing to herself on the obvious things: 'Why was the security so lax and that it was obvious that Rigby had left the firm. Had he been dismissed or left of his own accord? Or had he been made redundant?' She could only guess.

She knew the riverbank where Winnie had seen Rigby's car was quite a long way, so she cycled home. What should she do - confront Rigby, possibly in the presence of Winnie, or let the deception run a little longer in the hope that Rigby would come to his senses and confess the truth? Reluctantly she decided on the latter course as the truth would have to be revealed. She rang Winnie. From being just good neighbours they were now becoming more like friends.

"I'm just about to take Barney out. I'll come round in a quarter of an hour and we can go together."

"OK," replied Alice.

So fifteen minutes later they were off to try to solve the mystery. They soon found that Rigby's vehicle was indeed in the riverside car park, but there was no sign of the driver.

"Why don't we go and ask the owner of that sandwich bar about Rigby?"

"I think not" was Alice's robust reply. "Rigby might see us."

So without stopping they made their way home. Sitting down in Alice's lounge with yet another cup of coffee they discussed the situation.

"We could try praying about it."

Alice was horrified. First, she had thought that Winnie was not the praying type, too down-to-earth; and secondly, she had given up on prayers and church when her parents were killed in a plane crash many years ago.

"That won't be any good" was her quick dismissal, thinking in her heart of hearts Winnie might not be quite right. "I think I'll let it run for a week if you don't mind. Winnie, thank you so much for your help."

Winnie's only response was "It has to end sometime," as she let herself out the door.

'We could try praying.' Those words echoed round in Alice's brain as she readied herself to go to her part-time job, which extended over the lunch hours, but was OK in that Alice was home in time for when George came back from school.

"Had a good day at the office?" was Alice's usual opening gambit, knowing full well that was where he had not been.

"Very tiring" was Rigby's response, slumping in his favourite chair.

'Tired through all that walking, no doubt,' thought Alice as she prepared to get the supper, noticing that the newspaper which Rigby used to bring back in pristine condition was now in a crumpled state as if it had been read from cover to cover.

Throughout the meal George kept the conversation going with all the events of his school day – for example, telling them about his mates in his maths class ribbing him because he had come first in their test the previous day.

Rigby remained silent. He ate his food very slowly. Both George (who suspected something) and Alice (who knew something was wrong) held the peace just in case Rigby resorted to some verbal outburst.

As Rigby was clearing the plates away the phone rang.

"Villiers here."

"Villiers, my old mate!" Rigby as if woken from a deep sleep was now almost full of life.

After the usual banalities about health and families Villiers said, "Next week I've got a fortnight free. Have you any holiday left? Why not fly out to join us?"

"As a matter of fact, I have." (Not adding that life was all holiday at the moment – well, sort of.) "Alice . . ." George had now disappeared to his room. "Alice, it's Villiers. He wants us to go out to South Africa to stay for a fortnight."

"When?"

"On Monday!"

"Help! I packed many of our summer clothes away. What about your job? Can you get time off? I thought we had had all our holidays."

"I have some time due – remember all the overtime I did for those exhibitions."

"I will tell George. I guess that it's a once-in-a-lifetime opportunity."

"Yes, Villiers – love to. I'll book the tickets online straight away."

So the charade continued, Rigby pretending he was still working, Alice knowing he wasn't. And George noticed the tension.

Events moved very quickly. Winnie was kind enough to take on Alice's part-time job for three hours, three days a week. George rued the thought of missing his parents, but was delighted at the thought of staying with his rumbustious cousins across the other side of town. Janie, Alice's sister, was delighted at the thought of George coming to stay. Not knowing the other side of George, she said he would be able to keep the other two quiet for a while.

As Alice got into bed she said, "Why don't we try praying? It might be worth it."

Rigby was already asleep, tired out by all his exercise along the riverbank.

However, Monday soon came and the flight to Cape Town was delightfully smooth. Villiers and Patricia (she didn't like to be called Pat) greeted them warmly at the airport and drove them to their home in the shadow of Table Mountain.

After they enjoyed dinner together Villiers enquired about

Rigby's job. Rigby replied enthusiastically enough about being promoted, about arranging exhibitions and so on and so on. Alice sat there wanting to stop him, but let him ramble on. Villiers and Patricia listened quietly, but were beginning to suspect something wasn't quite true. When Rigby had gone to the loo, Alice shared her thoughts with Villiers and Patricia and they were not really surprised.

"We had a guy in our church like that – got the sack and didn't let his wife know for weeks, not until the company wanted the car back."

"Just like what? I only half heard what you said as I was coming out the loo."

"Oh, nothing, Rigby. It's just in my job I meet lots of people who spend their lives pretending to be something or someone else. I guess actors do it for a living." So, changing the subject quickly, Villiers added, "Do you know what? It's the mayor's annual ball on Saturday. Would you like to go?"

"What us – us all?" Alice replied timidly.

"Tomorrow Patricia will take you down to the best dress-hire shop. It's all on us."

Alice and Rigby could not believe what was happening to them.

"I've only been to discos, never to a dinner dance. Nor for that matter has Rigby, but he has of course attended plenty of formal and informal works dos."

Time flew by, Saturday evening was a whale of a time. Rigby and Alice had never danced properly before, but somehow managed it without stepping on each other's toes. The introductions to the mayor and mayoress were cordial without Rigby being able to say much except they were delighted to be in this lovely country.

Arriving back in Villiers and Patricia's home, they were tired and exhilarated.

"We are off to worship at ten tomorrow. I hope you will join us?"

"Not me, mate," responded Rigby. "I'll lay out by the pool if I may."

"I'll come" was Alice's quick response. "After all, you have been so kind to us it's the least I can do."

Whilst the other three went off, Rigby wandered about the house and discovered a tiny library. He noticed a couple of Bibles, books labelled 'Commentaries', and several paperbacks on the Christian life, all of which he thought well used. In the miscellaneous section he found a book called *Jeffrey's Shorts* written by an Englishman, with a picture which he supposed was Jeffrey in a pair of red shorts on the front cover. He thumbed through it and took it down to the pool to read.

Alice enjoyed the worship at the local church and was engrossed when the preacher introduced his sermon, 'What's the Point of Praying?'

"Had a good morning?"

"Wonderful!" was Alice's comment. "What about you?"

"Oh, I found this book called *Jeffrey's Shorts,* full of short stories and one a bit 'churchy'. Quite funny in places. I didn't know vicars have a sense of humour. What about you?"

Alice's head and heart were very full. A quarter of her thoughts were still at last night's sumptuous ball; the rest of them were on the sermon and a prayer she had absorbed and just a little on the prospect of lunch.

"Rigby, I've been thinking."

'Oh, no,' he thought.

"You have been conning me!"

"Me, Alice?"

"Yes, you have," she said, plucking up courage.

At this Villiers and Patricia thought it time to move into the shade and left them to it.

In no time Rigby was almost in tears as he told Alice the full story, including the incident with Imogen. After three-quarters of an hour he concluded, "There, you know every single bit. I've been a complete and utter fool. Oh, yes, we have enough money to live on for a while, but somehow I must get another job."

"You idiot!" was all the equally tearful Alice could say, coming closer and kissing him tenderly.

"Look, I'll show you the book I've been given. It says that Christianity is as easy as ABCD."

"Oh, yes!" Rigby responded.

"It says," Alice was determined to press home the fact, "A means accepting you are a twit (well, at long last you have recognised that); B means you have to believe Jesus can do something about it, and He has; C means commit yourself to this unseen Jesus; and D means to decide to follow Him in future. Look, here's Patricia and Villiers with some cold drinks."

"I see you have been rambling around in what I like to call a library? I'm delighted – I don't get the chance to read as much as I used to."

"Villiers and Patricia," – it was Alice's chance to open up the conversation – "that ball last night was just wonderful."

"Alice, you looked stunning in that blue dress. I'm glad I had a hand in choosing it. Didn't we take a long time?" Patricia giggled.

Alice politely ignored the compliment, but continued: "Rigby and I have a lot to tell you. Your hospitality has been absolutely wonderful."

So the whole saga was repeated.

"I don't know what to say," said Patricia, draining her last drop of iced orange juice.

"I do," replied Villiers as he tipped both Alice and Rigby in the pool.

"You brute," shouted Alice as she spat out water and then hauled herself to the side, where Rigby was already sitting laughing his head off.

So the four of them sat with their feet in the water and

incongruously, as it seemed, Villiers and Patricia prayed. Alice joined in with a repetition of what she had heard that morning.

All Rigby could say was "Lord, it's me," and left it at that.

More drinks were followed by a lovely barbecue.

The day flew by. Alice sent pictures to George by Skype, saying that she thought Daddy was becoming a new man. There were trips to the beach, an open-air concert, a game-reserve visit and then worship on Sunday, with both Rigby and Alice particularly enthusiastically rounding off the holiday. All too soon they were at the airport on their way home.

"Villiers, I always thought God was like an umpire in the sky. When His finger goes up you are out, no arguing, no ifs or buts. But now I know differently."

Villiers and Patricia's smiles outweighed their tears as they said goodbye.

Settled in their seats on the aircraft, Alice whispered to Rigby, "I never did ask you why your clothes once smelt of expensive perfume and Chinese takeaway?"

But Rigby was already asleep.

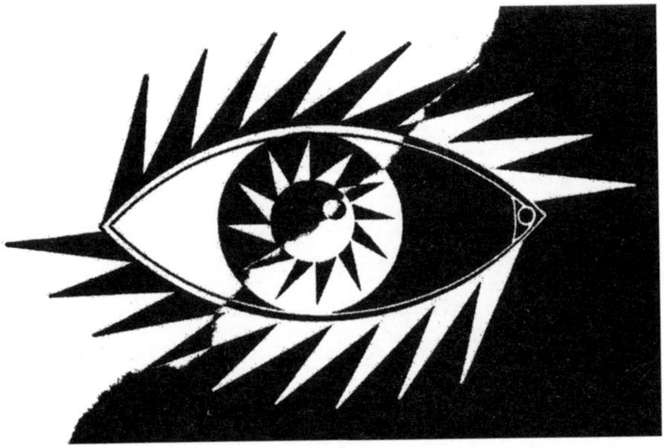

NOW YOU SEE HIM, NOW YOU –

It had been a tiring journey to the airport, and it had been just as exhausting through security and ticket checking. However, eventually Charlie settled down in her designated seat and found herself sitting next to a good-looking man of average height, obviously Middle Eastern in appearance - Egyptian, Jordanian or Syrian? He had blue eyes and a well-trimmed beard and he wore a long greeny-blue gown and sandals. Charlie thought he was a rabbi or some other sort of religious leader. Perhaps he was even Christian. But she did notice on his hands were what seemed to be dark bruises as well as on his feet. She concluded they must be birth defects. The stranger smiled and she managed half a smile back. He looked kind enough, but throughout her short life she had had an innate distrust of strangers.

The stranger did not introduce himself. He commented, but not in an obtrusive way, "I saw Luxembourg on your bag. Are you sure you are on the right aircraft?"

"Oh, that's my name," she replied. "My adoptive mother was living in the city of Luxembourg at the time I was born and she had studied the life of the anarchist Rosa Luxemburg in some detail, so I was named after her. It's a long story and it's very confusing.

"I'm going to Jerusalem - like you, I guess."

Formalities completed, light meal consumed, Charlie

was soon asleep, dreaming of this man beside her, telling him her life story even though he had not asked for it. She dreamed on, of her parents attached to the UN diplomatic service in a fairly minor role, of her mother as a very determined woman staying long enough in one place to scour orphanages to foster and then adopt children. There were five in total, of whom Charlie (short for Charlotte) was the last.

Of course they had all the privileges of the embassy staff, but her parents were well below the rank of an ambassador or even his deputy. Her father enjoyed his job, even though he did not have a lot to do. He gave help to tourists who had lost their passports, people taken ill, sometimes without proper insurance, the occasional lost student or someone whose romantic marriage had turned out to be something less.

Not having children of her own, her mother saw her fate as collecting others' children. She was in a way fortunate that her husband's posting in Kuala Lumpur was short as she did not know how any child she acquired could bear such a name. However, when Frank was posted to Addis Ababa she was almost spoilt for choice as to whom she could find to foster or adopt and she mulled over the name Addis Ababa. She thought of just Addis, but settled on Pia as in Ethiopia. Pia was a lovely six-year-old whose parents had died. Charlie's mother with her persuasive manner soon had Pia under her care.

Unfortunately as much as Pia wanted to be loved she didn't really fancy being under Barbara's wing.

"You would have been interested in Pia," murmured Charlie in her sleep to her companion. "Perhaps you have met her already? She grew up a flighty teenager and in spite of her adoptive mother's best efforts she, for some unknown reason, eventually wanted to be called Sami, which we had to accept. She got married at eighteen, but sadly it did not last. Another marriage and divorce followed in quick succession - so much so the registrar had tried to suppress his astonishment when she arrived a fifth time. By this time Frank and Barbara had retired back to the United Kingdom and had refused to go to any more of Sami's weddings.

"Guess what? She has another man, a water-board engineer!" exclaimed Charlotte. "She has given up on marriage, saying it doesn't work. She also has met another bloke, a bit like you but without the birthmarks on his feet and hands."

She briefly opened her eyes and found the stranger looking at her, but not in an unkind way. She looked out of the cabin window, but all she could see was clouds, and now fell back to a dreamlike sleep, wondering who this stranger was and if he was at all like the seventh fellow in Sami's life.

Sami had in fact texted Charlie saying she had met the other chap, who was so different from the others. She said she was interested in her new partner's job and that he had a vital role to play in a country short of water. 'He kind of knows me through and through and works for a different water company. Isn't that strange?'

Charlie replied, 'There are a few people, very few, that somehow can see right through us, warts and all.'

Sami texted back, 'Guess what? He has offered me a job in his water company, and it's permanent!'

Charlie dreamed on. "Then there was Berli – short for Berlin, where Frank and Barbara had been posted. It was terribly difficult getting past the German officials, who were very keen that his Germanic origins should not be subsumed into British ones. However, with the ambassador's help Barbara eventually succeeded: her adopted son was allowed to be called Berli, but the officials instructed Hans to be added as an additional name. Berli was very hardworking and was planning to join the diplomatic service – like Frank, his adoptive father.

"Then much to their disgust there was the story of Zac. Mum and Dad were posted to Guatemala and had to go on a trip to Zacapa. There they found a child in the street, a boy aged about nine, though looking older. He rushed up to them.

"'We can't take any more!' exclaimed Frank. We already have Pia (Sami) and Berli!'

"But despite all their efforts to trace the boy's family, enquiring at the police station and writing to the local authorities, no one could trace a single relative.

"Someone said, 'Oh, he is the Tree Boy. He seems to live up there. He only comes down when he wants something. He is a cunning little lad. Even at his age he can get money out of almost anyone. One or two people have said he is cleverer than a tax collector!'

"Not surprisingly many years later he found a job with HMRC.

"So without too much trouble Zac was duly adopted and named after his native town. He settled in well. The only trouble was he was always inviting other children into the home – something the ambassador's wife strongly disapproved of. Things came to a pass when a strange but kind man was invited in.

"Come to think of it," dreamed on Charlie, "he looked quite like you."

The man did not utter a word, but Charlotte half turned to her smiling fellow passenger.

"You will never be surprised that Zac, who gave up tax collection, has gone on to be a forester and has made a lot of money at it. Quite a lot he gives away – maybe most of it. He claims to be so grateful for all the kindness he has received. Something strange happened to cause his career change. You remember that man who invited Sami to join his water company? Well, he was working outside Zac's house. Maybe there were overhanging branches which might get in the way of the highway. Anyway, Zac had shinned up the tree (I always knew he would make a good forester), and before long the boss of the water company called him down and suggested they talk over the problem over a cup of tea.

"So they got to know each another really well. They are still very much in touch. They email or text each day. What a career change – taxman to forester! I guess he got a taste of the wooded world when that water-board engineer came by and he shinned up the tree to see what was happening.

"I haven't told you about Nic. He's the oldest."

Her next-door passenger observed Charlotte, and apart from her eyelids occasionally fluttering she slept on.

"Mum and Dad's first posting was to Cyprus. As I have said, Barbara had a passion for looking for lost children. This time she didn't have to look far. She was sitting outside the consulate enjoying the evening sun when a woman, possibly in her late thirties, was dragging this stubborn boy along the street. Her English was rather poor, but she noticed where Barbara was sitting, and without further ado thrust the child into Barbara's arms. Barbara could only make out something like 'His father doesn't want him and I don't either. I've got seven other children to look after, so you can have him.'

"The boy's eyes were tear-stained after hours of crying and so Barbara tried to give him a cuddle, which he eventually responded to, along with his eyes being gently wiped.

"'I guess you are hungry, little one. Let's go inside.'

"The British security guard was very puzzled, but after quizzing Barbara for a while dialled the security code and let them back into the compound. Try as they might, Barbara and Frank could not get a word out of the child, who was excited by lovely cream cake, biscuits and tea.

"Frank, who had gone to Greek lessons prior to the posting, asked him in Greek, 'What is your name?'

"The boy did not reply as such, but talked about all

sorts of things and especially said he wanted to be a lawyer when he grew up.

"So with the high commissioner's help Nic (as he became known) became the first one of the complex and strange family to be adopted. Don't ask me how it happened, but I guess you know how such things work."

'I certainly do,' thought the stranger, who had more than an inkling of what Charlie was dreaming about.

"Nic was a very bright lad. He sailed through school and university and had no idea why his parents had rejected him. With a first in law he began work as a junior partner in a local solicitor's, and before long he was on the lawyers' council.

"One night, quite late, he rushed out. Mum and Dad were watching TV (they were now retired and back in the UK).

"'Where are you going, Nic?' The question was more out of interest than a parental admonition.

"'Oh, I have to go and see a client.'

"'What – at this time of night?'

"'I'm afraid so.'

"Now 'client' wasn't strictly true, but it would have taken too long to explain.

"'Perhaps it's something to do with his adoption,' mused Frank. 'He is often saying it possibly wasn't legal! I even heard him uttering that if somehow he could get back into his mother's womb he could come out a different person.'

"Clever and sophisticated as he may be he does have some weird ideas from time to time.

"'Who is this man he is meeting?' Barbara was more than a little concerned. 'Ought we to follow him? I saw a book on his desk and it looked as if it was in Hebrew. He's not turning to be a Jew, is he? And there was another book about obstetrics, also a book on reincarnation, which he has thrown away. I also discovered he had one of those funeral plans. Yes, at his age. He even got the plot booked. Isn't that strange? What a wonderful collection of children we have – Nic, Zac, Sami, Berli and Charlie, three boys and two girls. That man Sami met seems to have had an influence – yes, more than an influence on the first three; less so with the other two.'"

Sounds of the food trolley woke Charlie up.

The stranger was still smiling. "Had a good sleep?" he enquired.

"Lovely" was all Charlie could say.

"I more than guessed it was pleasant by the times you smiled."

But then their reverie was interrupted by the attendant enquiring what they would like to eat and drink. The stranger asked for red wine, which when it came seemed the colour of blood, but he only ate a little fish and a dry biscuit.

The plane landed and the passengers were ushered through customs and security. Charlie looked for her new- found friend, but he was nowhere to be seen. She even attempted to ask officials, but no one had seen him.

'Strange,' she thought. 'He had a distinctive garb – surely someone would have noticed a rabbi.' It worried her and all kinds of speculative thoughts went through her mind. 'Has he been arrested? Is he still on the aircraft? Is there a special channel for rabbis?' And so on and so on, but such thoughts soon disappeared as she was helped into a taxi to her hotel.

She checked in and found herself in a comfortable room. She texted her family. Although she wasn't hungry she ordered a chicken sandwich and a small beer, enjoyed a shower and sat down to watch a little TV. The news came up in Hebrew, of which she knew little, but with English subtitles. The main news item was 'MAN DISAPPEARS FROM AIRPORT ROOF'. It went on at great pace. 'He was in his early thirties, slightly but strongly built, with a trimmed beard and wearing a grey-green gown. He had flown in on Flight IS 345, but customs and security had no record of him passing through. Nor, for some strange reason, did the aircraft company or the travel agents in the UK have any record of him. The report went on that around 6 p.m. a group of about eleven men assembled on the viewing platform. Security had decided that they were unarmed and thought they were a local football team, Galilee United, bidding farewell to their manager of the last three years. Rumours abounded. Someone said this so-called manager had 'J. C.' on his right shoulder. News got through and the police chief summoned his support staff and before long the international media were hot on the trail of what they saw as a newsworthy story. Was it just a fond farewell to a team boss who had led them to all sorts of victories, and who had dealt with their paltry disputes? For example, when two brothers had wanted to play centre forward, not the least of his problems was their interfering mum! More seriously he had to deal with the treasurer, J. I., who complained bitterly that he was always the sub and had falsely accused the manager to the IFA officials. This same manager at an away game when they were short of food got the kid at a burger bar to cough up so that both teams were fed and the spectators as well. His team picked up the bits and pieces and no one moaned. Now he was nowhere to be seen. One observer said he had been seen giving out instructions; others said they were the team sheets for the next match!

Anna sat in her office, deeply worried. As Police Chief she had responsibility for keeping law and order. Interviewed on state TV she said there was nothing to be concerned about. Curiosity, she said, should not be inflamed by rumour-mongers and sadly there were plenty of other things to worry about.

With some difficulty she got two of the leading players into her office – two brothers, who declined to give their names except to say they were P and J. P looked too old to play football, but despite one serious own goal and a certain amount of boasting he was obviously the captain of the team.

"Look, this isn't really a police matter, but a missing-persons enquiry. The manager has gone – we don't know where yet. Some of your team say he is still with you. We know he didn't jump off the roof as we would have found his body. The story goes that the manager of an opposing team once suggested he did that, but he declined. He was also offered bribes to throw matches, which would have given him untold wealth and power."

"Sounds like a case of abduction," said Levi, Anna's newly appointed deputy.

Levi, who knew nothing of the situation but had great ambition, started out from the point that he viewed everyone as a potential terrorist unless proved otherwise.

"Look," said P, "we have got a special meeting of the club in ten days' time. JC has said he will send his rep. As we are a winning team he should be very inspirational."

Anna and Levi shook their heads. "Not really our scene," they responded in unison. Levi and Anna looked at each other.

"You know what, Chief? I am becoming scared, very scared. This is becoming far too big for us to handle. I'm beginning to have my doubts that they are really a football team at all. It could be they are a political group. Did you believe that guy – what was his name now? Oh, Phil. He was saying he was going on a hitch-hiking holiday – to Gaza, of all places! Do you believe that?"

"No, I don't," replied Anna. "Now, is it a case of abduction? I'm all for lunch."

"So am I," replied Levi.

Charlie wandered down to the restaurant. There was a real buzz around the place. Reporters, TV crew, police – almost everyone was talking at once. A waiter enquired her name and found her a place at a side table, from where she dialled her friend Lance, who was due to meet her. He duly arrived armed with a bunch of flowers. She had not known Lance very long. They had met when he was studying in Jordan. She found him attractive, but knew little about him other than that he was a newspaper journalist and although not a Jew had just got a job in Israel as a tourist guide.

After the usual 'How are you?' etc., they soon engaged in conversation – so much so that they hardly noticed the waiter wanting their food order. Charlie had so much to say about her strange dreams, much of which she now realised was pure fantasy.

"Do you dream, Lance?"

"I do, but it's about gorgeous girls!"

"Not like me?" she blurted out.

"Why say that? I think you are OK," he added with a sly wink.

"Can you interpret dreams, Lance?"

"Dunno really" was Lance's first response. "I'll try." He was feeling he was really getting to know this strange girl.

"It's long and complicated."

"Well, it was a long flight!" interpreted Lance. "Go on."

So Charlie recounted her dream: the strange people claiming to be her adopted siblings, the taxman who became a forester and the promiscuous young woman whose life was changed by the water engineer, and so on.

"And is any of this true?" Lance wanted to enquire further.

There was a long pause. Charlie took a sip of her drink.

She was just about to say, "Yes, of course. I am one of five adoptees." But she checked herself just in time because it wasn't true. She, in fact, was an only child. Her father was an accountant and her mother a nurse. Luxembourg wasn't her real name; it was Jones. All this she gushed out on the verge of tears.

Lance did not know what to say or do. He was in a very public place with a girl he hardly knew. What was he to do? He looked around the restaurant. Everyone seemed engaged in eating, having their own conversations.

Was there a female on her own who could come to his/her assistance? Charlie began to sob. Nic, Sami, Zac and not forgetting Berli – they seemed so real with a common thread of lives being changed by encounters with strangers. Weirder still was that each of the first three men was so much like the rabbi-like fellow sitting next to her on the flight.

Lance eventually caught the eye of a female manager, who bustled across. She supposed there was something wrong with the meal. Lance got up and as briefly as possible explained the situation. Amanda thought at first she had in fact met this predicament before – lovers' tiffs and reconciliations that didn't quite come off were nothing new. However, this was something different. Amanda, fifty, short, confident and able, soon put her arm round Charlie and suggested she come and lie down in the staff restroom.

Confused, perplexed, in a strange country, the tearful Charlie could only mumble a stuttering "Yes, OK."

Once there, with a glass of orange juice in her trembling hands, Charlie spoke out her tale.

Lance, in the meantime, did not know what to do. Yes, in a way he was a friend of Charlie's, but he hardly knew her. For his part he had no real romantic ideas, but it was a situation he could not really walk away from. He went to the bar and ordered a large beer, and he was just about to take the first swig when he noticed a gentleman on his right with a well-trimmed beard and wearing a grey-green gown, like the man Charlie had described on the aircraft. He could not believe his eyes, but before he could speak there was a huge commotion as a dozen armed security guards rushed in. People fled in all directions. Was it a terrorist attack? Was it a bomb about to go off? There were a number of screams. Lance, a pragmatic character if ever there was one, looked into his beer and then turned to the stranger, but he was gone.

The PA system asked everyone to keep calm, announcing that it was a false alarm, and with no little confusion families and friends were reunited and some sort of order was restored.

Charlie, lying down with Amanda sitting beside her, telling her tale, was largely unaware of the commotion outside. If there were noises of chaos and people scurrying hither and thither she seemed unaware of it all. Amanda, however, saw everything on her monitor screen in the corner, but her professional training soon kicked in and she kept quiet and calm as Charlie told her lengthy story.

"I have to ask," said Amanda, "is Lance your boyfriend?"

"Oh, no," blushed Charlie. "He's just a friend. We met on the Net. He comes from New Zealand and he is willing to show me around Jerusalem."

'This girl is more naive than I thought,' pondered Amanda, wondering what to do next.

Order had been restored in the terminal building. Now there was just the usual hustle and bustle. Lance wondered where Charlie was when a female voice behind him said a demure "Hello."

"Charlie, how are you? Thank you, Amanda, for guiding Charlie back here."

"I could do with a beer" was all Charlie could utter.

Lance obligingly ordered two cold lagers. "Did you hear all the commotion with the security alerts?"

"No," replied Charlie, "I was with Amanda. Was it dramatic?"

"False alarm," responded Lance. "Say, what about that guy who sat next to you on the plane – the one with the smart beard and the grey-green full-length tunic? Do you know what?"

"No." Charlie was all ears.

"He stood next to me at the bar, and when I turned to speak to him he had disappeared. Isn't that strange? Who can it be? Is there anyone who can tell us?"

"We can try passport control," said Charlie, more in disbelief than out of real curiosity.

"Hey, there is a guy over there where it says 'Help Desk'. Let's try him."

So they hurried over with their query whilst Amanda went back to her office.

Eli had not had a good night. His young son Caleb was teething. Hazel, his wife, had been fretful. There was an air of tension in the home and Eli was glad to leave for work, only to find his frustration increasing through traffic jams and, to top it all, the security alert. However, he signed in and took over from Ronald, who had been running the desk until now and wondering where Eli had been. For the most part Eli enjoyed his job, especially reuniting lost children with their parents. Sometimes it was lost grannies, lost wallets, lost luggage - the whole panoply of human mistakes were often laid out before him. Today it would be different, or so he hoped. Despite his engaging nature, as he stood there at the desk in his smart uniform with 'Ask Me' in large letters across his chest he really wished that people for once would ignore him. Two paracetamols hadn't really relieved his headache. He thought he should have reported in sick, but realised his reasons for so doing were a bit thin.

"Anyway," he said to himself, "if I have a quiet day I can cope with my domestic problems much easier when I get home."

He was sadly disillusioned. Passengers came up to him in a steady stream. Where is this? Where is that? Some were polite in their requests, others less so, and one woman was quite aggressive, blaming poor Eli for missing her flight. Then came a quiet moment and he could take a sly look at his morning newspaper with the headline 'Man Disappears off Airport Terminal Roof'. His musings were soon interrupted by a pleasant-looking young couple.

Charlie spoke first: "We have a problem. It's not about lost children, lost money, tickets or luggage. It's about a man."

Eli's ears pricked up. This was different.

Charlotte explained about the man in the strange gown.

"Sure, I know about him," replied Eli. "It's in all the papers. Hang on a moment – I'll bet it's on TV!"

And sure enough it was, with all sorts of experts and pundits putting forth innumerable views. One claimed he had found an illusionist saying how it could be done; another had a biblical scholar saying that it was like Jesus after His Resurrection.

"Find him!"

Eli was incredulous. "Look, you two, I man a help desk. It is sometimes very stressful. You don't know how many people demand my services." And as he said that he was aware of a queue building up behind Lance and Charlie, some of whom were beginning to show signs of frustration at the delays. "Look, if the TV and the press and I daresay now the police can't locate him, how can I, poor old Eli, do it?"

"Well, thank you for your time." Lance was at his most apologetic. "Charlie, let's find your hotel. You are here for five days, right? I've an American tour party to take round tomorrow. I'll see if you can join them. Let's find a lift."

And as they did so they caught sight of the back of a man in a full-length grey-green gown. They screamed in unison, but he had stepped into the lift and was gone.

"Did you see that man?" they almost shouted to others standing around.

"Didn't see nuffin'," said one guy hastily.

"You know – the one the media are so agitated about."

"Oh, that!" said another cynically. "They need to fill up the space somehow."

Just at that moment a TV cameraman and a reporter appeared – one of a number who had been milling around the concourse. So Lance and Charlie were prevailed upon to tell their story. The reporter was particularly interested in what Charlie had to say and asked several pertinent questions. Charlie overcame her inner shyness and felt very confident in front of the camera. In no time the story had gone viral and Charlie's parents saw it in their retirement home in the UK.

"So, is he real?" The wide-eyed young reporter was intrigued as she signed off.

"Of course he is!" returned Charlie, but her words were cut short as the next item of news (a bomb blast in Gaza) took over.

"So much for thirty seconds of fame!" sighed Lance.

Eventually Charlie was installed in her hotel room. She said a faint goodbye to Lance, who went back to his flat, pondering all that had happened.

Charlie, with help, got to the restaurant, but could eat little. Soon she was tucked up in bed and dropped off to sleep.

Suddenly, she woke up, shot straight up in bed, and that man in the grey-green gown was standing beside her. She wanted to scream, but the words would just not come.

"It is I – don't be afraid."

But before Charlie could utter a word he was gone.

"Where's Lance's number?"

She fumblingly dialled.

"Hello," a sleepy male voice replied.

"Lance, he's here and he spoke to me. Lance, Lance, help, help! You've got to help me."

Lance looked at his digital clock and saw it was 2.30 a.m.

"Look, Charlie, try going back to bed. You have had quite a stormy twenty-four hours. It probably was just a bad dream."

"No, it wasn't a dream!" she shouted out enough to wake the couple in the next room, who banged on the wall loud enough to disturb other residents across the passage.

After a moment or two Lance's words sank in and she got back into bed and slept very soundly for the next six hours.

Over breakfast she pondered a great deal. 'Is he some sort of escapologist, mystery man or what?' The words "It is I – don't be afraid" were burned for ever deep in her brain. Where on earth had she heard that before?

As she finished her coffee, Lance appeared at her side. She looked up and smiled. He was such a reassuring person.

"I've fixed it – yes, you can join the tour party. We are going to the Mount of Olives this morning. Be ready at the front door in half an hour."

"But, Lance," she pleaded, "I want to talk about last night."

For the first time she saw a hint of impatience in Lance's eyes.

"Yes, OK, but can it wait?"

The tour bus duly pulled up and Lance introduced Charlie, saying that she was a friend who was joining the tour.

"Welcome on board!" was the heartfelt greeting from the fifteen or so tourists, who then went on talking among themselves.

One guy (Stan) did pipe up, "Bet you missed all the excitement at the airport?"

You mean the bomb scare, which had the police here running all over the place? It was scary, I can tell you. It was scary!"

"No!" Stan held his ground. "That man in the gown who just comes and goes, Charlie!" He thought it a strange name for a girl. "It is Charlie?" he wanted to reassure himself. "I bet you missed that."

"I did hear about it!" responded Charlie as she was

helped to find an empty seat by the window, for once keeping her thoughts to herself.

So Lance escorted the tourists around the sights.

"Do you believe all this?" a loud voice demanded from the back.

"Sure do," replied a slim attractive woman at the front, adding, "Christians have believed this for 2,000 years."

"And what about the trillions of years before that? What about all these wars and famines, earthquakes and tsunamis? He didn't do much to stop them!" Clarence was in full flight.

The other members of the group were shocked. They had come here on what they thought was a pilgrimage. Here was a very sacred site, and this guy was loud-mouthing his opinions for all to hear.

Lance ('What a nice young man!' more than one person thought) explained that this was where Jesus ascended into heaven.

"Hope His celestial lift works better than the one in our hotel!" Clarence had not eased off full throttle. However, again his offerings were cut short by Frances, his wife, giving him a sharp dig in the ribs. "Ouch, that hurt," he ejaculated. However, he did keep quiet so that Lance could finish his talk.

"Any questions, anyone?" This was the bit Lance hated, since it left himself exposed to covering up his ignorance.

"And do you believe this nonsense?" Clarence, forgetting the sharp pain in his ribs, wanted to know. Or did he? Wasn't he an agent provocateur? Perhaps he was just a stirrer-upper, not really needing a proper answer.

"Yes, I do actually," responded Lance to a considerable murmur of agreement.

"So do I!" said Veronique, a diminutive French student.

For once Clarence was lost for words, which even Frances thought odd. How they had come to go on such a trip was a mystery, but Emma at her bridge club had suggested it, hoping that it might help their marriage, which although it had lasted over forty years was more in a state of truce than the loving bond it should have been. Sadly, the trip (Clarence refused to call it a pilgrimage) had done little to improve their relationship. In fact, it had worsened and Clarence could not wait to get home.

When he recovered his composure he piped up again: "This guy, Jesus – what was he wearing?"

"I don't really know," replied Lance as he was at a loss for words. "Nobody really knows. Most pictures have him dressed in white as a symbol of purity."

"Not like this guy who just went past us – tall, bearded, with a grey-green full-length gown!"

At this there was a deep hush as every member of the party swivelled around to see whom Clarence was talking about; but there was nothing to see, only the city glimmering in the sunlight below.

Charlie could not contain herself and almost shouted, "There he goes again!"

The group almost fell upon her and questions flew thick and fast.

"So much for that!"

Lance, aware of the time, consulted his watch since he had to get the party back to the coach in good time for the next place to visit. Indeed the next group of spiritual tourists were climbing up the path to where he stood. Nevertheless there appeared to be something like a rugby scrum surrounding both Charlie and Clarence.

Charlie asserted herself. "I couldn't help seeing the TV programmes and reading in the press about these strange sightings – it's all over the place."

"Nope, we don't do foreign TV or papers" was the general viewpoint, though a couple did recall something they had seen.

Lance, aware of the animated discussion and recalling Clarence's previous outbursts, decided enough was enough and interrupted the group banter.

"Ladies and gentlemen, I too have seen the strange disappearing man."

"Have you?" The group turned as one on him. "Tell us more," they uttered in unison.

"Sorry, folks, I guess the authorities are dealing or will deal with the situation. We have to get back to the coach."

Charlie's admiration for Lance had begun to grow more than a little. He was a real man who despite his lack of years was growing into his role.

So with the others, and like so many sheep they were herded back to the coach and the next stop on the very full itinerary.

"Well, Clarence, what have you got to say for yourself?" It was Frances's turn to speak when they were safely aboard the coach. "As ever, you were an embarrassment to yourself and not least to me." The strain of bitterness in her voice was easily overheard by Charlie, sitting on her own in a seat behind.

"But I did see him!" was all Clarence could utter. "This young girl says she has heard about him several times - he's been on local TV and radio. This guy sat next to her on the flight here."

Frances was not only in her disapproving mode but in her disbelieving stance. However, she kept quiet and separated herself from Clarence as much as the seating would allow. She stared out of the window as the coach gathered speed.

The trip to Galilee was largely uneventful. Lance had briefed everyone on the need for security, not least in the way handbags should be carried and wisdom regarding the ostentatious display of jewellery, etc.

"That guy in the grey-green gown could be a thief!" Clarence said to himself, but for once shied away from expressing his opinion to one and all.

As the coach came to a halt, Lance gave all the usual

instructions about being back at 3 p.m. and set the scene, relating how important Galilee was to the life of the country and how it played a significant role in the life of Jesus and His immediate followers.

Clarence pondered, "This guy might be a Kiwi (their only religion is rugby), but he really does believe what he is saying. He's quite unlike lots of tour guides, who give out the spiel day in and day out and usually sound quite bored."

"There he is!" shouted Charlie as she struggled to get off the bus on the arm of Frances, with no one else really interested in helping her.

Twenty or so heads turned as one.

"Didn't you see him?" she almost screamed.

"No, we didn't!" The reply came back as one voice.

More than one person was getting the idea that this girl - what was her name, Charlie? - was seeing things. Well, if not things then this strange man!

Lance led the party to the water and told the story of how Jesus called His first disciples from fishing to follow Him.

"Crickey," murmured Clarence under his breath. "No way! I would never give up my job for what looks like a nutcase. Well, if not a nutcase, someone with such strange ideas."

Frances was well aware that Clarence was muttering things under his breath. She broke the icy silence between them: "Come on, Clarrie." (She always reserved 'Clarrie' for when their relationship was not all it should be, which was most of the time.) "Speak up!" And with more than a hint of sarcasm she added, "Everyone is dying to hear what you've got to say."

"I was only speculating that this girl seems to see things that others don't. Is she some sort of clairvoyant or what?"

"Well, back at the Mount of Olives you claimed to have seen the same guy!"

"Maybe, maybe not. I don't want to believe things I haven't seen!"

With that the frosty relationship continued.

Visit over, the party got back on the coach and headed back to the hotel. All the other passengers chatted away about all they had seen and heard - all except Charlie, who sat alone. More people were beginning to show her it wasn't a novel experience, young as she was, and of course Clarence and Frances continued their wall of silence, which one or two of the other tourists were beginning to notice.

'Holidays like this are a prelude to divorce!' thought Fred. 'Blimey, I should know. That fortnight with Julie in Malaga was sheer hell. Two weeks in the sun and all will be well! Turned out to be a disaster. I don't hold out much hope for these two!' he thought as he half turned round and looked at Clarence and Frances, who were lost in their own private world.

Dinner over, lots of grateful thanks were expressed, especially to Lance. As it was to be an early start the next day most guests retired early.

Clarence and Frances did manage a civilised "Goodnight" to each other.

"Did you enjoy the trip, Clarence?"

"Sort of" was his mumbled reply as he sank into sleep.

Very early the next day they woke with a start.

Clarence said, "I had such a strange dream. I dreamt that guy - the bearded one in the long grey-green gown - was calling!"

"That's very, very strange," responded Frances. "I had exactly the same dream!"

The ice had melted as they shared their joint experience in the early hours of the day.

"Do you think he has some claim on our lives?" uttered Frances.

"I certainly do, but I don't know what. We will have to ask someone, but who?" Clarence for once was all confused.

Fred could not believe his eyes when Clarence and Frances stepped out of the lift holding hands and looking at each other as if they were a honeymoon couple. He stared in disbelief, but was really grateful, for here was one holiday couple who on the face of it were not heading home and straight to the divorce solicitor.

Charlie meanwhile had returned to her room and began packing her case when there was a knock on the door.

"Come in, Lance," she responded.

"How did you know it was me?" he asked.

"I know your footsteps anywhere," she smiled.

"Just came to say goodbye. It's been wonderful meeting you. I'd never met a girl named Charlie before!"

"It's really Charlotte, but I like Charlie!"

"Don't suppose we are going to meet up again?" Lance was almost tearful.

There are always one or two female tourists who get a crush on a tour guide, especially the good-looking ones like Lance.

"I don't understand - did you really see the gentleman in the grey-green gown on the plane and at the Mount of Olives?"

"Yes, I did," replied Charlie enthusiastically. "You see, blind people can often see much more than sighted ones!" she added as they fell into each other's arms.

RECOMMENDATIONS OF *JEFFREY'S SHORTS*

'I cannot stay long without reading *Jeffrey's Shorts* again and again. They won't let me go! The characters are so much alive. . . . Perhaps I'll meet them around the corner some day. It's a book from and for the heart.'

Hervé Mousset, former lecturer in English, Paris

'I thoroughly enjoyed reading these delightful stories. Geoffrey has the gift of making ordinary everyday incidents reveal something of the interconnectedness of our lives. Written with a quiet humour, they are a reminder of how chance encounters can have surprising consequences and open up new possibilities.'

Dr Margaret Ives, former Reader in German at Lancaster University

'In these stories the author has been bold enough to address issues not usually touched upon. The reader is never sure what subject is coming next. His characters are interesting and believable. They sometimes return, and the story continues; it makes for compelling reading.'

Jeffrey Baker and Dr Carole Baker, Awre, Gloucestershire

'Geoffrey's book of short stories is imaginative and an enjoyable easy read with characters, faith and places embedded throughout the book, and I look forward to the next instalment.'

Debbie Russell, Forest Sweets, Cinderford, Gloucestershire

'I enjoyed reading *Jeffrey's Shorts* very much. Some stories were amusing, others challenging and thought-provoking.

'Well worth reading!'

Mary Cresswell, Chaplaincy Team, Gloucester Royal Hospital

AUTHOR'S PROFILE

Geoffrey is an energetic retired Anglican minister, living with his wife in the Forest of Dean (when they are not away in their motorhome). He is passionate about cricket, gardening, music, swimming and God - not necessarily in that order! He sees life as it really is and uses this in his stories.

Pam and Malcom Britton, Mitcheldean, Glouctershire